CARDINAL HILL

Cardinal Hill is a beautifully written novel, rich in authentic setting and memorable characters. Raised in the South in the 1930s and 40s, young Margaret Norman explores the secrets of family bonds and discovers the depth of true love as she arrives at womanhood.

—Michael K. Brown, 2015 Georgia
Author of the Year for *Somewhere a River*

Cardinal Hill is the delightful first novel by Mary Anna Bryan that chronicles the journey to adulthood of Margaret Norman. Told with the sureness of a Eudora Welty story and the subtle wit of a Flannery O'Connor tale, the book follows the main character as she grows up in rural Georgia during the 1930s and 40s. The characters are rich, the story is compelling, and the denouement is more than satisfying. *Cardinal Hill* is an undiscovered gem of Southern fiction. I recommend it, and I am looking forward to Bryan's next offering.

—Raymond L. Atkins, author of
South of the Etowah and *Sweetwater Blues*

Mary Anna Bryan has written a plaintively beautiful coming of age story set in the South of the 1900s.

—Jackie K Cooper, author of *Memory's Mist*

Mary Anna Bryan's novel, *Cardinal Hill*, is a coming of age tale set in rural, pre-World War II Georgia. Her protagonist is the delightful Margaret who is curious, daring, precocious, and insecure. Bryan is pitch perfect depicting that time and place with the "clean scent of pine," and "mockingbirds in the crepe myrtle bushes." Margaret and her African-American friend Lilly May find little more to do than pick up bottles along a country road to trade for candy and Double Bubble gum at the country store or to have contests to see who can spit watermelon seeds the longest distance. It all rings true. But it is the family dynamics that reel you in—sibling rivalry, adolescent love, but most of all the family secrets—and Margaret's big secret. All in all, it is a wonderful Southern novel about finally finding those two most important things in life— love and acceptance.

—Carolyn Curry, author of
Suffer and Grow Strong: The Life of Ella Gertrude Clanton Thomas 1834–1907 and founder and director of the non-profit, Women Alone Together®

CARDINAL HILL

A Novel

Mary Anna Bryan

Mercer University Press | MACON, GEORGIA

2016

MUP/P530

© 2016 by Mercer University Press
Published by Mercer University Press
1501 Mercer University Drive
Macon, Georgia 31207
All rights reserved

9 8 7 6 5 4 3 2 1

Books published by Mercer University Press are printed on
acid-free paper that meets the requirements of the American
National Standard for Information Sciences—Permanence of
Paper for Printed Library Materials.

ISBN   978-0-88146-573-0
Cataloging-in-Publication Data is available from the Library of
Congress

Winner of the 2014 Ferrol Sams Award for Fiction

To those whom I hold dearest:

Anna

Sarah

John

William

In memory of Gainer

ACKNOWLEDGMENTS

I could not have completed this book without the insights, guidance, and patience of my longtime writing partners, Farrar Atkinson, Mike Brown, Barbara Connor, and Ron Vigil, to whom I am forever grateful.

I am indebted to George Weinstein, Clay Ramsey, and Valerie Connors of The Atlanta Writers Club, each of whom offered encouragement and opportunities for growth.

Thanks to Judge Jim Henderson for sharing his knowledge of the workings of the Georgia legal system and to Helen Jenkins who assisted my efforts to capture the flavor of the African American dialect of a former era.

Thanks also to Kathy Holmes Benson, Judy Brown, Alice Clinesmith, Jeff Cropley, Mary Frazier Long, Margie Kersey, Casi McLean, Joslyn Ogden Schaefer, Marlene Sexton, and Rosemary Stewart, who moved my work forward in countless ways.

Finally, I offer my deepest appreciation to Barbara Rogers, fiction consumer par excellence, who never wavered in her support of my efforts.

CHAPTER 1

I grew up in a family with secrets. One secret involved my mother. No one would ever talk about her, and I couldn't understand why. Another secret involved me. I understood a lot about that one.

It was the summer of 1938, and I was eight. For weeks there had been no rain on Cardinal Hill. Papa said we had to conserve water because the well might run dry, so I used water from my Saturday night bath to pour over my moss garden. It didn't help. The moss died anyway. Then the weather changed. On Independence Day, it rained so hard I could barely see out the window. For nine days it rained like that off and on, and when it finally stopped, the world was green again.

On the morning after the rains, I lay in bed listening to a mockingbird in the crepe myrtle tree outside my window. The room was cool, and the top sheet was pulled up to my chin. Opposite my bed on the gray tongue-and-groove wall, a patch of sunlight was alive with colors swimming and twirling together. It made me think of fairies in rainbow gowns, dancing on emerald green moss.

The hall clock struck the half hour, and the mockingbird flew away. I got up, dressed, and went to the kitchen where Maggie, my great-aunt, had left a bowl of cornflakes on the table. I took the pitcher of cream meant for coffee from the refrigerator and emptied it over the cornflakes. Then I sat in my chair and slurped down my breakfast. Cream dribbled onto the table. I licked it up like a cat. How pleasant to eat with no grownups around to complain about manners.

After breakfast I went back to my room for Maggie's

old sewing basket. I dumped its contents—sycamore balls, okra pods, locust husks—onto the bed and took the basket outside. Ida was hanging up wash near the chinaberry trees. She nodded at me and I nodded back.

Ida had been with our family since before my mother died, seven days after I was born. She had helped Maggie raise my sister Louisa, now fifteen, and was helping Maggie raise me, too.

Ida was tall with lots of flesh on her bones. She never let on how much she weighed, but once when Lily May and I were in the barn loft, we spied her below on the feed scales. "Momma, how much you weigh?" Lily May called down. "None of your business," Ida replied. And when she got off the scales, she shuffled the weights. Naturally, Lily May and I made it our business. We kept an eye on the scales till the day Ida forgot to shuffle. Two hundred and seventeen pounds!

As I passed near the sugarberry tree with Maggie's basket in hand, I noticed that my mother's little green car wasn't parked in its usual spot.

"Where's the car?" I called over to Ida.

She took the clothespins out of her mouth. "Louisa done got Sam to drive her to town. She going shopping with Betsy."

I had wanted to go shopping myself (I needed barrettes and a jump rope), and Betsy, my cousin, would have been happy for me to come. But Louisa wouldn't have stood for it. She and I did not get along. No surprise she'd left without letting me know. I stepped off the sidewalk and turned toward the pasture.

"Where you headed to, Biscuit?" Ida called.

"Moss time!" I sang, holding up my basket. "Going down in the woods and get fresh moss for my garden."

"Moss time nothing." Ida shook out a towel, making it

snap like a firecracker. "This here be snake time. Day like this, every snake on the hill out looking to bite you. You stay home."

I glanced at the ground before I caught myself up. "Aw, there aren't any snakes around here. Just that old rat snake, and Sam says leave it alone 'cause it does good and not harm." I'd been roaming Cardinal Hill for as long as I could remember. True, I'd been scratched several times picking blackberries and occasionally stung by a bee, but nothing *really* bad had ever happened to me.

I reached the fence and climbed the stile into the pasture. The chickens around the feed trough made a to-do as I passed, my basket swinging. Farther on, the cows and Proud Beauty, Papa's mare, ignored me; they were too busy munching fresh grass sprouts. At the far side of the pasture, I followed the fence to a gully where, crouching low, I waddled under the barbed wire and set off down the hill.

The day was golden, the air fragrant with the clean scent of pine. Passing a clump of huckleberry bushes, I jumped when a rabbit darted out at my feet. I paused to search the bushes for its babies. All I found was a pile of fresh droppings.

Near the bottom of the hill where scrub oaks gave way to white oaks and hickories and where I expected to find moss for my garden in low, spongy places, I heard a noise like a squeaking gate. I paused. The noise came from my left. Stealthily, like an Indian, I slipped from tree to tree toward it. Tall bushes lay directly ahead. I circled them, darted behind a hickory, and waited. There wasn't another sound, not even a bird chirp. I peeked out.

A few yards away, a girl squatted on the ground, the skirt of her plain blue dress spreading out like a tent. Her hands were locked around a pine sapling, and her face was turned so all I could see was thick orange hair that fell in a

3

mat on her shoulders.

She was still as a rock. Then she groaned and pushed against the sapling. She pulled back, let go of the tree, and sat on the ground, drawing her knees up like a frog.

Something was jabbing my ribs and I looked down. The basket was wedged between me and the tree. I set down the basket, and when I looked again at the girl, she was sitting on the ground, leaning back on her arms, her legs stretched out in front. She began to sway side to side and whimper. Not like a dog whimpers. This was something more fearful.

I stepped out from the tree and she turned. Her eyes were bleached blue, her skin as pale as skimmed milk. Something about her—her dress, her expression—looked familiar. Then I knew who she was, or rather where she was from.

Cardinal Hill was six miles from The Georgia Instructional Institute for Mental Defectives, or Hope Forest, as most people called it. I'd gone there one Christmas with Maggie to deliver mittens knitted by the ladies at First Presbyterian Church. Sam let us out in front of a building where we were met by a lady with a big mole on her nose. She took us inside to her office, and while she and Maggie talked, I watched girls milling about in a room across the hall. They all wore plain gray or blue dresses along with vacant expressions.

The orange-haired girl turned away and moaned loudly. She tossed her head all around, hair flinging about like a rag in a dog's mouth. Then she hunched over, squeezed her arms to her chest, and let out a deep growl.

My heart pounded my ribs; my breath came in gasps. She must be in terrible pain. I started toward her to help. Then I stopped. What could I do? I didn't have pills. I couldn't give her a shot. And she might be having a fit—I'd

4

seen a kitten have one. If I got close, she might bite me or claw at my eyes. I slid back behind the tree.

When I peeked out again, the girl was squatting once more, growling and pushing the sapling so hard that its needles scraped the ground. I ran up the hill toward my house, then turned and ran back to the tree. The girl screamed, and when I peered around the tree again, I saw that she had collapsed on her side. Now, all I heard was my own shallow panting and the heavy thud of my heart.

After a few seconds, there came a new sound like a weak kitten crying. The girl pulled herself up to a sitting position and, muttering softly, bent over something that lay on the ground. She poked at it with a finger and seemed to move it about. Then she lay back and curled into a ball.

Finally gathering my courage, I stepped out from the tree. "Are you all right?" I asked softly.

The girl didn't stir. I tried to see what she had poked, but she must have been curled up around it.

From the top of the hill came the faint clang of the dinner bell. If I wasn't home soon, Ida would be in the yard yelling "You Margaret!" loud enough to be heard six counties away. I picked up my basket and started toward home. When I looked back, the girl was still curled in a ball.

* * *

"Your face done got all speckledy out in that sun," Ida said when I walked into the kitchen. Glancing at my empty basket, she went on, "Where all that moss you was going to get for your garden?"

"I guess the drought killed it."

"Well, wash up and go eat. Miss Maggie already in the dining room."

I ran my hands under the spigot at the sink and wiped

5

them on my skirt.

Maggie, who had come up from Savannah after our mother died to look after Louisa and me, stood at the buffet, putting napkins into the drawer. She wore her usual high-necked, long-sleeved black dress with black laced-up shoes and black stockings. She dressed that way both winter and summer, and the funny thing was that no matter how hot the weather, she never perspired. I always thought it was because she was such a fine lady that she didn't sweat like the rest of us. Papa had named me for Maggie, whose given name was also Margaret. She had taken care of him when he was a boy just as she took care of me now. Only his mother hadn't died; she'd been consumptive and confined to her bed.

I sat down at the table. I wasn't hungry; I wanted to get back to the woods. But if I didn't eat something, Maggie would start asking questions. So I nibbled some of the ham sandwich that Ida set on my plate and swallowed a few spoonfuls of soup.

As soon as Maggie laid her napkin back on the table, I hopped up and said, "Please excuse me."

She held up her hand. "Before you leave, child, you need to slip on your new dress, so I can measure for the hem."

"Could I— Oh, all right."

We went to her room, where she sat in her rocker and picked up my dress and a needle and thread. "It will take just a minute to catch up this edge."

"Good grief," I mumbled under my breath.

I flopped across her bed and stared at the ceiling, with its stucco flower clusters linked by long beaded strips. The design reminded me of decorations on a cake, and when I was younger, I thought it was made of sugar. Someday I'd planned to climb a tall ladder and break off some to eat. I would start in a corner where no one would notice.

I closed my eyes for a moment, and when I opened them, Maggie was darning a sock.

"Why didn't you tell me you were ready for me to try on the dress?" I asked, sitting up.

"You can try it on now."

It was pale pink and sprinkled with flowers, a Sunday school dress and unusually pretty. I had asked Maggie to make the skirt extra full, and now I was sorry because it would take forever to pin up the hem. As I slipped the dress over my head, she knelt on the floor to measure and pin. After a moment, I started to fidget. Maggie jerked back her hand.

"Mercy, child! All this wiggling, I've stuck myself." She pulled a handkerchief from her sleeve and blotted her finger. "Go ahead, take off the dress. I'll measure the rest from what's already pinned and just hope it hangs even."

An uneven hem didn't trouble me. I just wanted to get back to the woods. I couldn't cut through the pasture again; Ida might see me and wonder what I was up to. So I walked down the drive toward the mailbox on Cardinal Hill Road. Halfway there, I veered into the trees and headed for the pine sapling. It was not there. I walked up the hill to the fence and tried to retrace my earlier route. The huckleberry bushes were in the right place, but where was the tree that the girl pushed over? I wandered about looking for it.

Soon I was sweating all over, and a blister popped out on my toe. I was about to give up and go home when I spotted the small tree. The girl wasn't around, but sand was piled up where she'd been. Looking around for a stick to poke at the sand, I noticed footprints leading down the hill. I followed them until they disappeared in a carpet of pine needles, then I turned to go back to the sapling.

Passing a scrub oak, I noticed something that looked

7

like a crumpled newspaper lying beneath it. When I went closer, I realized it was a bundled-up petticoat. I knelt and unfolded it carefully. Inside, asleep, lay the tiniest baby girl I'd ever seen. Her head was the size of a baseball; her arms and legs were no thicker than twigs. Across her tummy, the cord lay like a big mangled worm.

Blood stained the place where the baby was lying, and I shifted her to a clean spot. She made a small squeaking sound.

"It's all right, little girl," I cooed. "I'll stay with you till your mother comes back. And if she asks why I'm here, I'll say it's to make sure no bugs crawled on her baby."

I sat down beside her. She went back to sleep, but I hummed a sweet tune to assure she had pleasant dreams.

My toe stung fiercely where the blister had burst, and I took off my sandal to brush away the grit. The baby kept sleeping. A tall-crested blue jay landed nearby. I sat perfectly still. The jay hopped around for a bit, pecking at ants and an unlucky beetle that crawled from under a leaf. My leg started to itch, and I eased a hand down to scratch. But the jay saw me move and flew off with a squawk.

The sun's rays had begun probing under the scrub oak, and I moved the baby deeper into the shade. She frowned but didn't open her eyes.

"Sorry, sweet thing," I said, "just trying to keep us from roasting alive."

Her little face twisted as though she might cry.

And if she did cry, what could I do? I couldn't feed her. I didn't even have water with me. I looked around for signs of the mother. If she didn't come soon, I'd have to take the baby home and let Maggie and Papa to decide what to do. They'd probably send her to an orphanage.

Or to Hope Forest?

Oh no, not to that place. I wouldn't let them. Those

people wouldn't know how to treat a baby. Not one like this who needed someone special to care for her. Again, I looked around for the mother. She was not coming back; I had suspected as much from the start. I got up. If that mother had wanted her baby, she wouldn't have gone off and left it. I stooped down, picked up the bundle, and started toward home.

"Finders keepers!" I announced to the world.

CHAPTER 2

I paused when I reached the fence around the pasture, not sure of what to do next. I *was* sure, however, of what the grownups would do if I gave them the baby. And it didn't seem right. Grownups didn't always understand things. The baby shifted in my arms, and I opened the petticoat. She was so small, even my doll clothes would be too big. She smiled as though having a pleasant dream, and a warm feeling surged through me.

Now, it so happened that I knew a lot about caring for babies. Ever since April, Ida's sister Junie and her baby, Dexter, had been living with Odell and Hazel, Lily May's grandparents. And every chance Lily May and I got, we rode over in Sam's mule-drawn wagon to help take care of Dexter. I knew how to burp him and rock him to sleep. I could change his diaper and bathe him. In fact, I knew about all there was to know about tending to babies.

But if I tended to this one, where would I keep her? Not in my bedroom with Ida and Maggie coming back all the time. Not in the barn loft where Sam might hear her cry and climb up to investigate. I decided the lockup would be the best place.

The lockup, a whitewashed building across the drive behind my room, used to be the kitchen. It had a fireplace big enough for me to stand in straight up, stretch out both arms, and still not touch the sides. The front door was boarded up, but the back door was not, and I could come and go without being seen.

Nowadays, the lockup was used for storage, and Lily May wouldn't go near it. She said it had rats. I'd never seen rats, although I had come across mouse droppings. Boxes and furniture were piled everywhere, and I'd made a path through them that came out at a back window with a missing pane. Under a table beneath the window, I had created a little room with cushions on top of a rag rug. I kept a pickle jar filled with hard Christmas candy, and sometimes I went there to read. Other times, I brought out my dolls to play house.

Since Ida might see me crossing the pasture with my bundle, I walked through the woods and came out at the water oak not far from the lockup. Folding my arms over my chest to hide as much of the petticoat as I could, I casually strolled to the back door. When I laid the baby on a cushion, she started to cry. Not with Dexter's lusty howls but with soft little mews.

"There, there, little girl," I said, brushing a finger over her cheek. "You hold on a minute, and I'll get you warm milk to drink."

After pushing boxes against the four sides of the cushion—Junie said you had to make sure your baby couldn't roll off from wherever you left it—I went to the kitchen. Ida was at the counter, stirring up cornbread.

"What you doing dirtying my pot?" she said when I poured milk into a saucepan.

"Heating milk for a barn kitten," I said.

"Barn kitten don't need no milk from you long as it got its momma to nurse."

"But I'm trying to tame this one, so it'll come when I call."

"Get out of here. I fixing to start supper on that stove."

Back in the lockup with a freshly washed doll bottle full of warm milk, I found the baby sleeping again. I picked her up, holding her close the way Junie held Dexter when she nursed him, and poked the nipple into her mouth. The baby frowned but didn't open her eyes. Milk ran down her chin, and I wiped it off with my skirt. She coughed and I lifted her to my shoulder and gently patted her back. But she wouldn't burp.

I thought about how Junie always gave her baby a bath in the morning. But since my baby was busy getting born that time of day, she would have to have an afternoon bath.

Back in the kitchen, I hung around till Ida stepped out. Then I grabbed the bowl she used for mixing cakes and went through the house filling a big grocery bag with washcloths and towels, an old sheet to tear up for diapers, safety pins, doll clothes, and blankets. I ran warm water into the bowl and sneaked out the front door with my supplies. Ida was none the wiser.

Junie always stuck her elbow into Dexter's bath water before putting him in. She said if you couldn't feel anything on your elbow, the water was just right for the baby. I stuck in my elbow; the water felt hot. We'd have to wait till it cooled.

I laid the baby in my lap. She opened her eyes like she was curious to see who held her. Leaning down, I kissed one soft cheek.

"What a sweet little girl you are," I said. "You're like Moses, only I didn't find you in the bulrushes; I found you under the scrub oak.

"You know what I'm going to do? I'm going to take care of you and raise you, and you'll be my own little girl, and no one can take you away. I promise I'll never go off and leave you or die or anything like that." I put a hand over my heart to show I was serious.

"Now, what shall I name you? After somebody in the Bible? Esther? Mary? Martha? How about a movie star like Shirley Temple or Deanna Durbin? No, those names don't fit.

"Know what I'll do? I'll give you the most beautiful name in the world: Alicia. Patricia? Which name do you like the best?"

The baby made no response.

"Okay, I'll give you both names."

Alicia Patricia lifted her forehead a little. I could tell she liked her new name.

I tested the water again, and it felt right on my elbow.

When Dexter was tiny, Junie bathed him by patting him all over with a damp cloth. She said a new baby's skin was too tender to rub. I bathed my new baby that way. And after patting her dry and placing a cloth pad over the cord (like Junie did), I put on her diaper and gown. By then, Alicia Patricia was sound asleep.

I stayed in the lockup till suppertime. Alicia Patricia slept all the while. But I talked to her, anyway, and sang songs, which she seemed to enjoy.

At supper, Louisa, who had already been away most of the day, announced that she'd be out for the evening. She was going on a hayride with the Methodist church youth group.

Papa should have known she was lying; nobody goes on hayrides in July. But all he said was that he hoped she had a good time.

I knew where my sister was going; I'd heard her tell Betsy her plans on the phone. She was going to the home of Mimi Fuller's rich uncle, who was vacationing with his family in France. Mimi's uncle had a swimming pool in his back yard, and Louisa and her friends planned to swim.

On evenings when she went out, Louisa was usually excused early from supper. That evening as soon as she left the table, I asked to be excused, too.

"No," Papa said. "You sit at your place until the meal is over." He glanced at my sister's empty chair. "All right, just this one time."

I had to get away before he did. I needed the flashlight

from his nightstand and a pillow and sheet from the linen closet. If Maggie found me gone from my room the next morning, she'd think nothing of it; I often went outside early to play. But if she found my sheet and pillow gone too, she'd suspect something was up.

Alicia Patricia was still asleep when I got back to the lockup. I checked her diaper. It was damp, so I changed it. She opened her eyes and seemed to be looking at me. Then she closed them again and went back to sleep.

Junie always said, "When my baby sleep, I leaves him be." But if Alicia Patricia didn't take in more food, she'd never grow big. I picked her up and gave her the bottle. Again, milk ran down her chin, but I couldn't tell if any ran down her throat. The problem might be the size of the doll nipple. There was a real baby bottle and nipple in the pantry. Tomorrow, I'd get them to use.

And I needed one more thing from the house: the orange crate Maggie used to store paper bags. It had strong wooden sides that would keep my baby safe. Ida knew a woman who'd slept with her baby and killed it when she rolled over on it. I wouldn't let that happen to Alicia Patricia.

When it was time for bed, Maggie only had to tell me once. Later, when she came back to kiss me good night, I pretended to be almost asleep.

"Child, you feeling all right? It's not like you to skip dessert and go to bed so readily."

"I'm fine." I gave a huge yawn. "Just tired. And I don't much like rice pudding dessert."

It was dark when I crept from my room to the lockup. Alicia Patricia lay like a pearl in her crate. I added one more "God bless" to my prayers, then I kissed the small head and settled down for the night beside her.

Something was poking into my side. Reaching down, I felt the flashlight. I sat up and groaned. My whole body ached from sleeping on the hard floor. Outside, the sky was pale gray; inside, the room was still black. I turned the flashlight onto Alicia Patricia. She lay exactly as she had when I kissed her good night, except for one hand that had worked out from the doll blanket. If she cried during the night, I hadn't heard.

When a runt was born to a litter of pigs, Sam always brought it to the house and put it in a box on the back porch. Maggie fed it with a rag dipped in sugar water and later added milk to the mixture. Soon the piglet was strong enough to go back to its mother. My baby might benefit from sugar water.

I tucked her hand under the blanket and went to the house. It was important to be out of the kitchen before Ida arrived.

I'd just finished cooling a pot of boiled sugar water under the tap when I saw her leave her house and start out across the field. Quickly, I poured the water into a jar and slipped down the hall and out the front door.

Alicia Patricia's eyes were closed, but she opened them when I touched her mouth with a rag dipped in sugar water. She raised her chin and I squeezed the water into her mouth, laughing when she stuck out her little pink tongue.

"You like sweet things, do you?" I said, squeezing a few more drops into her mouth. "Well, so do I, darling Alicia Patricia."

* * *

"What you doing out so early," Ida called through the

15

window.

"Looking for that hen's nest to see if the biddies have hatched." Why did Ida think she had to know everything that went on in the world?

In the kitchen, I got a banana to cut up over the raisin bran Maggie had set on the table. The outside of the banana looked fine, but when I peeled back the skin, the inside looked mushy.

"This banana is rotten!" I said, throwing it toward the slop bucket under the sink. It missed and slid along the floor till it hit the wall. "Now, what will I put on my cereal?"

Ida picked up the banana. "Ain't nothing wrong till you done gone and ruined it. Besides, you don't need banana on that cereal. It already got raisins."

"I don't like raisin bran without banana."

I picked up my bowl and was about to empty the cereal into the slop bucket when Ida took my arm and ushered me back to my chair. "You set back down and eat what you got."

She took milk from the refrigerator and poured it over the cereal. "How come you so prickly this morning? Ain't you got enough sleep?"

I sat down and ate. But when milk dribbled onto the table, I did *not* wipe it up. And when I finished my breakfast, I did *not* take the bowl to the sink. I sat and scowled till Ida left to take food scraps to the chickens. Then I got up.

I took the baby bottle and nipple from the pantry, washed them, and went back to the lockup where I filled the bottle with sugar water. I picked up Alicia Patricia. The nipple was so large it would hardly fit in her mouth, and she wouldn't suck it. I tickled her foot. It twitched, but she still wouldn't suck. She kept her eyes closed.

"You're awfully good at sleeping, little miss," I said,

"but you've got to learn to take your bottle. You've got to grow big, so I can teach you all the things I know about."

I wiggled the bottle; she made no response, so I set it down and unbuttoned my blouse. Gently pressing her mouth against the flat brown spot on my chest, I said, "Dear, sweet little girl, please nurse me. I love you so much."

* * *

"How come you keep fooling around that lockup?" Ida said when I came in for lunch.

"There's sour grass growing back behind it. I'm picking the seeds."

"Sour grass is growing near the top of the drive," Maggie said. "You could pick seeds there without getting into tall weeds."

"I believe I have all I need."

While Ida washed up after lunch, I stayed in the kitchen, helping Maggie polish silver to use when the church circle ladies met at our house. Ida could see for herself I wasn't fooling around the lockup all the time.

Finally, we finished the silver, and Maggie went to her room for a nap. Ida took the vacuum cleaner to the parlor, where she'd be for some time. I warmed milk on the stove.

Back in the lockup, I poured the warmed milk into the bottle with the sugar water.

Alicia Patricia's eyes were still closed when I picked her up. "Now, here's something you'll really love." I smacked my lips. "Sugar water *and* milk. You'll want to drink every drop."

I held her close. She felt different somehow. I opened the blanket and tickled her foot. It wouldn't twitch. I tickled her other foot. No response. Leaning down, I kissed the top of her head…her fingers…her toes….

My heart started racing. I felt dizzy and weak. My baby was as cold as a lamb on a tombstone.

"Please, God, make her move! Make her open her eyes! Don't let anything bad be wrong with Alicia Patricia. Make her all right. Please, please, dear God, don't let her be dead!"

I slumped back against the leg of the table, covered my mouth with both hands, and heaved great, silent sobs.

CHAPTER 3

I lay in bed with the pillow over my eyes to blot out the light. It did not blot out the terror. Thoughts swirled through my head like birds in a frenzy. Was it my fault she died? Had she suffered? Why hadn't I turned her over to Maggie? The police will be after me. They'll put me in jail. Maybe worse!

Deeper and deeper, I sank into the dark.

The clang of the dinner bell brought me to the surface. Pushing the pillow aside, I got up. The memory struck me like lightning, and I dropped back to the bed, an enormous weight pressing upon me.

"Breathe slowly," Maggie had said the time ceiling plaster in the hall fell with a crash that half scared me to death. "Breathe slowly. It will calm you."

So far, I was the only one who knew what had happened. At this moment, the others were busy about their own affairs: Maggie and Ida seeing to the final preparations of supper; Papa at his desk, tending to business; Louisa primping in front of her mirror. I went to the bathroom and splashed my face with cold water. Dear God, what should I do?

One time when I accidentally bumped Louisa while she was painting her toenails, she'd started fussing, and I, not wanting to hear, began to sing in my head. Staring straight at her and not moving my lips, I sang, "I've Been Working on the Railroad." I thought of a picture in a geography book of Chinese laborers laying down track. I became one with the laborers, banging the rail with my mallet. "I've been working on the railroad—ping! All the livelong day—ping! ping! ping!" The song filled my head, crowding out everything else.

"I've been working on the railroad," I sang on my way to the supper table.

The others were already seated, and when I sat down, Papa frowned. Then he took a deep breath, a sign he was about to say grace. I bowed my head.

"Child, are you feeling all right?" Maggie asked after Papa had finished.

"Yes, ma'am."

She looked doubtful.

"Only I found this little bird that had fallen out of its nest, and I tried to take care of it, but it died."

"I sure hope you washed your hands good before you came to the table," Louisa said.

Papa began serving pork chops onto our plates. "I heard sad news on the radio driving home," he told us. "Six infants died in a fire in the charity ward of a New York hospital."

Infants? Died? "I'VE BEEN WORKING ON THE RAILROAD—PING!" I roared in my head. "ALL THE LIVE LONG DAY—PING! PING! PING!"

Maggie reached her hand toward me. "Child, terrible things happen in this world. We must put our trust in a loving God."

Louisa curled up her lip. "She's upset because there aren't enough chops for her to have seconds."

"Oh, I don't think that's the case," Maggie said mildly.

Turning to Papa, she asked, "Jim, how was the ground-breaking ceremony for the new city auditorium?"

"Mercifully brief. The mayor's allergies were acting up, and he had to keep his speech short."

The conversation had moved to safe ground. My chest muscles eased.

After supper, I went to my room for the box I'd recently covered with flowered wallpaper. It held my treasures: the Bible Maggie had used as a child; my Sunday school pin for perfect attendance; a snapshot of my mother with her brother, Max, and another snapshot of Betsy holding me as a baby. I transferred the treasures to a dresser drawer and left the house with the box. I stopped by the lockup and the barn and then made my way back to the spot where my baby had come into the world.

The hole had to be deep enough so that no animals could dig up my baby. I'd learned the importance of that the time I'd watched Sam bury a dead calf. I dug till the hole came past my knees when I stepped into it. Then I put down the shovel and opened the box.

Alicia Patricia lay inside, tiny and gray, wearing my baby doll's prettiest gown, white batiste with blue tatting at the neck and the wrists. A few grains of sand had fallen on her face. I blew them away, replaced the lid, and set the box in the hole. My eyes got blurry, and I blinked a few times.

"Good-bye, dear little girl. Don't be afraid." I picked up the shovel, then put it down and pushed the sand into the hole with my hands.

Standing, I looked down at the grave. So bare and forlorn. I chewed strands off a jessamine vine and wove it into a wreath to put on the mound. Then I knelt and folded my hands.

"Dear God, you know how much I loved Alicia Patricia and didn't want her to die. But she did die and now she's with You. If You need someone special to look after her, I'm sure my mother will be happy to do it. Remember she never had a chance to look after me. Please tell her that Alicia Patricia likes warm sugar water and enjoys being sung to. Amen."

Standing again, I saw that the pine sapling was already beginning to straighten. Someday, it would be a tall monument for the little girl who had lived for less than two days.

Trudging back up the hill with the shovel, I dug another deep hole, this one in the back of my mind. Into it I crammed all my memories of Alicia Patricia. All my love and plans and concerns. I should never think about the baby again. For if I did—

"I'VE BEEN WORKING ON THE RAILROAD! PING! PING! PING!"

CHAPTER 4

The night after I buried Alicia Patricia, I couldn't sleep. I'd done something terrible—taking a baby that wasn't my own and then letting it die. I'd heard of a place where bad girls were sent. They were closed up in cells and given nothing but water and bread. Some of them probably died in those cells. I scooted down in the bed, drew up my knees and covered myself with the sheet, but it didn't help. The fear was inside me; I couldn't hide from it.

Early the next morning, I went to the lockup and cleared away all signs of the baby. If police came snooping around, they wouldn't find anything to show she had been there. What I couldn't understand, though, was that while I worked hard to hide what I'd done, I still wanted to tell Maggie about it. For days, all I thought about was getting caught. Then, gradually, other thoughts started creeping into my mind.

* * *

The heat returned to Cardinal Hill with a vengeance, and most days I played in the house. One afternoon while Louisa was gone somewhere, I was in her room, surveying the lipsticks arranged on her dresser. I picked up a bright red one called Passion Flame and, leaning close to the mirror, painted my lips, going a little outside the natural lip line.

After returning the lipstick to the exact spot where I'd found it, I glided across the room to stand in front of the full-length mirror. I was wearing the ballet costume Louisa had worn in her recital, "The Dance of the Flowers." She and two other girls had been columbines. The costume was blue with a net skirt layered over with wide satin panels. It came to my knees and was tight at the waist. But above my waist, to my delight and amazement, my bosoms stood out firm and high. If I lowered my head, I could almost touch the tops with my chin. Stepping back from the mirror, I extended one arm in front of me and the other behind me. Then I turned to nod at my beautiful mother, who beamed at me from the front row of the vast auditorium. Humming a tune, I rose to my toes and began to sway back and forth. Then to dance. Kick! Pirouette! Leap! Kick some more!

"What in the *world* are you doing?" Louisa stood at the door, her face gathered into a storm cloud.

"Nothing," I said.

"Get out of my costume this *instant*! You look *ridiculous*!"

I hurried as fast as I could; my hands were shaking and the hooks kept getting caught.

Finally, I got the thing over my head, and the two rolls of socks that had been my bosoms fell to the floor. I picked them up, put them into the dresser drawer, and hung the costume back in the wardrobe. As I leaned over to gather my clothes off the floor, Louisa delivered a kick to my bottom that sent me sailing through the door and into the hall where I sprawled flat. I lay, unable to move, the breath knocked from my lungs.

Louisa hesitated; she knew if she'd really hurt me, she would be in big trouble. But I sat up, and she threw my clothes out on top of me.

"Don't you *ever* come in my room again!" she yelled. "You hear me, you *brat*!"

Palms stinging, cheeks burning, I dressed and went to my room for Matilda, my doll.

On my way out of the house, Ida appeared and took hold of my arm.

"Now, Biscuit, don't you be going no more in your sister's room. You understand what I tell you?"

"Yeah, I understand." I wriggled loose from Ida and ran out the back door.

"I understand next time I go in her room, I'll make sure she's miles from home," I added once Ida could no longer hear me. When I came in for supper, my left palm still aching from smacking the floor earlier, my family was already seated.

"This is the second time you've been late for supper recently," Papa said. "Don't you know it's impolite to keep others waiting?"

"Yes, sir." I cut my eyes over to Louisa, whose nostrils were flared as though she smelled some bad air.

After grace, Maggie said, "Sister, it's too hot for you to be playing outside."

"I was under the water oak. It's not so hot there." I put a half tablespoonful of turnip greens—which I was required to eat—on top of a chunk of potato to make the serving appear larger.

"Aunt May Belle has invited me over to spend Friday night," Louisa said, helping herself to two biscuits from the basket Maggie held out. "And Uncle Ira is taking Betsy and me to the horse show on Saturday. I'll pick up pointers on how to handle Proud Beauty."

Louisa already knew how to handle Proud Beauty and had ribbons to prove it.

"What a nice thing they're doing for you," Papa said.

"Indeed," Maggie said.

I drew down my mouth. People always did nice things for Louisa. It never occurred to them that I might like nice things done for me. They treated her special because she was pretty—slender and small with wavy blond hair and skin as clear as a porcelain doll's. I was shaped like two

25

pillows stuffed into one pillowcase. My hair was stick straight and dirt brown, and my face was as speckled as a turkey egg. I planned to be a missionary when I grew up. That way people would be impressed by my goodness and not ask embarrassing questions about why no one wanted to marry me.

Ida came in with dessert, caramel cake that Papa's secretary, Doreen Hoyt, had made for his birthday. When she got to my place, she set down a slice with extra thick icing and nudged my shoulder before moving on. I glanced at Louisa's slice; my icing was definitely thicker. I broke off some and put it into my mouth. The warm, buttery flavor seeped through my nostrils, and I forgot about the nice things people did for Louisa. I broke off more icing and lifted my fork.

"Papa, Margaret was in my room this afternoon, dancing around in my blue ballet costume," Louisa said. "She had my lipstick smeared all over her face."

I lowered my fork. "I was just—"

"And she got all this stuff out of my dresser. Next thing she'll have Lily May in there rummaging through my wardrobe."

"I wasn't hurting anything."

The natural furrow between my father's eyes deepened into a trench. "That's not the point, Margaret. Your sister is entitled to her privacy. I don't want to hear any more about your getting into her things. Do I make myself clear, or need I take firmer measures?"

"Yes, sir—I mean no, sir. It's clear."

I slumped in my chair, my stomach squeezed into a fist. I had lost my appetite for the cake.

After supper, I wandered out to the front porch and sat on the steps. Seven miles away in Fredericksboro, Georgia, the lights were beginning to come on. Straight ahead, the beacon glowed on top of the Southern Exchange Building where Papa's law offices were. Beyond the building, to the north, tiny lights glinted across the low hills of South Carolina. To the west, on Fredericks Hill where Betsy and Aunt May Belle and Uncle Ira lived, an occasional beam danced among the dark trees. Those lights were as far away as the stars. I was alone in the world. In the whole universe. I drew up my knees and hugged them to my chest.

"You sure got yourself in a fix."

I turned. Lily May was coming around the side of the house. She climbed the steps and sat beside me.

"I thought Hazel and Odell were taking you to church meeting tonight," I said.

"That's tomorrow night." Lily May smoothed her dress. "And it ain't church meeting. It's revival meeting. Anyway, how come you go messing around with your sister?"

"How do you know what I did?"

"I be in the kitchen. I hear what all's going on."

"I wasn't hurting that old costume. Louisa will never wear it again anyway." A mosquito whined near my ear. I grabbed at it and missed.

Lily May poked out her lips. "What make that girl so mean, saying I get in her stuff? I don't want nothing she have."

"Yeah, and everybody thinks she's so nice."

"Me and you know how hateful she be." Lily May faced me and rubbed her left eyebrow with her finger. I rubbed my left eyebrow. It was our sign; it meant we're in this together.

She turned to look at the lights. "Reckon how come folks treat her so good?"

"'Cause she's pretty."

"Naw, it ain't that. They feel sorry for her 'cause she

27

half orphan and— 'Course, you is too. Half orphan, I mean."

I said nothing. Louisa and I may have both been half orphan, but we weren't equally half orphan. She'd had our mother for eight years; she'd gotten her love all that time. I'd had Mother for just a few days, only the smallest sliver of her, none of which I could remember. If either of us deserved pity, I did, not Louisa.

I drew in a breath and let it out as a sigh. "If I could have just gotten to know her."

"My momma knowed Miss Weezie real good. She come to work here right soon after her and Mr. Jim marry."

"Yeah, but Ida won't tell me anything, except how it was in the very beginning."

"Your kinfolk got mouths. It be their business to tell."

"But they won't." I leaned down to scratch an itch on my foot. "Maggie would, but she met Mother just that one time Papa took her to Savannah to visit. Aunt May Belle won't tell. She said she doesn't like to bring up the past. And Louisa sure-fired won't. She can't stand me and I don't know why. I never did anything to her."

"How 'bout your papa? He know plenty."

"I never asked Papa. Well, he's told me her favorite color was white and her favorite flower was the gardenia and that she could paint good."

"That ain't nothing." Lily May chewed on a fingernail. "Reckon there's stuff 'bout your momma folks oughtn't to know?"

"What? Of course not." What right had Lily May to imply there might be things that should stay hidden? "It's probably because it's not polite to talk about people after they die."

I nudged her shoulder. "Tell you one thing, though, I'll find out about Mother if it takes me the rest of my life."

Lily May nudged my shoulder back. "It be your right to know, and it be your folks' business to—"

Maggie opened the screen door. "You girls sitting there in the dark? Aren't mosquitoes eating you up?"

"I does feel a few bites," Lily May said.

"Then why don't you come inside?"

* * *

I had not told Lily May the truth when I said I'd never asked Papa about my mother. I had when I was five. Louisa had gone off to summer camp, and I'd cried because I couldn't go. Papa told me he wanted me to stay home so he could do things with me. And he did. He taught me to ride Proud Beauty, showed me how to prune roses, read me stories he'd liked when he was a boy. I enjoyed his reading the best, even though I didn't always understand what the stories were about.

One evening, I went to his study and said, "Papa, you haven't read to me in five days 'cause you've been working on Uncle Ira's business."

He pushed his papers aside. "This would be a fine night for a story."

Leaning over his bookcase, he ran his finger along the spines of books on the bottom shelf. I sat cross-legged on the floor at his feet.

"Let me see...Crusoe, Gulliver, Sawyer? What was I reading?"

"King Arthur."

He drew out a blue volume and flipped through the pages. "I believe I left off with Guinevere and Lancelot."

He had not; he had left off with Sir Gareth, right after Sir Gareth struck the puce knight to the ground. But I didn't correct him. Anything he read was just fine with me.

29

The story was long, but he read all of it. And when he had finished and laid the book on his desk, I said, "Papa, was my mother as beautiful as Queen Guinevere?"

A glow came into his eyes. "More beautiful by far."

"Will you tell me about her?"

He took off his glasses and laid them next to the book. "So, little Margaret wants me to tell her about her mother," he said as though to himself. "To tell her about Anne Louisa…"

Gazing up at the ceiling, he began in a low, singsong voice:

> She walks in beauty like the night
> of cloudless climes and starry skies
> And all that's best of dark and bright
> Meets in her aspect and her—

"But, Papa, that's a lady in a poem. That's not my mother!"

"Ah, but Anne Louisa was—" He mumbled something I couldn't understand, got up, and rushed from the room.

Later in bed, I pretended to be asleep when Maggie came back. But as she straightened up after kissing my cheek, I reached my arms around her neck. "Maggie, do you think Papa's mad because I asked him about my mother?"

"Of course not, child." She sat down on the bed.

"He started saying this poem. It wasn't even about Mother, but he got real sad. Why did he get so sad?"

"He loved your mother. He misses her so."

"I miss her, too. It's like this hollow place all inside me. Why won't people ever tell me about her?"

"Anne Louisa was a beautiful woman," Maggie said, stroking my hair.

I turned onto my stomach. "But why, Maggie, why…?"

"Time to rest, child." Maggie gently kneaded the hard places between my shoulders, the tight spots on my neck, and I drifted into a deep, velvet sleep.

CHAPTER 5

Ida was at the kitchen sink peeling peaches when I wandered in, wearing my blue pinafore and nothing else. The back of her dress was wet and sticking to her skin. Her shoes with slits in the sides to allow for her bunions were kicked off under the sink.

"Keep your hand out of my bowl." She bumped me with her hip as I grabbed a chunk of peach and popped it into my mouth. "With all these here bruises and wormholes, I ain't hardly got enough to do my cobbler for supper."

I grabbed another chunk and pulled over a stool to climb up and watch. "You're not cutting up any worms, are you?" I asked, fanning my skirt up and down to stir a breeze.

Maggie appeared in the doorway. "Mercy, child! You go right now and put on some underclothes."

Instead of going directly to my room, I decided to detour outside by my moss garden. Moseying down the hall, feet sliding along the smooth, wide pine planks, I noticed the door to Louisa's room was opened a crack, probably to allow for a cross breeze. Pausing, I peeped inside. My sister was sitting on the floor on the far side of the room, skirt hiked up to her hips, her hair, which earlier had been pinned on top of her head, falling in hanks to her shoulders. The bottom drawer of her dresser was pulled out and lying on the floor beside her, and she was shuffling through things I couldn't see. I watched a moment before moving on.

It wouldn't do for Louisa to catch me spying on her. She could be mean, and I'm not just talking about when she caught me wearing her ballet costume. Once when she and

Betsy were playing Rook in the parlor, I came in to show off a new dress. Betsy went on about how pretty it was and how much she wished she had a little sister like me. Louisa snarled and said, "Go ahead and take this one." She meant it, too. Another time when I was really small, Lily May and I were chasing each other around in the kitchen. Louisa came in, and I, without thinking, ran up and hugged her legs. "Stop it, you brat!" she screamed, ramming her knees hard into my stomach. I stumbled backwards and started to cry. Ida made her apologize for hurting me. But it wasn't so much the ram that had hurt as the look on her face when she did it.

No, it wouldn't do for my sister to notice me watching her. But what she didn't know wouldn't hurt.

A few days later while I was sitting on the carriage steps in the back yard, sorting through flower seeds I'd collected, Maggie came out to ask if I'd like to ride to town with her and Louisa.

"Oh, yes!" I cried, jumping up.

Then I paused and thought better of it. "No, I believe I'll stay home and read."

I knew Maggie thought I meant read my new Nancy Drew mystery. And I let her believe it, although I did hate to deceive her. She was so trusting, so eager for me to do what was right.

After Sam had driven them off, Ida and I were the only ones home. She was on the back porch, ironing clothes and singing "Give Me Jesus," not paying attention to me. I went to Louisa's room, closed the door, and opened the bottom drawer of her dresser. After poking through underwear and finding nothing of interest, I pulled the drawer out and peeked into the deep empty space. In the back were four ballet slipper boxes, which I took out and opened. Inside were Blue Horse composition notebooks filled with Louisa's handwriting.

One book looked different, short and thick with a green leather cover and "My Diary" printed in gold letters. A shiver passed through me. If Louisa ever discovered... I squeezed the book, half expecting secrets to ooze out like juice. Then I picked it up and opened it to the first page.

Jan. 1, 1929

Dear Diary,

I got this diary for Christmas. I am going to write in it every day. My name is Anne Louisa Norman. I am named for my mother Anne Louisa Goulding Norman. Only she is called Weezie and I am called Louisa. I am seven and everyone says I am pretty. I live on Cardinal Hill with my mother and my papa. Ida cooks for us. Sam takes care of our farm.

Love, Louisa

P.S. Papa helped me spell the hard words.

She had written that before I was born. Nineteen twenty-nine was the year Uncle Max died. A slip of paper tucked in the corner of his portrait that hung in the parlor read, "Max Goulding, 1906–1929." Mother had painted his portrait when he was fourteen. He was down on one knee, his arm around an Irish setter. He looked like Mother had at that age—large dark eyes, thick dark hair. In pictures of him when he was older, ones like the snapshot I kept with my treasures, Max looked like a movie star, a cross between Tyron Power and Gary Cooper.

I'd always felt a special tie with my uncle, even though I'd never known him. He had once used the same bedroom I used now. A few of his clothes—an argyle sweater full of moth holes, a white shirt, a pair of gray trousers—still hung in the back of my wardrobe. I'd tried them on once. I'd pulled back my hair and stood across the room from the mirror, squinting until things looked all fuzzy, and imagined it was Max standing there in those clothes. He had been killed in an automobile accident the year before I was born, and the person with him had been badly hurt. No one ever told me the details.

I turned to the next page in the diary.

Jan. 2, 1929

Dear Diary,

This is what all I got for Christmas. A baby doll that cries when you tip it and a blue cradle and a dress and some books and some games and 2 pictures Mother painted.

Love, Louisa

The pictures hung on either side of Louisa's dresser. They were of fairies dancing amidst flowers and birds. I'd always wished those pictures were mine.

I was about to turn to the next page when I heard Ida coming through the back door.

Quickly, I put everything back in its place and slipped from the room. Not that she would tell Louisa, but she'd fuss and keep an eye out to make sure I didn't go into Louisa's room the next time she was out.

It was almost two weeks before I could get back to the diaries. Then, one Saturday, I found myself alone in the house. Louisa was visiting Betsy, Ida and Lily May had gone to a funeral, and Papa had driven Maggie to town. I didn't even bother closing the door. I took out the diaries and started to read where I'd left off.

Jan. 3, 1929

I had to go back to school today. It was real cold and

me and Betsy got our feet wet walking home. Miss Woods gave me too much arithmetic homework. I hate <u>A</u> <u>R</u>at <u>In</u> <u>T</u>he <u>H</u>ouse <u>M</u>ay <u>E</u>at <u>T</u>he <u>I</u>ce <u>C</u>ream.

Louisa wrote every day, mostly about school, ballet lessons, birthday parties, and times spent with Betsy. She wrote about Max:

> Jan. 14, 1929
>
> Max took me to ride in his new car. It is black and has a rumble seat. He said he will take me and my beau to ride in the rumble seat. He is fooling. I do not have a beau. He drove real fast and bumped me all over.

> Feb. 8, 1929
>
> Max tried to eat my pie at supper. I kicked him under the table. He said I broke his leg. He looked like he was going to cry. Papa said Tom Foolery has no place at the table.

> March 21, 1929
>
> Max and his friends went on a trip. I told him to take me but he said he had no room unless he strapped me on back with the trunks. He bought me some rock candy. It fell on the floor and got dirty. I washed it off and ate it anyway.

The entry for March 26 was partly erased, but I could still make it out:

> Max is the nicest person I know. I am going to marry him when I grow up.

On April 3, Louisa wrote only one line:

Max got killed last night.

It was a month before she started writing again, and then not every day and not as neatly as before. It was as though her heart wasn't in it.

I put the diary away, went to my room, and took out the picture of Max and my mother. I studied their faces for a long time.

***

It was dangerous to read those diaries, but I did every chance I got. I was trying to find out about my mother—which I had every right in this world to do. And since my family wouldn't tell me anything, I'd find out the best way I could.

So far, though, the diaries hadn't been much help. A few times Louisa mentioned that she and Mother went shopping together or visited friends. Once, she wrote that Mother offered to teach her to paint but that she wasn't interested: "When I grow up I'm going to be a ballet dancer. Dancers don't have to know how to paint."

As the time drew nearer my date of birth, Louisa began to write more about Mother.

> Aug. 13, 1930
> I asked Mother to buy me some new ballet shoes. She said she can not drive to town. She has to rest. I said are you sick. She said no.

> Aug. 17, 1930
> Mother stayed in her room till supper time. I told her I helped Ida make the pudding. She said she knew it was good but she did not eat any.

37

Aug. 23, 1930
Mother is closed up in her room again. She will not let me in. She does not love me.

I reread the last sentence. Surely, Louisa didn't mean what she wrote. Mother was probably tired or sick that day. Ida said her cousin Lavelda was sick as a dog the whole time she carried her baby. Louisa should have been more understanding.

Aug. 29, 1930
Mother said she was going to the hospital to get me a baby brother or sister. I said do not bring it home. It will holler all the time like Lily May. One baby around here is enough.

So my sister hadn't even known I was on the way. And when she found out, she hadn't been pleased.

Sept. 7, 1930
Ida was here when I woke up. She said Papa and Mother went to the hospital to get the baby. I wanted to go. After supper Papa called and said I had a sister. I said bring Mother home. He said she had to rest. When he hung up I cried. Ida said be a big girl. I hate Ida.

During the week that followed, Aunt May Belle gave Louisa a baby doll; Maggie mailed her a nightgown with lace; Ida made macaroons, her favorite cookies. All that done for Louisa. Was anything done special for me?

Sept.13, 1930
Aunt May Bell asked me to spend the night and go to a movie with Betsy. I said I want to go see my mother.

Papa said she was not strong. I told Ida to make her some cookies to help her get well.

The rest of the diary was blank. I figured the dates. The last entry, September 13, was six days after I was born. September 14, the seventh day, Mother had died. I looked through the other diaries for the next closest date. It was January 1, 1931. Louisa started off writing about what she had gotten for Christmas. Then she wrote about a party she'd gone to. She wrote about a visit with Betsy. Page after page with no mention of Mother. Just as it must have been after Max died, Louisa found it too painful to write about Mother. But there was also no mention of me. Not a word. Nothing about what she thought when she saw me, whether she held me or fed me a bottle. I closed the diary and put it on the floor with the others.

I remembered how sad I'd felt after Alicia Patricia died, but I wouldn't have written about it in a diary for fear someone would find out what had happened. That was different from Louisa's not writing about me. If I had died as a baby, she would have been glad.

I pushed the diaries aside and lay down on the floor. My sister wished I'd never existed.

CHAPTER 6

Summer was finally over and I was glad. I would be in fourth grade at Smithson Elementary School, a block from Betsy's house on Fredericks Hill. Louisa also had gone to Smithson. Papa dropped her off there in the morning on his way to work and picked her up at Betsy's house on his way home. But when it was *my* time to start school back in first grade, he had planned to send me to Slocum, the country school two miles from Cardinal Hill. That is, until Aunt May Belle heard about it. We were at her house, celebrating Uncle Ira's birthday.

"Slocum!" Aunt May Belle exclaimed. "What kind of education could the child possibly get at that jerkwater place?"

"But things have changed, May Belle," Papa said. "With Betsy away at Ward Belmont and Louisa at Garrett High School, you don't have responsibilities keeping you home anymore. I'm not going to bother you with watching after Margaret when school lets out."

"Posh!" Aunt May Belle said with a flick of her hand. "If I need to run out, Nellie's always around." She fixed her dark little eyes on my father. "You know, Jim, Weezie would have wanted Margaret to attend Smithson. Good heavens, the thought of her going anywhere else is unnerving."

Papa protested no further.

And I did end up liking Smithson. The teachers were nice; I had lots of friends. The only hard part was the long wait afterwards at Aunt May Belle's house. She was always away doing the kinds of things that got written up in the newspaper's society section, and Nellie, the housekeeper, made it clear from the start that my presence was a great inconvenience to her.

Aunt May Belle had set up my routine. When I arrived after school, I had cookies and milk in the kitchen. Then I went down the hall to the library to do homework. After that, I was free to play. If the weather was nice, I played outside, climbing trees, yodeling in hopes of attracting neighborhood children, feeding bread crumbs to the goldfish that lazed in the backyard lily pond. A few times, trying to pet a fish, I leaned over too far and fell into the water. But it wasn't deep, and I climbed out and dried myself in the sun. If the weather was bad, I stayed in the library and looked at Uncle Ira's books, especially his art books with pictures of naked people, mostly plump women lying around looking bored.

Every afternoon from three until four, Nellie took a nap in the room off the kitchen, and that was when I explored the house. I discovered a stack of old movie magazines in Betsy's closet and read every one. I sprayed myself with Aunt May Belle's perfumes, remembering to scrub off the scent before I came back downstairs. I climbed steps to the attic and rummaged through everything up there, including a box of pictures of Mother and Aunt May Belle and Uncle Max when they were children. In one picture, Mother and a girl were standing with their arms around each other's waists while Aunt May Belle stood off to one side, looking sour. The faces of Mother and the girl were scratched out, but I knew they were laughing. We had the same picture at home.

That evening, I showed *our* picture to Papa and asked who the girl was. He mumbled something I didn't catch and took the picture away. I never saw it again.

Louisa's diary told about the things she and Betsy had done after school, which sounded like fun. They had dressed in Aunt May Belle's fine clothes and given themselves parties. Once they had a cocktail party and drank Uncle Ira's whiskey from wine glasses. That evening when Papa picked her up, Louisa claimed she was sick and rode home in the back seat because she was afraid Papa would smell the Scotch on her breath.

They also played jokes on the upstairs telephone. They called fire stations and said they wanted to report a blaze. When the firemen asked what was burning, one would say, "My heart! It's aflame over Douglas Fairbanks!" Or they called drug stores and asked if they had olive oil in a bottle. If the druggist said yes, they'd say, "Let her out! Popeye wants her." And when they hung up, they'd laugh till they cried. I played those same jokes on the phone, but they weren't fun for me. I had no one to laugh with.

When Betsy was in sixth grade and Louisa in fifth, Betsy got a crush on a boy named Bannister James. She called him every day, pretending to be one girl or another. Sometimes she just breathed heavily into the receiver. One Saturday, Betsy called Bannister and a man answered the phone. Louisa wrote about it in her diary:

> I can't put down what he said. It's simply too awful! But he called her something that starts with a <u>B</u>!!! I said go right downstairs and tell her father. Nobody should talk to a nice girl like that. She said she couldn't. He'd get mad because she wasn't supposed to play on the phone. One thing for sure, we won't call that Bannister James anymore!!!!!!

* * *

The Monday before Halloween, a new girl, Sue Lee Wright, showed up in my fourth grade class. She had a round face and blond, bouncy curls. At recess she said,

"Let's be best friends," and I said, "Okay." The next morning, she was in the desk next to mine. "I just told the teacher I couldn't see the board from that other desk," she explained.

During class, Sue Lee kept poking the eraser ends of two pencils into her cheeks. At recess I asked why she did it.

"To make dimples," she said. "Just look." She lifted the ends of her skirt, cocked her head to one side and curtsied. "Well, who do I look like?"

"I don't know."

"Watch."

Shuffling her shoes in the dirt, she began singing, "On the go-oo-od ship—"

"Shirley Temple!" I cried.

"Everybody says that." Sue Lee wiped the dust off her shoes with the underside of her skirt. "Except I don't have enough dimples. I'm getting some, though. See." She drew back her lips into a tight little grin. Two indentations appeared where she'd stuck in the erasers.

"You sure are!" I exclaimed.

Sue Lee fluffed out her skirt. "Any day I expect a talent scout to discover me and take me to Hollywood to be in the movies. I sing real good, and I can dance, too."

"My sister dances," I said. "I sure wish I could."

"Get her to teach you. My sister taught me."

"Oh, I don't think Louisa would do that."

Sue Lee looked puzzled. Then she gave her tight little grin. "Ginger will teach me anything I ask. She thinks I'm as cute as a button."

"Louisa thinks I'm a brat."

"Oh? Well, *I'll* teach you to dance. And once I'm a movie star in Hollywood, I'll send for you and let you dance in my pictures."

A warm feeling passed through me. How proud Papa would be. He'd be at the movie show with his friends, and I'd be up on the screen. He'd say, "That's my daughter up there, singing and dancing. Everybody wants her to be in their movies." His friends would all say, "How beautiful she is. How talented!"

I said, "We can bring my great-aunt along to sew up our costumes."

"Oh, they have special trained people for that," said Sue Lee. "But my mother will come out to drive us around."

A week before Christmas holidays, Sue Lee invited me to spend the afternoon at her house. "It's that huge one on Washington Way," she said.

Since all the houses on Washington Way were huge, I had no idea which one was hers. But I said, "Oh yeah, the huge one."

"Where do *you* live?" she asked.

"On Cardinal Hill."

"What kind of name is Cardinal Hill?"

"Some great-grandmother named our place after her favorite bird. Papa said—"

I was prepared to tell how my house sat on an ancient sand dune that stretched all through Georgia and into South Carolina. How the house had been built in the 1830s by a grandfather as a wedding gift to his daughter and how Papa had inherited it from an uncle. But Sue Lee wouldn't have listened; she only wanted to hear about things that concerned her. She started to practice a dance step.

Sue Lee's house was indeed huge, although her bedroom was small and quite plain. She explained that her mother was redecorating it and that it would be fabulous when it was finished. She showed me her autographed picture of Shirley Temple, her three Shirley Temple dolls, her six Shirley Temple cream pitchers that came out of

44

boxes of Wheaties, and her record of Shirley Temple songs.

"Let's get Ginger's phonograph and play my record," she said.

"Ginger's not home?"

"She's probably in her room."

"Won't she be mad if you take her phonograph?"

Sue Lee gave a sassy twitch to her shoulders. "Why should she? I'm her little sister. She thinks I'm cute as a button."

A scrumptious thought popped into my head. Wouldn't it be grand if Sue Lee dropped Ginger's phonograph and broke it? Then maybe Big Sister wouldn't think Little Sister was quite so cute.

I followed her down the hall to a door that she opened without even knocking. A plump girl about Louisa's age lay propped up on the bed, reading a movie magazine.

"That's Margaret." Sue Lee nodded toward me as she crossed the room to where a phonograph sat on a table. "We're going to play my Shirley Temple record."

Ginger barely gave me a glance. She hopped off the bed and started toward Sue Lee, her arms spread wide. "Come here, little button, and give me a hug."

I felt a hard squeeze in my chest. Why were some little sisters lovingly called little buttons while others were only referred to as brats?

* * *

The last day of February was sunny but bitterly cold. I finished my homework, took one of Uncle Ira's art books from the library shelf, and turned to the picture of a naked woman lying on a couch. I copied the picture into my notebook, sketching it as best I could. Then I tore my drawing to bits and dropped them into the wastebasket.

45

I left the library, looking for something to do. Passing the music room, I noticed how sunlight shining through a cut-glass vase had created rainbows on top of the piano. I went to the piano and tilted the vase. Rainbows appeared on a table. I tilted the vase farther. It slipped from my fingers and crashed to the floor. Before my heart resumed beating, Nellie stood at the door.

"Uh, uh, uh! You done fixed yourself now, missy." She left and returned with a dustpan and broom. "What Miss May Belle going to say about this?"

Later, on our ride home, Papa said, "You're so quiet. Do you feel all right?"

"I'm just tired." I leaned my head back on the seat to look more convincing.

After supper, I went to my room and lay on the bed. Maggie came back and put her hand on my forehead. "You don't feel feverish. Still, you may be coming down with something. Rest now; I'll be back shortly to see how you are."

The telephone rang and my blood froze.

"Please, God," I prayed, "give me the lockjaw or a ruptured appendix. Please, let me get sick right away!"

Papa appeared at the door. Pointing to a spot on the floor, he said, "Get up. Stand there. Look me straight in the eye."

I crawled off the bed; my legs felt like mush. "I didn't mean to," I said. "It was sitting crooked on the piano. I was trying to straighten it, and it slipped—"

"You shouldn't have touched the vase. And you certainly should have told me before May Belle called."

"I'm going to pay for it. I have two dollars and . . ."

My chest began heaving; I gasped a few times like a fish. I was trying to say I was sorry.

Papa's face softened. "Come here," he said.

I stepped forward and he put his hands on my shoulders. "Oh, little Margaret, what a pickle you're in."

The next morning, neither of us spoke as we rode into town. Two blocks from the school, he said, "It appears the broken vase incident has reached some sort of resolution. Maggie has offered to replace May Belle's vase with her pitcher."

Maggie's cut-glass pitcher was one of the few possessions she had brought with her from Savannah when she moved to our house after my mother died. It was larger and far prettier than Aunt May Belle's vase.

"What did Aunt May Belle say?"

"She accepted the offer."

The next morning I waited until Papa had stopped the car in front of the school. Then I said, "She shouldn't do it."

"Yes, I know and it troubles me. But Maggie has a heart of gold and she wants—"

"No, Papa. Aunt May Belle. She shouldn't take Maggie's vase. It's wrong of her to."

Papa narrowed his eyes and said, "Hmm."

That Friday afternoon he withdrew me from Smithson. At first, I felt relieved. No more long afternoons by myself. No more annoying Nellie or upsetting Aunt May Belle. But by Saturday night, I felt anxious. I got out of bed and went to Maggie's room. She was buffing her shoes for church the next morning.

"Maggie, can I sleep with you?"

"Of course, child, if you like."

She stopped buffing and studied my face. "You're worried about changing schools?"

"I don't want to go to Slocum."

"Your papa believes it's for the best. And with Sam picking you up after school instead of having to wait for your papa, you'll have more time at home."

I slid into Maggie's bed and watched her put away the shoe polish and rag. She got in beside me.

"Change brings new opportunities," she said and switched off the lamp.

* * *

A baby doll in a white gown lay on top of Aunt May Belle's piano. I picked it up, wanting to cuddle it, but it slipped through my hands to the floor where it shattered. I started to cry.

"There, there, child," Maggie was saying. "It's all right."

I opened my eyes. She was sitting up in the bed, her hand on my shoulder. "You were just having a bad dream," she said.

She smoothed down the covers and kissed my cheek. "Who is Alicia Patricia?"

CHAPTER 7

"I wouldn't go to that Slocum school for no amount of money in this world," Lily May said.

It was an unusually warm day for early March, and we were sitting on the carriage steps behind the house, finishing the lemon meringue pie left from Sunday dinner. I'd divided the pie into two slightly unequal pieces and given her the smaller one, which was only fair since at dinner, Louisa's slice had been larger than mine.

"Whoever divides, the other gets first choice," Lily May quickly reminded me, but not quickly enough to keep me from licking the amber beads off the top of my meringue.

She wrinkled her nose. "You worse than a hog."

I ignored the remark. "Why wouldn't you go to Slocum?"

"Bad things go on there."

"You don't know."

"How come I don't? Don't my cousin Guy Nell work for a lady what's best friend teach there? Weren't my Uncle Jasper janitor there for two years? I know last week one of them Pirkle boys sneak a six-foot rattler in his teacher's desk and liked to give her a heart attack."

"That's not true and you know it." I shifted uncomfortably.

"Huh, you ask Guy Nell if a boy didn't bring a snake in that school. It bit three children 'fore they got it killed. Seem like to me she say they all be in fourth grade."

"I don't believe that. It would've been in the newspaper if it'd happened."

"Don't everything be in the newspaper. Weren't in no newspaper when them big boys hung the substitute teacher

49

out the window by her heels."

"Lily May, you know it's a sin to lie, and it's a double sin to lie on Sunday. You better quit before the devil snatches you up."

"And I reckon you don't believe about that crazy boy what tried to burn down the school."

I did believe that. I'd heard the story from both Ida and Maggie. A family nobody knew had moved into a shack not far from the farm of Odell and Hazel, Lily May's grandparents. One day, the truant officer picked up the boy and brought him to school. During recess while everyone was outside, he sneaked back to the classroom and started a fire in the wastebasket. It had spread to papers on the teacher's desk before the janitor got it put out. In the meantime, the boy had disappeared, and the next day when police went looking for his family, they had disappeared, too.

"Well, that happened long ago before I was even old enough to be going to school."

Lily May had finished her pie and was eyeing mine. I'd eaten off the meringue and was about to start on the custard.

"You didn't get no spit on that part," she said, rubbing her finger over some filling.

I broke off what she had touched and gave it to her. Maybe that would keep her from telling more lies about Slocum. I was already uneasy about the children who went there. Some of them hung around Stumpy's Store where Papa bought gas, and they didn't act friendly.

"When you does get to that school," Lily May said, licking my custard off her fingers, "don't make nobody mad 'cause if you does, they'll get you. And if they don't get you at school, they sneak around here at night and then get you."

I didn't respond to her warning, but I did promise myself to be extra careful.

* * *

"Time to get up." Maggie switched on the light in my room.

I rolled onto my stomach.

"Don't go back to sleep, child. You don't want your papa having to wait on you. Remember, he has to register you before he goes on to work."

Now I was awake. Awake and aware of a potential pain in my stomach.

"Ooh, I feel awful!" I turned my face so Maggie could see my distress. "I think I'm going to throw up."

"You'll feel better once you've had breakfast." She turned toward the door. "Wait, I'll be right back."

While she was gone, I stuck my finger down my throat, trying to make myself vomit. But nothing came up. She returned with the dress she'd just finished making, lavender with a full skirt that stood out when I twirled.

"Why don't you wear this your first day? You look so pretty in it."

Sighing, I got out of bed.

Maggie had fixed pancakes the way I liked best, extra flat with lacy, crisp edges. I ate six, slathered with butter and soaked in Georgia cane syrup.

Papa came in with his briefcase. "Ready, Margaret?"

"Please Papa, can Maggie come, too?"

"No sense in that. I'd have to drive her back home."

I turned pleading eyes on my aunt, but she shook her head. I put on my coat and picked up my book satchel.

On my way out the door, Maggie pressed two nickels into my hand. "Lunch money," she said. "The extra nickel is for a treat."

I slipped the coins into my pocket and walked out the door, not bothering to thank her.

Slocum Elementary was a one-story brick building at the corner of Flowering Peach Road and Highway 25, where the backwash of the city ended and the farming community began. On one side of the school were modest frame houses set on a latticework of gray, dusty roads. On the other side, across Flowering Peach Road, was Robert's Gas and Grocery where children bought cookies and candy for lunch. Directly across Highway 25 was Kenyan County Home for Men, a cluster of mustard-colored buildings set in a grove of hackberry trees.

Papa turned onto the dirt drive in front of the school and drove up to the entrance. The pancakes shifted uncomfortably inside my stomach.

"I'm not feeling so good," I said.

"You're fine," Papa proclaimed, getting out of the car.

Reluctantly, I followed him up the three concrete steps to the entrance. He was about to open the door when a narrow man whose stomach stuck out like a cushion burst through it.

"Langley Hudson, sir!" he boomed, grabbing Papa's hand and pumping it up and down. "Been looking forward to meeting you since our phone conversation on Friday."

Then he smiled down at me, exposing front teeth that would have felt at home in a beaver's mouth. "I can assure you, sir, we'll take good care of this fine little lady here."

He led us to his office and invited us to make ourselves comfortable in two straight-back chairs while he jotted down information about me.

When he finished, he said, "Granted, some of our youngsters may not have the advantages those in the other school have, but they're mighty fine all the same. And our teachers? Top notch, sir, top notch. Little Miss Margaret will learn a whole lot at old Slocum."

He stood up. "And now, if this young lady will come with me, I'll show her to her class."

Outside the office, Papa shook Mr. Hudson's hand, patted my shoulder, and left.

As I walked down the hall beside the principal, I noticed the open transoms over the classroom doors, emitted various levels of racket.

"Your teacher is Miss Sewell," he said, stopping under the transom with the loudest noise. "And a finer one you'll never have. Completely dedicated to her profession."

"Clive Pinkard, get yourself out of that window!" a woman's voice shrieked through the transom.

Mr. Hudson flung open the door, and a resounding hush fell over the room. With a wave of the hand, he ushered me in. All eyes were upon us. All eyes, that is, except those belonging to the boy standing on a chair in the back of the room. His legs and rear end were inside; the rest of him hung outside the window. I watched as his top half reentered.

"I was just calling howdy to Grandpa over yonder—"

"Sit down, boy!" roared Mr. Hudson.

Clive Pinkard bolted to his seat like a rabbit trying to outrun buckshot.

Mr. Hudson turned his beaver smile on Miss Sewell. "We've brought you a new pupil: Margaret Norman. She's transferring from Smithson up yonder on Fredericks Hill. I told her daddy she can get as fine an education here at Slocum as anywhere in the state."

Miss Sewell, a slender young woman with wavy, bobbed hair and straight, black-penciled eyebrows, offered me a strained smile. "We're so glad to have you," she said. "Let's see now, where we can put you?" She looked over the room. "I believe you can sit there in the desk near the window. Jimmy, you go back and sit behind Clive."

"Huh uh, I ain't gonna—" Jimmy, a skinny boy with meanness written all over his face, stopped when he cut his eyes over to Mr. Hudson. With no further protest, he slouched to the back of the room.

I sat in the vacated desk, its top covered with drawings of monsters and body parts generally thought of as private, and attempted to slide my satchel inside. But it wouldn't slide. The desk was too full of trash. I put the satchel on the floor at my feet.

"Now, I know y'all will make this young lady feel right at home," Mr. Hudson said, his eyes roaming over the class. And after one more beaver smile at Miss Sewell, he was gone.

Mr. Hudson was right about one thing that day: I did learn a lot at old Slocum. By the end of first recess, I'd learned that Clive Pinkard's grandpa lived at the county home across the highway and that every day in one way or another Clive communicated with him. I'd learned that the father of Jimmy Bunger, the boy whose seat I had taken, was serving time on the chain gang for knocking out a man's eye, and that it was best not to mess with a Bunger because he always got even. I'd learned that Lester Timmons, the runty boy across the aisle from me, had dipped snuff since he was four and that if you aggravated him, he'd spit tobacco juice on you. These things and more I'd learned from the girl who sat directly behind me, Pearl Hubert Norton.

Pearl Hubert smelled like a mattress that had been wet many times. Her hair and her skin were the color of dust. At second recess, she showed me how to get the most for my nickel at Robert's Grocery and Gas. And since she had lost her own nickel on the school bus and I had two nickels,

I bought her lunch. It was the least I could do.

Pearl Hubert kept folks in their place. "I don't take guff off nobody and don't let none of my friends take it neither," she said. She proved it coming in from recess when a girl, nodding toward me, said, "Don't she dress funny!" Pearl Hubert shoved her into the wall. During arithmetic when a boy asked, "Teacher, what's that rag the new girl got on her head?" referring to the ribbon Maggie had tied in my hair, Pearl Hubert shot back, "Shut your mouth 'fore I slap your head off!"

The boy did shut his mouth, and I was grateful. But as I glanced around the room, I saw that I was the only girl wearing a ribbon. I wish Maggie had known that fourth grade girls were too old for such things.

After recess, Miss Sewell assigned the class a story to read silently. The room was hot—and quiet, for once. I finished the story and looked at the teacher. She sat at her desk, grading papers. I looked around. Not one person was reading. Most had their heads on their desks. Across the aisle, Lester Timmons snored softly, mouth open, brown saliva drooling onto a page in his book.

Something stroked the back of my head, and I turned. Pearl Hubert held up a purple comb, the inner sides of its teeth coated gray.

"Want me to comb your hair?" she whispered.

"That would feel good," I whispered back.

It did feel good. So relaxing. The next day after recess and every day from then on, she combed my hair while the class slept.

By the end of the second week, I had head lice.

CHAPTER 8

Lily May discovered the lice. We were in the back yard, playing hopscotch, and I was taking my own sweet time aiming the rock at the spot where it needed to land. Lily May kept bumping me, trying to make me miss my throw.

Suddenly, she leaned forward and scrunched up her eyes. "What's that thing on your neck?"

"Hush, and quit bothering me."

She leaned closer, then jumped back. "Girl, you got cooties!"

"You crazy as you look."

"Naw, I ain't. You got 'em. Now you gonna get your head shaved and go around bald for a year."

I narrowed my eyes and gave her my most hateful stare. She nodded imperiously. I threw down my rock and stormed off to the house.

"I'm not playing with you anymore!" I yelled over my shoulder.

By the time I'd reached my bedroom, a spot on my head itched like crazy. I clawed at it with my fingers, and after a moment, it felt fine. I took the kaleidoscope down from my bookcase and sat on the edge of the bed. Turning toward the light from the window, I looked through the scope at a six-pointed star. When I twisted it, the star bloomed into a flower with blue, red, yellow, and green petals. I didn't have cooties; it was Lily May's talk that had caused all the ruckus. I returned the kaleidoscope to the bookcase and went to Maggie's room. She was sitting in her rocker near the window, looking through her Walthourville book.

"Can I look with you?" I asked.

"Of course, child."

I pulled the footstool over and sat down.

The Walthourville book had a brown leather cover tooled in a floral design and coarse, gray pages joined together with a ribbon. On the first page was written:

The Deserted Village
Walthourville, Georgia
1829–1909

According to Maggie, an itinerant photographer had gone through her village, taking pictures of houses, both occupied and deserted. He glued them into books, pairing a house where a family still lived with one that was abandoned. Beneath the pictures he pasted typewritten messages: "Where once reigned gaiety and merry laughter— is now still as a grave." "Where great men were born and reared—is now the home of snakes and insects."

Pointing to a sepia photograph of a dilapidated house in a yard of tall weeds, I read, "'—has nothing to offer but sad associations and loneliness.' This was your home, wasn't it, Maggie?"

"Yes, but we had moved to Savannah years earlier." She turned to the next page with a picture of a well-kept country home.

"And this was where you would have lived if you'd married your sweetheart."

I knew the story by heart. Maggie and Benjamin Cay planned to share the house with his widowed mother, but a week before their wedding, he died of a ruptured appendix. I'd seen his grave in the Walthourville Cemetery the summer Papa, Maggie, and I rode out from Savannah where we'd been visiting a cousin. While Papa and Maggie pulled weeds from the family plot, I had wandered about, reading tombstones. When I found one with Benjamin

Cay's name on it, I ran back to tell Maggie. "And there's a vacant place right next to it," I said. "Is that where you want to be buried?"

"Wherever my body is laid, there will I rest content. But my heart lies forever with Benjamin." Maggie's words sounded like poetry.

A spot on the top of my head started itching, and I scratched it while Maggie put her Walthourville book back in the dresser.

When she returned to her rocker, I asked, "What does a person do if they have cooties?"

"Get rid of them, naturally. Why do you ask?"

"Oh, just somebody said you have to shave your head if you've got them."

"That's the surest and quickest way to be rid of head lice and nits, and it's fine for a boy. But for a girl, I'd use a different treatment."

"What are nits?"

"The little eggs glued to the strands of hair."

Now a place near my ear itched. I brushed it hard with my hand. "What if you leave everything alone?"

"Margaret, let me look at your head."

I knew she'd say that. I put my head in her lap, and she passed her fingers through my hair.

"Oh, Aunt Jemima! Your hair's full of them!"

I lifted my head, raking my fingernails across the itch near my ear. "What will you do?"

"Comb your hair every day with a fine-tooth comb to catch the lice and dip them in alcohol. Snip off any hair with nits attached. Wipe alcohol on your hair to kill nits that I missed."

"You won't tell Louisa, will you? She said she knew a girl who was nasty enough to hold a cootie convention. If she found out about me, she'd want Papa to move me down to the barn."

"I'll treat you before Louisa comes home from school. She won't have to know. Where do you think you picked up the lice?"

"This girl at school, I suppose. She combs my hair every day with her comb."

"Don't let her do it again. And stay away from her if you can. Head lice can travel." Maggie got up and walked to the fireplace where she shook out her skirt and brushed off her hands.

The next day after second recess—and before Pearl Hubert could take out her comb—I passed her a note: "I guess you better not comb my hair. It gives me a headache." I waited a moment and then turned around. Her eyes were glued to her book.

After dismissal bell rang, I said, "Pearl Hubert, I wish you could keep combing my hair. It's just these headaches I get."

She got up from her desk and started toward the door. I hurried after her. "I've got fifteen cents I'm going to bring tomorrow for lunch. Will you help me decide what to buy at the store?"

She paused. "Yeah, I reckon," she said.

* * *

I could keep Pearl Hubert from combing my hair, but I could not stay away from her. She was the only friend I had at school. Certain fourth graders were outcasts. Lester Timmons, the snuff-dipping runt, was one. Jimmy Bunger, whose daddy worked on the chain gang, was another— although Jimmy was more feared than shunned; he liked bloodying noses. Pearl Hubert Norton was an outcast. She was called Pick-Her-Nose because of her initials and her disagreeable habit. I was an outcast because I was different. I never wore dresses made from chicken feed sacks or said things like "Me and her ain't got no paper," or "Hit don't make no never mind." Also, I didn't catch on to the dirty jokes people told, and they thought I was stupid.

But I knew dirty jokes, too. One day at recess, Pearl Hubert and I were standing near Laverne Pruitt and Doris Wilkins at the water fountain, a raised rectangular pipe with holes spurting water.

"Pearl Hubert," I said loudly, "have you read that new book, *The Golden Stream*, by I. P. Freely?"

Doris and Laverne looked over and giggled.

Pointing to a stream arching up from the fountain, Laverne asked, "Did that gold stream look like this here?"

The four of us shrieked.

I motioned Laverne and Doris to come closer, and they did, although they left space between themselves and Pearl Hubert.

"Now, this one is really, really bad," I said in a low voice. "Have you—"

"What's going on?" bellowed Lola Jean Thrasher.

Lola Jean was eleven and the biggest, meanest girl in fourth grade. She had two broken front teeth, which, according to Pearl Hubert, happened the time her momma whopped her in the mouth with a chunk of coal.

Laverne, Doris, and I took a step back. Pearl Hubert took a step forward. "Ain't nothin' to you!" she snarled up into Lola Jean's face.

"It sure ain't if you're in on it," Lola Jean said.

She turned as though to walk off. But as soon as I leaned over to drink from the fountain, she whirled back and flipped up my skirt. Pearl Hubert grabbed for her hair but missed, and Lola Jean ran off screaming, "Y'all see that! That girl got lace on her pants!"

The next day in class while Pearl Hubert was excused to go to the restroom, Clive Pinkard, who had moved himself up to Lester Timmons's seat while Lester was out with measles, whispered to me, "Hey, fancy pants, how come you got lace on your drawers?"

I ignored him and went on labeling the New England states on my ditto sheet.

Clive leaned out farther. "Answer me, Frilly Bottom, what makes you—"

"Clive!" Miss Sewell said sharply. "One more word out of you and you'll go to the office."

Clive poked his lip out. "I ain't done nothin'," he said and started scratching heavy lines all over his map.

I finished my work and put my head on my desk. It hurt when people made fun of me. Could they tell I was not a good person? That I had done something terribly wrong?

I had tried hard to forget about the baby, but I didn't succeed. Once, I'd gone back to the place where she was buried. The pine sapling had straightened itself, and the wind and the rain had flattened the mound. There was a tangle of dead jessamine vines near the base of a scrub oak, and I picked it up, thinking it might be what was left of the wreath I had placed on Alicia Patricia's grave. Sitting down with the dead vines, I had started to cry. I couldn't even make a proper grave marker for my little girl.

* * *

The summer between fourth and fifth grades was a wet one, which meant that Lily May and I had to spend a lot of time in the house. We played games—Monopoly, Rook, checkers (both Chinese and regular). Lily May, being a year older than I, presumed she knew all the rules. She did not, and we squabbled a lot. I was glad when school started again.

On the first day of fifth grade when Miss Howard assigned seats to our class, Pearl Hubert and I ended up on opposite sides of the room. But she still looked out for me when I needed help—although by then most classmates had stopped teasing me. And some even were friendly.

But not Lola Jean Thrasher. She still picked on me whenever she could. On the night of the March P.T.A. meeting, while fifth graders waited outside the school auditorium after presenting a program of songs about springtime, she stepped over to me.

"Hey, Pantylace, that old woman you came with?" (She was referring to Maggie, who sat in the auditorium with Papa.) "That shriveled old woman, she your pretend momma? No wonder you act so peculiar."

Something inside me exploded, and I started to swell, my fingers drawing up into claws. I'd rake the skin off that ugly face.

But as quickly as my rage flared up, it burned out. What good would it do to fight Lola Jean? It would only hurt Maggie. Pearl Hubert, who had overheard Lola Jean, lunged toward her, growling, "I'm gonna snatch that nasty head bald!"

I put my hand on her arm. "Don't do that, Pearl Hubert. Leave her alone. She doesn't know any better."

Pearl Hubert Norton, true friend and protector. I was deeply indebted to her. Yet by the end of the school year, I'd betrayed her.

It happened on Monday during the last week of school. She and I were sitting under a privet during second recess, finishing the cinnamon rolls I'd bought for our lunch when Laverne Pruitt and Doris Wilkins walked up.

"Margaret, you want to play dodge ball?" Laverne

asked.

I jumped up. "Yeah, I sure do!"

I glanced down. "Can Pearl—"

"I don't want to play," Pearl Hubert interrupted.

"That's 'cause she knows we won't let her," Doris said.

Pearl Hubert stood up and brushed the crumbs off her skirt. "I got better things to do with my time than get knocked around by a ball."

She started toward the water fountain. But before she had gone very far, she turned and gave me a look, proud and yet pleading. I knew what I should do: tell Laverne and Doris that if Pearl Hubert couldn't play, I wouldn't play. But it was the first time other girls had asked me to join them. I did so want to have friends. And I did so love to play dodge ball.

Doris tugged at my sleeve. "Come on, we've got to get started."

"Okay," I said and ran off with her and Laverne.

I felt bad all day for deserting my friend. The next day I brought a slice of pound cake wrapped in waxed paper to school. At first recess, I went up to Pearl Hubert and said, "My aunt made this pound cake, and I thought you might like some." I held out the cake.

She glanced at it and then looked away. "I don't like cake," she said.

I moved closer. "Pearl Hubert, I hope you'll still be my friend. You've always been so nice to me and all."

She hesitated a moment. Then she smiled sweetly, and, without saying a word, walked away.

I took the cake home and put it back into the cake box. I couldn't eat it.

CHAPTER 9

"I's bored," Lily May said. It was only the second week of summer vacation after I finished fifth grade and she finished sixth grade at her school. We were sitting on the steps outside her door, watching a hen in the yard scratch up bugs for its biddies.

"What do you want to do?" I asked.

"Something what's fun. And I don't mean no tree-climbing or Rook."

"We could hunt drink bottles on Cardinal Hill Road, and next time we're at Stumpy's, trade them in for candy and stuff."

"Ain't no bottles on our part of Cardinal Hill Road. Folks with drinks done finished them off long before they gets to the top of the hill."

"Then let's ask Maggie and Ida if we can hunt bottles on the path down to Stumpy's."

Lily May stood up and stretched out her long, skinny arms. "Why we be worrying the grown folks? Don't we know our way down that path?"

By the road, Stumpy's Store was two miles from our house; Lily May and I often rode down it with Papa. By the path through the woods—which started across Cardinal Hill Road from our drive—the store was much closer. Lily May and I occasionally walked it with Ida.

Stumpy's Store, a long whitewashed building with two Sinclair gas pumps out front, was not clean and orderly like Robert's Grocery and Gas across from Slocum school, but it was far more interesting.

Besides groceries, Stumpy stocked pocket watches, knives, patent medicines, overalls, work shoes, hammers and nails, five flavors of chewing tobacco, and seven brands of snuff. He also had twenty-three canaries in cages that hung from the ceiling. He called them his babies and twittered to them in bird language. They twittered back. They weren't for sale.

But even more interesting than the merchandise and canaries was Stumpy himself. He was a midget who had once worked in the circus.

"What did you do in the circus?" I asked him one day when Lily May and I had ridden down to the store with my father.

"Oh, lots of things," he replied.

"Ever get shot out of a cannon?" Lily May asked.

"Never that, Lily May. Mainly, I worked with the clowns."

Papa, who was getting a Coke out of the ice chest, said, "Stumpy, why don't you show the girls your pictures?"

"Happy to oblige," Stumpy said.

We followed him to his living space, a room in the back of the store. Tacked to the walls were large photographs, yellowed and curled at the edges: Stumpy in a little convertible, smiling and waving a glove; Stumpy in a baby carriage, wearing a bonnet and being pushed by a big poodle in a nurse's cap; Stumpy in a cowboy suit, riding a miniature horse.

"But this one's my favorite." He pointed to the photograph over his bed. "That's me sitting on Emmett Kelly's lap. Emmett Kelly is the most famous clown in the world, you know. See his hand is up under my coat? He's pretending to make me talk. Then we start fussing, and I jump down and run off, Emmett chasing after me."

Stumpy began running in place, little arms swinging. Lily May and I giggled.

"That act always brought down the house," Stumpy said, "because up till then, see, the audience thought I was a dummy."

As I was leaving the room, I noticed newspaper clippings on the wall near the door. "What are these, Stumpy?" I asked.

"Stories about folks who visited my store."

"Look, that's Governor Talmadge!" I pointed to a picture of a man with dark-rimmed glasses and black hair falling over his forehead.

"Sure is," Stumpy said. "Old Gene stopped by back in '32 for a little politicking and tobacco chawing. That picture came out in the paper right soon after his visit."

I was about to move on when another picture caught my eye. The cut line read,

LOCAL ARTISTS AWARDED AT ART SHOW
Anne Louisa Norman and Tallulah Cassels were recognized for...

The rest of the line was torn off.

In the picture, my mother and another woman smiled into the camera. Mother wore a snug-fitting hat with a large flower on one side. A *red* flower, I knew. Ida used to wear that hat when she dressed up for church. Mother must have given it to her. Or maybe Papa had after Mother died.

"What you looking at?" Lily May asked.

"Just these old newspaper pictures," I said.

"Well, you better come on. Your papa ready to leave."

I followed her to the front of the store and stopped. "You go on to the car. I want to see if Stumpy will swap my grape sucker for a cherry one."

Stumpy was standing on the stool near the cash register, arranging cans of Tube Rose Snuff on a rack. As soon as the door closed behind Lily May, I said, "Stumpy, you got a picture of my mother on your wall. Can I have it?"

"That old newspaper clipping? 'Course you can."

I ran to the back of the store and returned with the clipping. "Did you know my mother?'

He nodded. "Would come in with your daddy right soon after they married. Beautiful lady. Made me think of this ballet dancer with the circus. Graceful and light.

"Now, that other lady in the picture, she was the one with your mother when they—" Stumpy coughed and touched his hand to his mouth.

"When they what?"

"It's a long story and I'm not the best one to tell it."

Lily May stuck her head through the door. "Your papa waiting."

I slipped the picture of my mother into the sack with my candy and hurried out of the store. When I got home, I put it with my other pictures, the ones of Mother and Uncle Max, of Betsy and me, and a new one I'd cut from a magazine: one of Woodrow Wilson standing alongside a girl. The girl looked a little like me. Woodrow Wilson reminded me of my father.

* * *

On our first trip down the shortcut to Stumpy's, Lily May and I found four drink bottles each, and we traded them for enough candy and bubble gum to last almost two days. On our second trip a week later, we found only three bottles between us and couldn't agree on how to spend the six cents deposit. Since I'd found two of the bottles, I had every right to insist we spend five cents on a Mounds candy bar and each take half. Lily May insisted she spend three cents on gum. The day was hot, and by the time we reached the grove of trees behind Stumpy's we were both steaming.

"All right," I said, "we'll buy the Mounds bar and you

67

can spend the leftover penny on whatever you want."

"Huh uh," Lily May said. "I ain't spending *none* of my money on mushy, melty old coconut."

"That's what you think," I muttered under my breath.

Behind the store, Hubert, who did odd jobs for Stumpy, was propped against a pile of old tires, sound asleep.

"Phew!" Lily May fanned the air in front of her nose. "That old sot smell worse than a billy goat. Reckon how come Stumpy keep him around?"

"Papa says he feels sorry for Hubert's family. If Stumpy didn't help out, they would starve."

Lily May glared at the sleeping Hubert. "Your family ain't got to starve, you stinky old white man. They could get out and chop cotton like other folks does what need money."

Hubert replied with a resonant snore.

As we rounded the corner at the front of the store, Lily May and I quickened our pace. We reached the door at the same time and both tried to push through it, causing me to skin my elbow. Now, I *knew* I wouldn't let her have three cents for gum.

Stumpy was in back on a stepladder, taking cans off a shelf.

"Be with you in a minute, girls," he called.

Lily May couldn't wait. She marched herself up to the candy counter and called back, "I wants me three cents worth of that Double Bubble Gum, please, Mr. Stumpy."

"Got a customer right now, Lily May." He nodded toward a girl standing with her back to us. She glanced around briefly and pulled her skirts tight.

The girl looked familiar, but I was too irritated with Lily May to pay much attention. I walked to the aisle farthest away where two canaries were building a nest from the twigs Stumpy had put into their cage.

"All right, young lady," I heard Stumpy say. "Reckon this fixes you up."

The girl started toward the front of the store with a sack of groceries. As she drew near me, she turned her head as though looking at the shelf with cookies and crackers. But I saw who she was—Pearl Hubert Norton.

As soon as she was out the door, Lily May cried, "Mr. Stumpy, that girl done forgot to pay for her groceries. Want me to run catch her?"

"No, it's all right." Stumpy walked to the cash register. "Her pa he works here. I'll settle with him."

"Her pa? Who he?" Lily May asked.

"Hubert Norton."

"Hubert?" I said. "That's Pearl Hubert's father?"

"One and the same," Stumpy said.

Lily May came over to where I was standing and stuck her face into mine. "So, *she* be your best friend in school!"

"She wasn't my *best* friend," I mumbled. "Just she helped me out sometimes when I first started to Slocum."

"Naw, you say she your best friend and look out for you all the time. What *I* say is you sure don't mind associating yourself with white trash. I be shamed of myself going around with dirt like that there."

She walked back to the candy counter. "Mr. Stumpy, we got us three drink bottles, and I wants all my refund in Double Bubble Gum, please."

I knew what Lily May was up to, trying to shame me into forgetting about the Mounds candy bar. I did not forget, but I did feel shame. Shame over the way I had treated a loyal friend. But even more, pity for the girl with such a poor excuse for a father.

* * *

69

Several old men lounged on the benches in front of Stumpy's Store. Occasionally, one or another sold a can of oil or a fan belt for Stumpy. If a lady customer or a stranger pulled up to the gas pump, an old man would fill up the tank. Regular customers like Papa were expected to wait on themselves.

The old men talked about crops and politics and what other old men were up to. Clyde Craddock talked about all of that and also sang songs. He sang about darling Nellie Gray who got taken away, never to be seen anymore, and about Bohunkus who died and went to heaven while his brother went to—"DELL!" When Clyde sang "DELL!" he'd cut his eyes over to me. As if I didn't know he really meant "HELL!"

Clyde urged the other old men to join in his singing, but they seldom did. Lily May and I did, though. He gave us pennies.

The next week as we were starting for home after our third trip to Stumpy's, Clyde said to us, "Come here, you young 'uns. I'm gonna learn you a new song."

We obliged him.

"Now, this here's what my pappy learnt me when he got back from fighting Damnyankees."

Clyde got up, cleared his throat like a backfiring car, and began to march up and down. To the tune of "Pop Goes the Weasel," he sang:

> *Jeff Davis rides a pretty white horse.*
> *Lincoln rides a mule.*
> *Jeff Davis is a gentleman,*
> *And Lincoln is a fool!*

On the second round, Lily May and I joined in, marching and singing. The old men started cackling and slapping their knees.

After we had gone through the song several times, Clyde batted some winks at his friends and said, "All right, you young 'uns done it real good," and he reached into his pocket for pennies.

On our way home, Lily May and I made up a dance to go with the song. It involved lots of twitching and kicking. When we arrived, we found Ida sitting on a crate under a chinaberry tree, shelling peas. We ran over to her.

"Momma, look-a-here what we can do!" Lily May said.

We performed our song and dance to perfection and ended by bumping our hips together on the word "fool!" But instead of praising our performance, Ida growled, "Who learnt you that?"

"Nobody," said Lily May. "We made it up from various sundry things what we heard."

"You didn't make that up. Who you been messing with?"

I thought Ida was mad because we'd used the word "fool," which the Bible says puts you in danger of hellfire and damnation.

"Where you two been taking yourself?"

"I've got to go to the bathroom." I said, starting toward the house. But Lily May grabbed hold of my skirt and wouldn't let go.

"You been going to Stumpy's where you ain't got no business going," Ida said. "You been picking up mess you ain't got no business picking up. President Lincoln weren't no fool. Nobody what freed the slaves a fool." She got up and took the bowl of shelled peas to the house.

After she'd gone, Lily May said, "It's all your fault. You made me go to that store."

"I sure as heck didn't! You made *me* go."

"You lying." Lily May stalked off to her house.

I went to sit on the little porch off my bedroom. I was in trouble and not exactly sure why. I hadn't meant to slur President Lincoln; when I sang, I wasn't even thinking about him.

That evening when Ida served supper, she acted as though nothing had happened. I thought my troubles were over. But afterwards, when Papa said, "Margaret, come to my study," I knew she had spoken to him.

He sat behind his desk; I stood in front of it. "You girls were foolish to go to Stumpy's without letting anyone know. Something unfortunate could have happened to you. Don't do it again. You understand?"

"Yes, sir," I said. Which was half true. I understood we weren't to go to Stumpy's again, but I did not understand what unfortunate thing could have happened to us.

Papa did not mention the song Lily May and I had sung, so I assumed Ida had not told him about it. I'd already figured out why the old men thought it was funny—Lily May, a colored girl, singing about Abraham Lincoln that way.

I went to my room, took out construction paper and crayons, and drew two pictures of a robin perched on a mimosa branch with a worm in its mouth. The next morning I gave one picture to Ida, who said she was going to pin it to the wall in her house. That evening I propped the other picture against Papa's water glass at the table.

"What's this?" he said, sitting down for supper.

"I did it for you, Papa. You can pin it up in your study, if you want to."

Across the table, Louisa rolled her eyes.

"Very nice," Papa said, laying the picture flat on the table.

He did seem pleased, but when he left the dining room later, he left the picture behind. I slipped back to get it.

Louisa, who happened to pass the door, looked in and saw me. I ripped the picture in two. She widened her eyes. I ripped it again.

"It wasn't all that good, anyway," I said, balling up the scraps in my hand.

CHAPTER 10

I didn't see Lily May for several days after the incident at Stumpy's. Then one afternoon I was sitting on the carriage steps in the back yard, threading honeysuckle blossoms onto broom straws when I looked up to see her crossing the field from her house. Moments later, she was sitting beside me, the bucket of honeysuckle blossoms between us.

"What you doing?" she asked.

"Making bookmarks for Christmas presents." I bit off the tip of a blossom, sucked out the nectar, and threaded the blossom onto a straw. "When I get the straw filled up, I'll press it under a book."

Lily May picked up a blossom and straw. "I'm going to do me a decoration," she said.

We worked a while without speaking. Then she said, "Momma sure got on me about going to Stumpy's."

"Not as bad as Papa got onto me."

"He didn't say nothing about tearing you up next time you does something bad."

"But he got mad and fussed a whole lot."

"Huh. He don't fuss at you." Lily May coaxed the straw down the throat of a blossom. "Seem like to me your papa don't stir hisself much whatever you does, good or bad."

"He most certainly does." I picked a yellowed flower out of the bucket and threw it onto the ground. The bees had already stolen the nectar. "He just stays busy with important—"

"'Course now," Lily May interrupted, "he don't know about most of the bad what you does. And the good, you don't do enough of that to make him take notice."

I reached across the bucket and pushed her with my

elbow. "Lily May, you don't know what you're talking about."

She ignored my push and went on. "Louisa the one your papa notice. Them ballet recitals. Them horse-backing ribbons."

"I could win ribbons in horse shows if I wanted to. I know how to ride."

"You don't never do it."

"I'm planning to ride before the summer is over. I'm planning to do lots of good things, you'll see."

Lily May snorted.

Sam came around the side of the house, carrying a bucket of milk. I jumped up and ran toward him. "Sam, will you teach me to milk?"

"Sure thing. Be at the barn at five in the morning."

"I believe I'll start tomorrow afternoon."

"Sure thing," Sam said.

Lily May was wrong about Papa. He got after me when I did something bad, just not when she was around. As for the good things I did, I'd just have to make sure he knew about them. Sam would teach me to milk, and one day soon we'd walk into the kitchen, Sam carrying the bucket of milk too heavy for me to lift. Papa would be there, and Sam would say, "She milked all this by herself. Didn't nobody help." Papa would be proud and amazed. I only hoped Louisa was around to see it.

* * *

Sam usually showed up at the barn around four in the afternoon. The cows and Proud Beauty showed up much earlier, and the closer it came to the hour, the more impatient they grew. Franklin, the Black Angus steer, would stretch out his neck and bawl loudly. Geraldine and

75

Trippylou, the big Guernseys, were almost as bad, but they had a reason. They needed milking. Yet during all the commotion, Cherry, the little Jersey that would drop her first calf any day now, stood to one side, quietly waiting.

Sam came from the feed room with two buckets of feed. "Got them milking hands ready?"

I held up my hands. "Ready for action!"

I opened the barn door and stepped aside quickly. Geraldine and Trippylou rushed past me to their stalls. Sam followed, poured feed into their troughs, and closed the stocks. Then he went back to tend to the other animals.

I had decided to milk Geraldine, who was better tempered than Trippylou. I wiped down her udder with a rag and clear water the way Sam always did and set the bucket and stool in position.

Sam usually leaned the side of his head against the cow's belly while he milked. I leaned my head against Geraldine. I could barely reach the teats. I pulled the stool closer, but it didn't help.

Sam came back inside. "You ain't got to go nestle on her," he said.

I straightened my back and gripped the two nearest teats. They felt warm and spongy. Gently, I squeezed them. Nothing came out.

"You got to squeeze harder than that," Sam said.

I did. Still no milk. I squeezed as hard as I could. Geraldine turned to look at me as though asking what I was up to.

"You ain't got to go pinch her," Sam said. He squatted beside me and took the teats from my hands. "Push up and draw down. Easy, like so." He nudged his fists into Geraldine's udder and pulled down on the teats. Milk pinged against the bottom of the pail.

"I see, I see! I can do it now."

Sam let go of the teats.

I did exactly as he had shown me. A few drops of milk dribbled into the pail.

"You getting the hang of it," he said and walked over to Trippylou.

I pushed up and drew down, pushed up and drew down until my hands ached. Only a few drops of milk had trickled into the pail.

Ida Claire, the barn cat, wandered in and sat down beside me. Sam always gave her a few squirts of milk. High, low, left, right—wherever he aimed, she jumped around and caught the squirts in her mouth. I aimed straight at her and squeezed. Milk dribbled onto my knee. Ida Claire got up and walked over to Sam.

Sam finished milking Trippylou and set his pail on the shelf. He opened the stock. Trippylou backed out of the stall and turned toward the door. Just as she reached me, she paused and let down her manners in soft, fuming plops. I gagged.

Sam came over. "How you doing?" he asked.

"Fine," I replied. The bottom of my pail was barely covered with milk.

"Want me to strip her out for you?"

"I guess so."

I got up from the stool. Sam took my place and grasped the teats I'd been holding. White jets hit the side of the bucket like the sound of a drum roll.

"Thanks for teaching me to milk," I said and turned toward the barn door.

"You be down in the morning?" Sam called after me. "I sure needs the help."

I kept going, not looking back. Learning to milk cows was not a good idea. My hands would get calloused like Sam's, and the barn odors couldn't be good for my lungs.

Besides, if I spent all my time milking, I couldn't practice my horseback riding. I pretended not to hear Sam.

* * *

I was down on my knees, leaning over a box of old clothes, when Lily May came into the room, eating a bacon and mayonnaise sandwich. "Now what you up to?" she garbled.

"Looking for Louisa's old riding habit. I'm riding Proud Beauty today."

"Let's play Rook."

"Don't have time. Got to practice my riding so I'll get really good."

Lily May took a bite of her sandwich, leaving a streak of mayonnaise across her cheek.

She chewed thoughtfully a moment. Then she said, "Uh *huh*."

"What?"

"I know what you up to. I sees it plain. You aiming to outdo your sister. You pitched up 'cause you think your papa prize her more than you."

"You don't know what you're talking about. I already told you I was going to practice horseback riding this summer." I hated it when Lily May acted like she knew everything going on inside my head.

"Oh yeah, oh yeah," she nodded. "You thinking about how your sister get bragged on when she bring home them horse ribbons."

I reared back on my knees. "Lily May, you got mayonnaise smeared all over your face. Why don't you go clean it off?"

Louisa's old riding habit was in the bottom of the box. I took it out and put it on. The jodhpurs wouldn't quite close at the top, but the jacket covered most of the gap.

When I arrived at the barn, I found Sam sitting on a crate, honing a scythe.

"I'm riding Proud Beauty today," I announced.

He frowned. "You remember your papa say it be all right long as you mind what he learnt you."

"I remember everything."

Sam followed me into the feed room, where I took down the bridle. He threw a few handfuls of oats into a bucket and hoisted the saddle onto his shoulder. Outside, Proud Beauty was standing in the middle of the pasture. Sam whistled and she trotted over. He fed her the oats.

"I don't mind if you help me get started," I said, handing the bridle to Sam, "but I know what all I'm supposed to do."

"Sure hopes you does." He saddled the horse and held the reins while I mounted.

"Come on, Proud Beauty, we're going for a ride." I gently nudged my heels against her sides, and she jerked forward.

A week later while I was riding around the house, Maggie stepped into the yard.

"Mercy, just look at you!" she exclaimed.

I urged Proud Beauty into a canter.

The next time around, I found Louisa, dressed for town, standing with Maggie.

"Doesn't she look splendid!" Maggie exclaimed.

Louisa snorted. "The horse or the rider? Proud Beauty looks splendid. The rider looks like Sancho Panza without windmills."

Louisa probably thought I didn't know who Sancho Panza was, but I did. I'd seen pictures of Don Quixote's fat little squire in books.

Fat little girl, that's how she still saw me. But I had grown. Maggie had to let out the hems of my skirts, and she said if I got any thinner, she'd have to take up seams in the waists. I turned Proud Beauty around and rode down to the barn, where I stayed until Louisa drove off.

Two days later, I gave up horseback riding. Proud Beauty was getting old, and along the way had picked up bad habits. She nipped at me when I put the bit in her mouth. When I mounted, she tried to kick me. Sam must have noticed and reported to Papa, for that morning as he was leaving for work, he said that I wasn't to saddle the horse unless he or Sam was around. I protested, of course, but it did me no good. This new restriction along with Louisa's unkind remarks—I didn't even want to practice riding anymore.

As I watched Papa drive away in his car, I felt tears well up in my eyes.

On one side of our drive stood an old cedar tree with low, wide-spreading branches. I climbed to the top and straddled a branch. If I treated Proud Beauty the way Louisa did—yelling at her, slapping her with the crop—she'd behave for me, too. But I couldn't be mean; I didn't even carry a crop. I leaned my back against the tree trunk and stared out at the sky. An ant crawled onto my hand. I carefully brushed it back onto the branch.

A thought popped into my head. There was one thing I did better than Louisa could ever hope to do. I climbed down the tree.

* * *

"Papa, will you buy me some paint and art paper?"

He looked up from the work on his desk. "So, you'd like to paint, would you?"

"Yes, like my mother."

A light went on in his eyes. "Ah, yes, Anne Louisa,

such a fine artist. Those sketches of Ida in the hall, she did them soon after Ida came to Cardinal Hill. The one with Ida hanging out laundry, the wind billowing her skirt, is especially beautiful. That oil of Max in the parlor. Did you know it took first prize in an art show?"

"No, sir."

"And there's this one." He swiveled his chair around to look at the landscape hanging on the wall behind him. It was of trees twisting in the wind with a vast, stormy sky above them. "A present to me the first Christmas after we married."

He studied the painting a moment, then turned to me. "You know, daughter, you just may have inherited your mother's considerable talent. Perhaps you'd like to take art lessons someday?"

"Oh, Papa, I would! I most certainly would!"

It was later that doubts settled in. I would never be able to paint as well as my mother. It was foolish even to think it.

But Papa had said I might have talent. I—not Louisa—may have inherited my mother's gift. He said he'd let me take art lessons, and, oh, how proud I would make him.

A few days later, he brought home watercolors and brushes and art paper, and the next day I painted three pictures: two ripe tomatoes, a hen with her biddies, and a rabbit nibbling huckleberries off a low bush. The rabbit picture was my best, and I put it on Papa's desk. That evening after supper he brought it to the parlor.

"Good work, Margaret," he said, holding up my picture. "Very creative."

I felt warm all over.

After he'd left for work the next day, I went to his study and saw my picture propped on his bookcase.

Mother's picture over his desk, mine on his bookcase—he would see them both every day.

I worked hard on my pictures, always showing the best ones to Papa, but he never said anything more about art lessons. One Saturday morning, I followed him out to the car.

"Papa, it's been over a month since you said I could start taking art lessons."

"Did I say you'd start right away?" He opened the car door and got in.

"But I have lots of spare time this summer."

"I haven't located a teacher yet. And there's also the matter of your transportation."

"Sam could drive me in Mother's car."

"I'll think about it." He reached for the door handle. "Stand aside, Margaret. Right now I've got to buy hinges so Sam can repair the barn door."

After he left, I crossed the yard to look at the sunflower I had planted that spring. A worm had eaten away half its leaves. Only the puniest bud was on top.

Maggie called from the porch, "Sister, come in out of the sun. Ida has made lemonade. We'll have a glass in my room."

The drink was cold and sweet, but I drank only half before setting the glass on the table.

"Is something wrong, child?" Maggie asked.

"Louisa gets to do whatever she wants. She gets to ride Proud Beauty in horse shows. She gets to take dance lessons. She told Mimi Fuller she's going to be a debutante next year."

"And what do you want?"

"I want to take art lessons. Papa said he'd let me. But he hasn't and the summer's almost over. He's probably decided I don't have enough talent to waste money on."

"Now, you know that's not so." Maggie sounded impatient. "You paint very well. And if your father promised lessons, he'll keep his word."

"He didn't keep his word about giving me ballet lessons. He said he'd look into it, but he never did."

"Did you remind him?"

"Yeah. Once.

"Sometimes your father forgets."

"He didn't forget to give Louisa dance lessons. He knew I wanted them, too."

"Margaret, your father tries to be fair. He tries to do right by both of you girls."

I picked up my lemonade glass and took it to the kitchen. I wanted to believe Maggie was right, but deep down, I wasn't so sure.

CHAPTER 11

While I spent my summer being frustrated, Louisa spent hers having the time of her life. In the fall, she would enter Converse College near Spartanburg, South Carolina, and every other day she drove into town to buy things for school. Once when she was about to leave, I offered to go with her. "I could carry your packages and—"

"Never mind. I'm in a hurry to meet Mimi for lunch." She pushed past me on the porch, almost colliding with Ida who was coming in with a basket of laundry.

Ida paused to watch Louisa rush to the car and speed off. She chuckled, "Second Louisa drive just like the first."

"Yeah, and she'll have Mother's car all worn out before it's my turn to drive," I said.

"Oh, I 'spect Mr. Jim have something for you."

"I doubt it." My lower lip quivered.

When Louisa wasn't shopping in town, she was attending parties for Betsy and other Fredericksboro girls who would make their debuts later that year. A newspaper article reported the opening party: "The debutante season got off to a dazzling start when more than one hundred guests assembled in the rose gardens of the John L. and Beverly Burton's handsome estate on Sand Dust Road." Above the story was a picture of debutantes seated at a picnic table, and behind them, mouth open, stood Louisa. That afternoon, I showed her the picture.

"Horrors!" She grabbed the newspaper out of my hand. "That stupid photographer deliberately waited till I was about to bite into a sandwich."

She tore out the page, crumpled it, and threw it into the wastebasket, even though neither Maggie nor Papa had read the paper.

After she left the room, I fished out the page and cut out the picture. I started to put it into the box with my other family pictures, then changed my mind and slipped it into the dresser drawer with my underwear.

Louisa planned to have a luncheon for Betsy at the Forest Lake Country Club and invite twelve guests. Then she raised the number to twenty. I was outside Papa's study when she told him about the change.

"Look, Louisa," Papa said, "if you want more people, you can let them come here. Ida serves a better meal than any of those at the club."

"Oh, Papa, nobody wants to drive out to the sticks. I'd be embarrassed to ask them."

"But you're talking about nearly doubling the cost of this thing. You're forgetting that sending you off to college is expensive. I'm not a rich man."

"But I don't see how I can leave a single name off the list. See for yourself. I'm inviting only the people I have to invite." There was a pause; I moved closer to the door.

"What about this name, Sue Lee Wright?" Papa asked. "Wasn't she Margaret's little friend at Smithson school?"

"I don't remember. Maybe she was. Her sister, Ginger, is president of the debutante club. Sue Lee has already been to several parties. Some people have to be invited because of their connections."

"Then what about Margaret? She has connections. And I don't see Maggie's name on your list."

"Since they wouldn't know anybody there, except Betsy and Aunt May Belle—oh, all right, I suppose I could leave off Sue Lee and let Maggie come."

"And Margaret?"

"Heavens, Papa, she'd embarrass me to death! She has such terrible table manners."

What a lie! It was all I could do to keep from bursting

into the study.

"I hadn't noticed," Papa said blandly.

"She burps at the table."

Well, maybe I did, occasionally, silently. Louisa did something far worse. She didn't close her eyes during grace. Time and again when my eyes happened to open a second, I'd see her looking around. Once she even pinched off some roast beef and ate it while Papa was praying.

"You have to invite your sister," Papa said.

"Umm, I suppose I could leave off Mrs. Bilney, although I hate to. She gave such a nice tea for Betsy and would probably do the same for me when I come out next year."

"When *you* come out? This is the first I've heard about that. I tell you, Louisa, I don't go along with all this high society business. There are more important ways to spend one's time and money."

"But, Papa, I have to come out. Aunt May Belle's staying on the cotillion board another year just to make sure I get an invitation to the debutante club."

"We'll talk about this later," Papa said.

I slipped down the hall and out the front door.

I didn't even want to go to Louisa's old luncheon. And, as it turned out, I couldn't have anyway. Two days before the event, I sprained my ankle when I fell out of a chinaberry tree while trying to peek inside a robin's nest. Sue Lee Wright went in my place. That must have pleased Louisa immensely.

* * *

The first week of September, I entered sixth grade at Slocum. The third week, Louisa left for her first year at Converse, although she came home most weekends to attend debutante parties.

Near the end of November, Papa took his tuxedo from the closet, and Ida hung it outside to air. After she'd brought it back in and pressed it, he tried it on. Maggie and I were in the hall when he came out to view himself in the full-length mirror.

"It's tight around the middle." He pulled at the waistband.

"I can easily let out a seam," Maggie said.

"Thank you, Maggie." He ran his fingers through his gray hair. "I wish you could as easily remedy this. The last time I wore this suit, my hair matched its color."

"But gray is becoming, Papa," I said. "You look like Woodrow Wilson."

"How tactful of you." He smiled slightly. "I feel better now."

Maggie had made both my gown and hers and would have made Louisa's gown, too. But Louisa insisted that only Miss Moats, the most expensive dressmaker in Fredericksboro, be entrusted with that sacred task.

Maggie's gown was of navy crepe with a white lace jabot cascading down from the neck. She planned to wear her gold breast pin with it and afterwards shorten the skirt so she could wear it to church. My gown was of Christmas green taffeta with a full skirt, a tight-fitted waist, and a wide boat neckline. It, plus the crinoline petticoat, took a whole week to sew up.

The first time I put the gown and petticoat on and looked in the mirror, I squealed and hugged Maggie so tightly that she nearly fell over.

"Mercy, child, I'm glad you like it so much."

It *was* a beautiful dress. But what had excited me so— and what I couldn't dare tell Maggie—was the boat neckline. It puffed out so far in front that anyone who saw me would think I had a bosom!

On the morning of the cotillion, I washed my hair and rinsed it with lemon juice to make it shiny and soft. Maggie rolled it on rag strips, the way her mother had rolled her hair when she was a girl, and I went around all day with these little white corkscrews poking up from my head. Lily May said I looked like a tomato worm with those white seed-like things sticking out of its back.

Louisa stayed in her room the whole day, coming out only for lunch and later to drive into town to pick up her gown. When she arrived home with a white dress box under one arm, I was waiting near the back door.

"Let me see it!" I said, following her down the hall.

She hesitated, then said, "I don't have time," and rushed into her room, closing the door. I crossed the hall to the parlor. If she came out, I'd slip in for a quick peek at her dress. But she didn't come out, not even for the sandwiches Maggie made to hold us till the late dinner at the cotillion.

An hour before time to leave, Maggie helped me into my petticoat and gown. She took the rag strips from my hair and brushed out the curls. Then she pulled my hair back on top and tied it with a red ribbon, trailing streamers.

Taffeta swishing, I walked to the hall to stand in front of the mirror. My breath caught in my throat. Plain Margaret Norman existed no longer. In her place stood Scarlett O'Hara...Cinderella...Princess Elizabeth...

Papa paused on the way to his room. "What a vision of delight!" he exclaimed.

My feet rose from the floor, and I floated on air.

When it was time to leave for the club, Louisa was still in her room. Papa called twice, then he and Maggie went out to the car. I waited outside her door. Papa tooted the horn and she finally emerged, a curious look on her face. Her black velvet evening coat was buttoned up to her neck and hid every inch of her gown.

"Why are you standing there?" She rushed past, wafting the fragrance of hyacinths. "You're making us late."

CHAPTER 12

"Everyone in the world must be here tonight!" Louisa stared out the window at the cars lining both sides of the street in front of the Fredericksboro Country Club.

"There's a crowd all right," Papa said.

He turned his car in at the gate and pulled up under the canopy of the main entrance, where a doorman in a black uniform with gold epaulets opened his door. On the other side of the car, a white-coated attendant assisted Maggie out, then Louisa. I waited for my door to be opened. When it wasn't, I reached for the handle. But before I could turn it, the attendant sprang into the front seat and started to drive off.

"Wait! Wait!" I cried.

The attendant jerked his head around, eyes wide, whites shining. "Lord-a-mercy!" he exclaimed, slamming on the brakes.

He hopped from the car and opened my door with a flourish. "Sorry, ma'am!" he said, grinning so broadly that my consternation immediately melted.

As soon as we entered the foyer, Louisa said, "Something's wrong with my placket," and turned in the direction of the ladies' room.

Papa, Maggie, and I checked our coats and continued down the hall.

As we stepped into the ballroom, I gasped. Never had I seen it look as it did on this night. The theme for the evening was "Moonlight in a Winter Garden," and the room had been transformed. Holly laden with red berries banked the walls, evergreens clustered in corners, stars twinkled across the ceiling. The tables surrounding the dance floor were adorned with bowls of camellias encircled by candles. At the far end of the room near the orchestra stood a platform set about with camellia bushes in bloom. A trellis entwined with ivy stood in the center of the platform, and a full moon hung above it. My chest tightened; my eyes filled with tears. It was so magnificent, so wondrous, I could barely stand it.

The orchestra began to play "The Way You Look Tonight," and as we walked toward our table, my feet slid in time with the music. It was all I could do to keep my whole body from swaying.

I found my place card, sat down, and looked about me. Everywhere, gentlemen in handsome tuxedos and ladies in exquisite gowns were talking and laughing. All elegant and charming. All transformed by the evening.

Aunt May Belle, wearing a red gown sprinkled with sequins, arrived at our table. "Margaret, stand up. Let me look at you."

Gracefully—wavy hair caressing my shoulders, taffeta skirt billowing about me—I rose to my feet.

"How gorgeous you are!" Aunt May Belle exclaimed.

I glanced at Maggie and Papa. They were smiling at me, and from somewhere deep inside, my joy bubbled up in a laugh.

Betsy's three escorts arrived, and Aunt May Belle introduced them around. I accorded a dazzling smile to each of them. Two of the escorts, a Mercer University law student and a University of Georgia sophomore, were family friends. The third, a tall young man with wavy, blond hair, was Betsy's boyfriend, Rodney Bridgeman. He worked at Uncle Ira's furniture store.

The University of Georgia sophomore, a chubby young man with a prominent nose and insignificant chin, sat next to me, diffusing the odor of pine sap and cloves. He fooled with his cuff links, then adjusted his chair closer to mine.

"They've overdone this greenery bit," he said out of the side of his mouth. "The place looks like a damn jungle."

His confident tone, his use of a cuss word—he had assumed I was older!

"They could have used fewer hollies," I replied, my voice sultry and low.

I put an elbow on the table and rested my cheek on two fingers, the way movie stars often posed. The sophomore twiddled a wine glass.

"Oh, well," he sighed. "After a while, these comings-out all seem alike."

"I am sure." I pushed back a stray lock of hair.

The sophomore took a gold cigarette case from an inside pocket and flipped open the lid. "Care for a smoke?"

My head jerked ever so slightly as I glanced at my father. He was engrossed in whatever the law student was saying.

"Not at the moment," I smoothly replied.

But the sophomore narrowed his eyes and studied my face. Casually, I brought my hand to my neck, brushing my arm across my bosom. It stuck out reassuringly. I may have been only eleven, but with my bosom and all, I looked every bit of sixteen. And even if I'd been seventeen, the sophomore should have known I couldn't smoke with my father right there at the table. I offered a conspiratorial smile as though saying you know how fathers can be about their daughters and smoking. But he lit a cigarette, inhaled, and stared into the candles.

He had dismissed me. I couldn't care less; his profile resembled a gopher's.

The orchestra finished its song, the lights dimmed, and the last guests hurried to their seats. A hush settled over the crowd.

My eye was drawn to the other side of the room, and

there, shed at last of her black velvet cocoon, stood Louisa. Her yellow satin gown was cut appallingly low and clung to her form like a skin. Chin high, she glanced over the crowd. Then she saw us, smiled, and with the wave of a hand glided toward us, the moon highlighting her figure in gold. Gopherhead's eyes bulged from their sockets. The law student's jaw dropped. Papa and Maggie turned to see what had caused the interruption.

"Lou—!" Papa half rose from his chair and dropped back, shaking his head. "How in the world did she manage—?"

Maggie put a hand on his arm as, triumph written all over her face, my sister slithered into her seat.

The spotlight turned onto a barrel-shaped man whom I recognized as president of First Georgia Bank where Papa did business.

"Ladies and gentlemen!" the banker said into a microphone. "Good evening and welcome to th—" The microphone squawked and the banker jumped back. He twisted a knob and started again. "Ladies and..." His mouth kept moving, but no sound could be heard. A ruddy-faced man wearing a red cummerbund rushed to the microphone and made some adjustments. Still no sound. The ruddy-faced man rushed from the room.

"Ladies and gentlemen!" shouted the banker. "Can y'all hear me?"

Most people couldn't, but he kept shouting anyway.

"Welcome to this year's debutante ball, each and every one of you! As you know, the Fredericksboro Debutante Cotillion is a treasured tradition among..."

People started talking. The banker shouted louder.

"...when a group of socially-minded citizens met together to form the very first..."

The ruddy-faced man rushed in with another

microphone.

"Whew!" said the banker, wiping his brow.

A few people laughed.

"And now," he continued in a volume that set my ears ringing, "on this auspicious evening of December 6, 1941, it is my great privilege and distinct honor to present to you the crème de la crème of Southern womanhood, the loveliest flowers in the garden of our fair town's society—members of the 1941 Fredericksboro Debutante Club!"

Everyone clapped, and the orchestra began playing "Moonlight and Roses."

The spotlight turned to the trellis, where a brunette with a riveted smile stood beside the ruddy-faced man. Her name and her parents' names were announced and applauded. Then the father escorted his daughter from the platform, and the spotlight returned to the trellis and another debutante standing with her father.

Betsy was the fourth debutante to be presented: "Miss Elizabeth Goulding Goldsmith! Daughter of Mr. and Mrs. Ira Joseph Goldsmith."

I glanced at Aunt May Belle. She sat straining forward, eyes glittering, hands tightly clasped under her chin.

"Isn't she gorgeous?" she whispered loudly to Rodney Bridgeman, who was seated beside her.

Rodney looked startled. Then he said, "Yes, ma'am."

Now, I loved my cousin Betsy most dearly, but I had never thought of her as gorgeous; her face was too much like her mother's—narrow, eyes set close together. But at that moment, there on the platform in her dazzling gown, dark hair woven with flowers, face glowing with happiness, Betsy was gorgeous indeed.

After the last debutante and her father had stepped from the platform and the banker had led in a final round of applause, the orchestra struck up a waltz. A few hesitant steps, and fathers and daughters swept grandly across the dance floor.

"They're playing Strauss's 'Roses from the South,'" Aunt May Belle said, nodding in time with the music. "Appropriate, don't you think? Ira suggested it."

Halfway through the waltz, Betsy and Uncle Ira danced over to Aunt May Belle. Uncle Ira bowed low, and Betsy kissed her mother's cheek, although her eyes stayed on Rodney.

When the second dance started, Rodney and other escorts stood and walked onto the dance floor to break in on the fathers. The law student invited Louisa to dance; Gopherhead invited Aunt May Belle.

"May I have the honor of this dance?"

Maggie jumped. "Mercy, Mr. Goldsmith! Thank you, but my dancing days have long passed."

"Maggie and I are only spectators, now," Papa said.

"Now, Jim, I don't accept that. But I won't argue if you'll allow me the honor of dancing with your beautiful daughter."

I looked around for Louisa; she was on the other side of the room.

"I'm sure Margaret would be delighted to dance," Papa said.

Me? Dance? Oh, no! No, I would not be delighted. "I can't dance, Uncle Ira. I— I— No one ever taught me. I tried to teach myself once, but it...." I couldn't stop babbling.

Uncle Ira smiled. "You don't need lessons for this, Margaret. You can count to two, can't you? This is a two-step."

I looked to Maggie for help. She gave an encouraging smile.

Dancing with Uncle Ira was like being nudged into

doing what my feet wanted to do anyway. The only problem was that I kept bumping into his cushiony middle, which was embarrassing.

We two-stepped to the other side of the floor, and there, not ten feet away, sat Sue Lee Wright.

I had seen Sue Lee only once since Papa withdrew me from Smithson, the Sunday her family visited our church. She looked taller now and thinner, her Shirley Temple curls replaced by a sleek pageboy bob.

She saw me and waved, and the moment I was back at my table, she came over.

"Isn't this the most marvelous thing in the world!" she gushed, sitting in Gopherhead's chair. "That dress of yours is absolutely marvelous. Did you get it at Goldberg's? That's where I got mine and Ginger got hers. Did you see Ginger? Doesn't she look marvelous! She's president of the debutante club, you know."

"Your gown is really beautiful," I said while Sue Lee paused to sip wine from Gopherhead's goblet. "Let's go to the ladies room and freshen our faces. Be sure to bring your purse."

I'd started out with a purse, an old one of Louisa's, but decided to leave it in the car. All it had in it was a handkerchief and a nickel.

"Oh, dear," I exclaimed, looking around my seat. "I must have left my purse in the car."

"Never mind," Sue Lee said. "You can borrow my makeup."

Makeup!

The ladies' room was crowded, but we managed to work up to a spot near the mirror. Sue Lee took out a tube of pale lipstick and went over her lips.

"Mother says Tangee Natural is the appropriate color for girls of my age." She handed the lipstick to me.

96

I rubbed it over my lips and studied them in the mirror. They didn't look any different, but I felt much more self-assured.

"Need to powder your nose?" Sue Lee held out a silver compact.

Of course, I did.

She invited me to sit at her table a while; we had so much to discuss. She wanted to hear all about Betsy's escorts, and I told her what little I knew.

"Father made Ginger invite two family friends, too," Sue Lee said. "And then she got to pick one boy she wanted. She had the worst time making up her mind. There were so many to choose from. Finally, she decided on Bannister James."

Bannister James? The name sounded familiar. Then I remembered. He was the boy Betsy had a crush on in sixth grade. I had read about him years ago in Louisa's diary.

"I've heard about Bannister, but I've never met him," I said.

"Oh, Margaret, you simply must! He's the most delectable man you'll ever lay eyes on. Let me see if I can spot him... Yes! Look over there! He's dancing with Ginger."

He was tall, had shiny black hair, and I could not take my eyes off him. Bannister James was the closest I would ever come to seeing Robert Taylor in the flesh—down to earth and human-sized. My heart did a flip-flop.

"When we were coming in tonight," Sue Lee went on, "I nearly tripped on the carpet, and he grabbed hold of my arm." She held up the sanctified object. "I'll never wash it again."

When I returned to my table, Miss Camilla Lupton, a distant cousin, was standing there talking to Papa and blocking the way to my chair. Miss Camilla was made up of

97

two prominent parts: her behind and her bosom. This evening, her behind was suppressed, doubtless within a new girdle, tight as a balloon about to explode. But her bosom was a marvel of horizontal protrusion. And as she talked, it heaved and fell dangerously low over Maggie's head.

"Won't you please have a seat?" Papa kept saying, indicating the chair where the law student had sat. But Miss Camilla ignored his offer and kept talking. Or perhaps she was afraid that if she bent to sit down, something might snap like an overstretched rubber band.

I decided to go out to the car for my purse.

Crossing the ballroom, I noticed Betsy and the law student talking with another couple at the edge of the dance floor. Betsy kept looking around, probably for Rodney. As I neared the door, I spotted Louisa dancing with a wiry young man who seemed a bit older than most of the escorts. He was whirling her rapidly, eyes locked on her face.

Outside, the night air was cold and clear. Couples stood in small groups, exhaling pale smoke into the blackness. I headed in the direction that the attendant had driven Papa's car. Cutting between the rows of cars, I noticed a movement, a reflection of light, in the back seat of a car. I continued on till I found our car. It was locked and I had no key, so I turned to go back to the clubhouse.

As I approached the car where I'd seen movement, I paused in the shadows. Moonlight fell across the back seat where two men were tussling, wrapped all together. One man turned his head, and I saw it was Bannister James. The other one shifted so that moonlight fell on his wavy blond hair. I ran back to the clubhouse; I should tell Papa before someone got hurt.

But as I entered the foyer, I slowed. And at the door to the ballroom, I stopped. The expression on Bannister's face wasn't anger or fear. It was—something else.

No one knew what I'd seen; no one could blame me if I didn't report it. I continued on to my table.

"So there you are, Margaret," Papa said. "Maggie was beginning to worry. We've just come from the buffet. May I bring you a plate, or would you prefer to serve yourself?"

"I'll serve myself, thank you," I said.

The wiry young man whom I seen earlier dancing with Louisa was sitting with her at the table. He had stood when I came up.

"Frank," Papa said, "have you met Margaret, Louisa's sister? Margaret, this is Frank Varnedoe."

Without moving his head, he looked me up and down, a smile playing over his lips. "What a little beauty you are," he said. Then he gave me a wink that jolted me from the top of my head to the tips of my toes.

I went to the buffet and filled my plate with something or other. When I got back to the table, Papa and Frank were discussing cows. I sat down and lifted a green blob to my mouth.

Louisa leaned over and whispered into Frank's ear. He stood and helped her up from her chair. Passing me on the way to the dance floor, he winked again. It was as though a live wire had touched me.

As I rode home, half asleep in the back seat, impressions of people and music and gowns and conversation tumbled about in my head. Gradually, all of them faded but one—Frank Varnedoe.

Of course, he was interested in Louisa; everybody at the ball had been interested in Louisa. But I could tell she cared not a fig about him. True, he wasn't the best-looking man in the world. Certainly not movie star handsome. But something about him....

I slid between the icy sheets on my bed. Frank was older than I. But Papa was older than Mother. Rhett Butler was older than Scarlett.

If only he'd wait for me to grow up.

CHAPTER 13

The morning after the ball, Louisa and I were allowed to sleep in and miss church.

When I arrived at the dinner table, my head feeling as though it was buried in cotton, Papa and Maggie were already seated. Moments later, Louisa wandered in, eyes half shut, traces of makeup still on her face.

"Let us say grace," Papa pronounced solemnly.

I bowed my head, closed my eyes, and immediately lapsed into deep, regular breathing. For once I hoped the prayer would be long.

It was. And about the usual things: "Thank you, our Heavenly Father, for your watchful care over us, for this holy day set aside for worship and rest. Thank you...

"...and we ask you, Dear Lord, to bless those in authority over us, those with whom we work every day, those whom we love.... Keep watch over..."

I dozed on.

"Now, bless this food to the nourishment of our bodies...." He was headed down the home stretch; I prepared for my last somnolent breaths. But instead of "Amen," Papa went on at full throttle. "Almighty God, on this infamous day of December 7, 1941, we lift our nation to Thee. Protect her against her enemies. Confound the aggressors. Shield us from their heinous intent. Bless our servicemen as they go into battle—"

"What?" cried Louisa.

I was jerked wide awake. My sister was staring at Papa. She had interrupted his prayer.

"The Japanese have attacked our fleet at Pearl Harbor," he said. "Our nation is at war."

Louisa shoved back her chair. "That can't be true! Now

the boys will be sent off to fight and we'll be left all alone!"

I waited a moment. Then I said, "Papa, where's Pearl Harbor?"

"In Hawaii. We have a large naval base there."

"The Japanese and the Germans won't come to Georgia, will they?"

"They will if our men don't go there to fight them," Louisa said.

"We'll stop them, though, won't we, Papa?"

"I hope so, Margaret." He picked up the carving knife and fork and began slicing the pork roast. "Our nation has the potential for being a strong military power. We should be safe here."

"Jim, do you want to finish your prayer?" Maggie asked.

"I believe the Lord knows what I intended to say." Papa placed a slice of roast on a plate.

He had said we'd be safe. What a relief. I'd seen pictures of war: soldiers in trenches, bombs bursting in air. War could be awful. But Pearl Harbor was in Hawaii, on the other side of the world. There would be no fighting here.

The aroma of the roast mingled with sweet potato soufflé along with lima beans boiled with ham hock set my stomach to gnaw on itself, and as soon as my plate was served, I gave my full attention to eating. It wasn't until I was almost done that I noticed the others had only picked at their food. Perhaps they were too tired to eat; perhaps they were concerned over the war. Tonight, I would pray extra hard that our men would be safe. God would make everything right. After dinner I returned to my room. My green taffeta gown hung on a hanger on the open door of my wardrobe, its skirt still billowing, its boat neckline still beguilingly full. I ran my hands over the crisp emerald cloth, and it whispered delicious secrets to me.

I kicked off my shoes, crawled into bed, and closed my eyes. I was again at the ball, and the orchestra played "Moonlight and Roses." Aunt May Belle exclaimed over how gorgeous I looked, Gopherhead offered me a cigarette from his case, and Frank Varnedoe said what a little beauty I was and winked. Oh, yes, he most definitely winked.

* * *

"A good morning to you!" He stood at the back door, his gold corduroy shirt opened at the neck, his dark brown eyes twinkling.

It was the day after Louisa arrived home from college for Christmas holidays. Lily May and I were at the kitchen table, eating biscuits left from breakfast and squabbling over who had dripped honey onto the floor. I wore an ugly brown dress and a green sweater with the elbows worn through. My hair, tangles and all, was pulled back and fastened with a rubber band. I looked like a toad.

But if Frank Varnedoe was shocked by my sloppy appearance when I opened the door, he didn't let on. He grinned and bowed low. "And, Meg-o-my-Heart, how are you this beautiful day?"

"Oh!" I finally got out.

He glanced beyond me, and I turned to see Ida and Lily May standing there, Ida smiling hospitably, Lily May unabashedly gawking.

"Good morning," he said. "I'm Frank Varnedoe. I'm here to see Louisa."

"How do you do? I's Ida Robinson, this here's Lily May. Won't you please step inside?"

At least Ida hadn't forgotten *her* manners.

In the kitchen, Frank glanced at the mess on the table

and said, his eyes twinkling, "Did you save me a biscuit?"

"They's still some in the oven Momma keeping back for Sam," Lily May said. "She can make him some more."

Frank laughed. "I'm teasing, Lily May; I've already eaten." He turned to face me. "But I tell you what I would like. I'd like Meg here to let Little Lulu know I'm ready to take her for that ride whenever she's ready to go."

So he had given Louisa a nickname, too; I wished it was only me.

Still, mine was nicer. "Meg-o-my-Heart" came from a love song. "Little Lulu" came from a cartoon in the *Saturday Evening Post*.

When I went to her room, Louisa was still in pajamas, her hair still in rollers.

"Good heavens!" She glanced at her watch. "He wasn't due for another half hour. He'll just have to wait."

I went to her dresser. "Louisa, may I borrow your hairbrush and—"

"No, get out of here."

I went to Maggie's room and brushed my hair. Then I took her new blue sweater from a drawer and exchanged it for my ragged green one. She wouldn't mind.

When I got back to the kitchen, Maggie was sitting at the table with Frank, having coffee. Her eyes widened when she saw me in her sweater, but she didn't say anything.

Frank noticed the change and exclaimed, "Ah, the enchantress in blue!"

Lily May's eyebrows shot up through her scalp.

I pulled up a chair and sat down. He was in the middle of some tale about a mule that had gotten stuck in the mud and had to be pulled out with a tractor. It sounded kind of silly to me, but I laughed as hard as I could when he finished, and he smiled, obviously pleased.

Louisa appeared in the doorway wearing a yellow tamo-shanter, a yellow cashmere sweater, and a green and yellow plaid skirt. Frank sprang to his feet.

"Sunshine to rival nature's own!" He said, beaming.

Louisa gave a tight smile. She turned to Maggie. "We'll probably be gone most of the day."

When they left, the sunshine left with them. But it wasn't Louisa.

* * *

The diary lay in the bottom of the suitcase Louisa had brought home from college. I took it to the chair near the window so I could see when Ida or Lily May left their house and started toward mine. Maggie was taking a nap. Papa and Louisa had gone into town. It was a safe time to read.

Louisa had written over six pages about the debutante ball, mostly about who flirted with whom and whose gown was the tackiest. She listed the names of the boys she had danced with and wrote comments on each. All she wrote about Frank was that he danced well but wasn't her type.

Just as I had suspected, there was nothing between them. Naturally, like every other man at the ball, he was attracted to her. But she was not attracted to him and had said as much in her diary.

In a later entry, Louisa noted that she had gotten a letter from Betsy. She wrote,

> Poor girl's still besotted with Rodney Bridgeman. She's hoping for an engagement ring sometime around Christmas. Why she wants to marry that skinny nobody I'll never understand. She says he reminds her of Leslie Howard in *Gone with the Wind*. She's insane.

I skimmed through the next several pages, which were

mainly about schoolwork and professors. Then I came across this:

> Anna Grace Steele from across the hall in my dorm knows Frank Varnedoe's family. She says they own half of the farmland in South Carolina! And he'd led me to believe he was a common dirt farmer. I may answer his letter after all.

So he had written to her. I was hoping he hadn't. But he was probably just trying to be polite.

In her last entry before coming home for the holidays, she wrote,

> Betsy called long distance to say Rodney got his draft notice. He has to report to Fort Benning early in January. She's talking about their getting married before he leaves. He hasn't even asked her, for heaven sakes! But nothing makes sense any more. Here's Frank, a Citadel graduate who would enter the Army with a commission but hasn't heard one word from the draft. He's afraid they'll want him to stay home and grow food for the Military and is trying to get it all changed. Says his mother can run the farm as well as he can. Figures if she did it after his father died, she can do it again.

Louisa had answered his letter, and he'd written her back. Maybe even driven over to see her. I put the diary into the trunk and left the room. There was an uneasy feeling inside me.

* * *

The engagement party for Betsy and Rodney was on Christmas Eve at her home. I wore my green taffeta gown and touched up my lips with a little lipstick from a discarded tube of Louisa's. I also put some crumpled tissue in the front of my boat neckline to make it stand out even farther. I could have easily passed for eighteen.

The Goldsmith's house glowed with candles; the air smelled of cinnamon and cloves. Rodney Bridgeman's parents and his brother, Roger, had driven over from Birmingham to attend the party. Rodney and Roger were identical twins, but it was easy to tell them apart. Roger was heavier and smiled a lot more.

As soon as Nellie took my coat at the door, Betsy rushed up to give me a hug. "Dear child, have you seen my engagement ring?" She grabbed my arm and pulled me over to a small lamp. "Isn't it gorgeous!" she bubbled, holding her hand to the light. "You almost need sunglasses to cut down the glare."

The diamond did sparkle. But it was so tiny that I had to squint to see it.

"It's beautiful!" I exclaimed and looked up into her eyes, which sparkled far more than the stone.

The dining room table was extended full length and covered with white lace cloths. Four lighted silver candelabra surrounded by evergreens and silver balls were spaced down the center.

I had hoped to be seated near Frank Varnedoe but instead found my place card at the opposite end of the table next to old Mr. Saltus, a family friend.

Mr. Saltus had palsy, and when he ate, bits of salad and bread fell into his beard. I tried not to look because the sight affected my appetite. But he kept talking to me, and I couldn't be rude. Somehow, he'd gotten it into his head that I wanted to be a cotton broker when I grew up and took it upon himself to tell me everything he had learned during his fifty-four years in the business. Such exciting information as the grade and staple and preparation of cotton and how to get the best price in the market. Leaning close, he confided, "Now, the way to beat the game is to go into the fields before the cotton is picked and check out the crop for yourself. And steer clear of the futures market!" Mr. Saltus scowled and reared back in his chair. "That's where I almost lost my shirt. A *cotton* one, naturally. Hee! Hee!"

I rewarded him with a half-smile.

Finally, dessert—chocolate mousse with raspberries and crisp, lacy cookies—was served, and Mr. Saltus turned his attention from me to the food.

I was only half through my mousse when Uncle Ira stood up at the head of the table.

"Friends!" He raised his glass of champagne. "If I may, will you join me in a toast?"

As we rose, Mr. Saltus bumped my elbow, causing my ginger ale to slosh onto the tablecloth. I shifted my plate over the worst of the spill.

"Let us all join in drinking to the happiness of this young couple whose future welfare is so dear to our hearts!" Uncle Ira raised his glass higher. "To Betsy!" She giggled. "And to Rodney!" He slumped in his chair.

We clinked our glasses to cries of "Here, here!" and "Best wishes!"

A few men called, "Speech! Speech!" and Rodney slumped even lower. Betsy leaned over and whispered into his ear. Slowly, he rose.

"I...I...Er..." He stared down at his empty dessert plate as though it had been his last meal before facing the gallows. "Betsy and I thank you."

He dropped to his seat like a sack of potatoes and everyone clapped and shouted, "Bravo!"

While the grownups were having coffee in the library, I

wandered out to the sun porch and picked up a *National Geographic*. I was flipping through the pages when someone—Uncle Ira, I thought—put his hands on my shoulders. But when I turned and looked up, I was staring into the deep, smiling eyes of Frank Varnedoe.

"What are you doing out here by yourself?" he asked.

Stuttering something, I tried to replace the magazine on the table. It slipped to the floor, and we both reached down to retrieve it. He reached it first.

"Allow me," he said, winking.

My heart gave a flutter and I thought I might faint.

How was it that someone I'd known for such a short time could make me feel so wonderfully strange?

* * *

Betsy's wedding took place on New Year's Day at St. Matthew's Episcopal Church. Only family members attended. Betsy, wearing the lace gown Aunt May Belle had bought for her years earlier in Paris, looked radiant; Rodney, in his private's uniform, his blond hair shorn to stubble, looked weak-kneed and pale. After the ceremony the bridal couple sped away in Betsy's convertible for a brief honeymoon at the Cloister on Sea Island. Then Rodney set out for Fort Benning, and Betsy returned home to her parents.

CHAPTER 14

Summer vacation began. I had finished sixth grade and Lily May had graduated from seventh. Maggie gave her a new blouse and skirt to wear in the fall when she started to Rainey Institute, the high school for colored students in downtown Fredericksboro. Ida had high ambitions for her daughter. She wanted her to complete high school and go on to college so she could be a schoolteacher. Lily May said all that learning might put a strain on her brain, and she'd have to think about it. I hoped she was kidding.

"Rodney's back," Louisa announced as soon as Papa finished saying grace at supper. She had arrived home from college earlier that afternoon to start summer vacation and had been on the phone ever since.

"What do you mean Rodney's back?" I asked. "Betsy doesn't expect to see him for months."

"What I mean is he's out of the Army."

I turned to Papa for an explanation; he was busy carving the ham. I glanced at Maggie, who was adjusting her napkin.

"Did he get hurt or something?"

"He banged up his arm pretty badly on bivouac," Louisa said.

"Yeah, but that was months ago." I looked again at Papa and Maggie.

"Louisa, are you're still planning to help me in the office this summer?" Papa handed her a plate with a slice of ham on it. "I'm losing another law clerk to a job at Camp Walker."

Louisa scooped up *four* melted marshmallows with her dab of sweet potato soufflé. "I'll have to buy new clothes. I don't have a thing to wear in an office."

"But what about—" I looked at the grownups who continued to ignore me. It was apparent that they would talk no more about Rodney.

The next morning after Louisa left to go shopping for clothes, I went to her room to read her diary. But it was nowhere to be found, and I had to conclude that she no longer kept one.

Several times over the next few days, I brought up the subject of Rodney. But the only additional information I gleaned was from Louisa's comment that Aunt May Belle had said sometimes the Army makes a mistake. Whatever that meant.

The next Monday, Louisa started to work in Papa's office. She claimed to like the job, but when Papa wasn't around, she complained about Miss Doreen, his secretary, and her tacky ways. I understood that; I didn't much care for Miss Doreen, either.

The height of my summer vacation was visiting with Betsy. At least once a week, she invited me to come by Uncle Ira's stationery store, where she was supposedly in management training. I would ride into town with Papa and Louisa and cross the street to the store.

It was plain from the beginning that Betsy would make a terrible manager. She gave away more stuff than she sold. If a soldier walked through the door, she'd present him with a Waterman pen. If a child came in with its mother, she gave the child a tablet and crayons. And if her boss, Mr. Moon, suggested she do anything more complicated than stack boxes on a shelf, she'd smile sweetly and say, "Now, you know you can do that a thousand times better than me!" Mr. Moon's face would turn pink.

Also, Betsy would take off from work whenever she pleased. "See you later," she'd say to her boss as we walked out the door.

She was looking for things to put in the house Uncle Ira had bought for her and Rodney, even though Aunt May Belle had already furnished it from top to bottom. One afternoon, we were riding around in an old section of Fredericksboro, trying to locate an antique shop where she thought she might find a cradle.

"Are you having a baby?" I asked.

Betsy wiggled a finger at me. "Shh! Don't tell anyone I'm expecting, because I am not. I just want to be ready in case."

We came to an old cemetery surrounded by a brick wall, and she stopped at the gate.

"When was the last time you were here?" she asked.

"Never," I said. "I've never been here. Why do you ask?"

"Your mother's buried inside."

I stared at the gate. Old, rusty, lopsided. Apparently, it was supposed to be closed, but one side was pushed back far enough for someone to slip inside.

A thought stirred deep within me. "I may have been here when I was real little," I said. "I believe Maggie brought me. I remember running around with a stick, stirring up doodle bug holes and singing, 'Doodle bug, doodle bug, your house is on fire.' But I don't remember anything about my mother being buried here."

"Uncle Jim never took you when he put flowers on Aunt Weezie's grave?"

"What? No, I never knew he did that."

"Every year on her birthday, a dozen gardenias. For a while my mother went with him. Then she stopped. Said it made her too sad."

Betsy opened the car door. "Do you want to go see the grave?"

The cemetery was crowded with stones, some broken,

some leaning at angles, most smudged with dark mold. We followed a gravel path to the back, where Betsy stopped in front of a plot bordered by a low wrought-iron fence. Inside the fence, the grass—what little there was—had been mowed. Gravestones stood in two rows.

"There," Betsy gestured toward the front row, "great-grandparents, grandparents, great-uncles and aunts. Over there," she pointed to a thick granite marker on the second row, "Max. And next to him, Weezie."

It was a white marble obelisk at least six feet tall with a garland of fruit and flowers carved down one side. I walked over to it. The inscription read:

ANNE LOUISA GOULDING NORMAN
1897–1930

Warm Summer Sun, Shine Kindly Here
Warm Southern Wind, Blow Softly Here
Green Sod Above, Lie Light, Lie Light
Good Night, Dear Heart, Good Night

A shiver ran through me and I lurched forward. A hand grasped my arm.

"Margaret, are you all right?"

I nodded that I was. But I was shaken to the core.

So this was the place where it had ended. Here beneath that pale gravestone lay the link to my being, the essential connection I knew only through imagination and dreams. I stared at the stone, wishing it could answer my questions.

How many times over the years had I studied pictures of my mother as a child and as a young woman? Two of those pictures I had appropriated for myself alone: the one of her with her brother, Max, and the one of her on a beach standing against the sea and the sky, wearing a long white dress with a billowing skirt.

It was the one on the beach that had fixed my image of her, my beautiful mother, all love and perfection, the "best of love and light" of Papa's poem, the "Dear Heart" of the gravestone inscription. I stepped closer and ran my fingers over her name. My heart was too full for words.

That night, lying in bed in my dark room, I relived the moments of the afternoon. While I stood at the stone, Betsy had put her arm around me and drawn me close. Neither of us spoke. I didn't cry.

But I cried now. Tears of sorrow and loss and regret and love rolled off my cheeks and puddled inside my ears.

Finally, I dried my face and ears on the sheet, turned onto my side, and drifted into merciful sleep.

* * *

For the first time that I could remember, I fell out of bed. I'd been dreaming about chasing a moth through the woods. But it wasn't really a moth; it didn't have wings, and it wore a white gown. It fluttered into some bushes. I plunged in after it, and that's when I hit the floor.

Sitting up, I untwisted myself from the sheet I had dragged off the bed and crawled to the wardrobe a few feet away. I felt through the bottom drawer until my fingers touched the soft hair of my old friend, Matilda. I pulled her out and climbed back into bed. As I held her close, the words tumbled through me:

Warm Summer Sun, Shine Kindly Here
Warm Southern Wind, Blow Softly...

CHAPTER 15

On weekdays Louisa worked in Papa's law office, and on weekends she dated. She would have dated on weekdays, too, had Papa allowed it. But he said she wouldn't be fit to work if she'd spent half the night gallivanting around.

When Louisa had a date with Frank Varnedoe, which she often did, I made it a point to be the one to greet him at the door and show him to the parlor. Papa and Maggie were usually there, and the four of us sat and talked till Louisa appeared. In the fall, after she went back to college, I saw Frank only at Thanksgiving when Louisa was home and didn't expect to see him again till Christmas break. But one evening in early December, the doorbell rang, and when I opened the door, there he stood—minus his usual smile.

"Take a good look, Meg," he said lifting his arms from his sides, "because this is the last time you'll see me in civvies."

I led him to the parlor where Papa and Maggie were reading the newspaper. He had come to tell us good-bye and could stay only a minute. He was leaving for Fort Bragg in the morning.

Papa mentioned a young lawyer friend stationed at the fort, and Frank said he'd look him up. Maggie took down his address and promised to write. I also promised to write. Then we walked with him to the door, where he shook Papa's hand and kissed Maggie's cheek. As he turned toward to me, I said quickly, "I'll walk you outside." There was something I needed to ask him in private.

At the car, I turned toward him. The porch light illumined most of his face. But his eyes were in shadows, and I couldn't read what they were saying.

"Frank, would you—I wonder—"

"What is it, Meg?"

"Would you send me a picture of you in your uniform?"

"Sure, I will. Want me to be wearing my medals, in which case you may have to wait a while? Or will my plain khakis do?"

Even in the dark, I could make out a small, teasing smile. "Your khakis will do fine."

"Well then, little Meg, I suppose it's good-bye."

I extended my hand, but he pushed it aside and drew me against his chest. I heard the hump-*dup*, hump-*dup* of his heart.

He held me a moment, then stepped back and put his hands on my shoulders. "Now, don't you get all grown up and sophisticated while I'm away. Promise you'll stay just as sweet and innocent as you are right now."

Me? Sweet and innocent? I nodded, trying to muster my best sweet and innocent look.

Then he was gone. A roar of an engine, a shadow fading into the darkness.

Later in bed, I relived the parting. Over and over. The fresh country smell of his clothes. The warmth of his arms wrapped about me. The soft, steady thud of his heart.

* * *

The Rev. Jonathan Boyd Harper was called to be minister of our church, First Presbyterian, in the middle of January. Two weeks later, Sue Lee Wright's family moved their membership there. I wasn't surprised. Earlier, Sue Lee had told me that her mother had been offended by remarks made by their minister at Sandy Creek church about women who spent all their time playing bridge. Soon, Sue Lee and I were sitting together on the back pew during worship service. And we were usually the first ones out the door when the service was over.

"Isn't he simply divine!" Sue Lee exclaimed one Sunday as we stood outside the church, watching our minister greet parishioners as they came through the door.

"Oh, yes!" I agreed.

Mr. Harper was indeed divine—broad shoulders, thick, sandy hair, eyes deeply and beautifully blue.

"Papa was on the pulpit committee that recommended him to the church," I bragged. "At first Papa worried that the congregation wouldn't accept him, being so young and a Yankee and all. But everybody likes him just fine. Even her." I gestured toward a sallow-faced woman who kept shaking the minister's hand.

"You mean that lady with the crippled daughter?"

"Yeah, the one who always sits right in front of my family."

"The one who looks like she chews green persimmons?"

Sue Lee and I were still snickering when Papa and Maggie came down the steps. Papa frowned and I straightened my face. I didn't dare look at my friend.

* * *

Our church grew crowded on Sundays. Not only did more members attend but also soldiers from nearby Camp Walker. Papa said wartime brought out religion in people and that they were drawn to our church because of Mr. Harper's fine sermons. I certainly thought his sermons were fine. Short, and full of interesting stories.

He began preaching sermons on the Ten Commandments, which I already knew a lot about, having studied them in Miss Annie Taylor's Sunday school class. Miss Annie, however, hadn't been clear about the Seventh Commandment, the one I happened to be the most interested in. She read the Scripture: "Thou shalt not commit adultery." Then she read a story about a girl named Rose who kept herself pure until she was married. Miss Annie said we girls should keep ourselves clean and pure, too. Sue Lee, trying to be funny, asked, "Does that mean we have to bathe all the time?" Miss Annie turned red faced and said she was speaking of another kind of cleanliness. But she didn't explain what it was.

I had heard that only married people could commit adultery, and so I didn't much worry about breaking the Seventh Commandment—until Mr. Harper's sermon.

"Remember, dear friends," he said, eyes scanning his flock, "that even to *look* at another with lust is to commit adultery in your heart." For an instant his eyes locked into mine, and hot waves of guilt rolled over me. If I wasn't feeling lust in my heart at that moment, I was feeling something mighty close to it.

But it was the sermon the Sunday before on "Thou shalt not kill" that had truly disturbed me. My sweet Alicia Patricia had been dead for almost four years, and still there were times when I felt afraid. And the dreams. Some I couldn't recall upon waking—although their uneasy traces remained. Others so vivid they yanked me awake, and I lay in the dark, sad and anxious.

* * *

It became customary for church members to invite soldiers home for dinner after the morning service. One Sunday, Papa invited Private Eric Svendsen to come and eat with us. As we sat around the dining table, Eric, a large, pink-skinned young man with hair the color of cream, told us that he had grown up on a dairy farm in Wisconsin.

"So you know a lot about cows?" Papa asked. "I'd like to see what you think about our cows, especially our Jersey."

"Her name is Cherry," I volunteered. "Papa calls her his butter lady because her milk is so rich."

Eric, who had consumed everything on the table except a few pickles, daintily dabbed his mouth with the napkin. "I'd sure like to see her," he said. "Cows remind me of home."

The cows were standing in the middle of the pasture, soaking up the early spring sun.

Papa took a bucket of oats from the barn and said, "Cherry will come if you whistle."

Eric gave a shrill call and Cherry started toward us. The young soldier scooped up some oats and fed her when she arrived.

"Man, oh man!" he said, wiping his slobbery hand on the cow's neck. "She reminds me of this little heifer I raised in 4-H Club. Sonia took a blue at the county fair. So did one of her calves." He reached into the bucket for more oats. "It near 'bout killed me when Dad sold her off."

"So you'd say our little Jersey measures up to your Wisconsin cows?" Papa asked.

"Sure does. Look at the strength in the head. Look at the size of that udder. Give me time to groom her a little, polish them horns, I guarantee she'd take the blue at any fair in the state."

"I wish you could work with her, son," Papa said gently.

Eric pulled Cherry's ear, and she pushed her wet nose against his arm.

"Man, oh, man!" he said. He flung his arms across Cherry's back, and, leaning into her side, began choking out sobs.

After Papa left to drive Eric to town to catch his bus back to camp, I told Maggie what happened at the barn.

"It's so sad," she said. "A young man uprooted from home and being trained to kill or be killed in this terrible war. It's so very sad."

I thought of another young man being trained to kill or be killed, and my eyes welled with tears.

Eric Svendsen was not at church the next Sunday. Papa heard that his unit had shipped out.

* * *

The war intruded more and more into our lives. Gas was rationed and we were allowed only three gallons a week for the green car. That meant Maggie had to plan carefully for our trips into town. Tires and shoes were rationed, also sugar and meat. Meat rationing was no problem for us; Sam kept us supplied. But sugar rationing required a personal sacrifice on my part because Ida had to cut way back on desserts.

Pictures of servicemen killed or missing in action began to appear at the bottom of the front page of the newspaper, and every night, I looked for them with a mixture of curiosity and dread. So far I hadn't recognized any of the men. That changed one evening in March.

It was after supper, and I was sprawled out on the rug in the living room, studying for a history test, when I happened to glance up at the paper Papa was reading. "Bombs Over Schweinfurt," the bold print announced. And below it in smaller print: "Allied Bombers Launch Massive Attack on Ball-bearing Factories."

Papa shifted the paper, exposing pictures of two servicemen on the bottom half of the page. One was a sailor who looked no older than I. The other— I sat up abruptly.

"Bannister James!"

Papa lowered the newspaper. "What did you say?"

I pointed to the picture of the second man and read the cutline: "Corporal R. Bannister James, Jr., son of Mr. and Mrs. R. Bannister James, 131 Reid Lane. Killed in action, March 11."

"You knew him?" Papa turned the newspaper around to look at the picture.

"He was Ginger Wright's escort at the debutante ball. He went to Smithson Grammar School along with Louisa and Betsy."

Papa held out the newspaper for Maggie to see.

"Such a handsome young man," she said. "So very sad for his family."

I got up. "I'm going to call Betsy. She probably doesn't know about Bannister. She hardly ever looks at the paper."

Out in the hall, I picked up the telephone receiver. Then I paused. What if Betsy asked why I thought she had a particular interest Bannister James? She didn't know I'd read in Louisa's diary that she had a crush on him in sixth grade. I put back the receiver and went outside to sit on the steps. The air was brisk and clear. Seven miles away in the city, fewer lights glimmered than in the past. To the west near Camp Walker, bright yellow pencils crisscrossed the sky. From somewhere far off came the drone of a plane engine. I searched the sky, but the stars were fixed.

Bannister James, dead. I had never actually met him. Still, I felt sad. Would Betsy feel sad when she learned he'd been killed? And what about Rodney? Would he grieve over Bannister? I'd realized long ago that it was Rodney's wavy blond hair that I saw in the back seat of the car on the night of the debutante ball.

A sharp wind swept the last bit of heat from my

sweater. I shivered; I needed to go inside to the warmth, warmth that might ease my troubled heart.

CHAPTER 16

From the beginning, I supported the war effort in every way I could. I bought saving stamps with my allowance, turned off lights that weren't being used, collected kitchen grease to be made into bombs. I'd have willingly done even more.

What I couldn't understand was Lily May's attitude. She wouldn't raise one finger to help bring peace to the world. Slocum school had a contest with a prize of a $25.00 war bond for whoever brought in the most scrap metal. I asked Lily May to help me gather pieces of old machinery lying around the barn. She said, "Huh uh, totin' that stuff put a strain on my back."

"I'm not asking you to help with the real heavy stuff," I told her. "Sam will take care of that. Tell you what, if I win the bond, I'll give you half when it comes due."

"When's that?"

"Ten years."

"Ten years! By then I be so decrepit I won't be needing no money."

"Well, how do you expect us to win this war if you won't do one thing to help?"

Lily May snorted. "Why I'm worrying about a bunch of white folks killing theyselves on the other side of the world?"

"Lily May! That's a terrible thing to say. Besides, colored people are fighting, too."

"I don't care if they is. I don't care nothing about no war." She closed her eyes, lifted her chin, and intoned, "They always be wars and rumors of wars and blood in the horses' nostrils."

"What are you talking about?"

"What the preacher say about war. It be in the Bible,

the Book of the Revelation."

"Well, the preacher didn't say we weren't supposed to help stop this war, did he?"

"This war stop, another war start. I ain't wasting my time on no war."

She was acting so hateful I almost didn't tell her about the important visitor who was coming to see us the next day. Miss Camilla Lupton, the bosomy lady who'd blocked my way to my seat at the debutante ball, was bringing her nephew to visit. She had told Maggie that after all Fenton had been through (his father was wounded in the North African Campaign), he needed to get out amongst the trees and the flowers. Maggie said I'd be his hostess—a great honor, I thought. What a privilege to help this poor boy forget the horrors of war.

I only wished Miss Camilla didn't have to come too. She would arrive at our house in her big limousine and, nose pointing skyward, proceed to the parlor where she'd wedge her vast bottom into the flimsiest chair and hold forth for hours on her illustrious ancestors. Maggie always had to lie down after she left.

The next day at four, the limousine drew up in front of our house. Octavos, a raisin of a man in a uniform three sizes too large, got out and opened the back door with a flourish. Miss Camilla emerged and turned to help Fenton. But he was already out and coming around the side of the car. Lily May and I followed Maggie down the front steps to greet them.

Fenton Lupton didn't look at all the way I had imagined. He was about a year younger than I, and shorter, and—well, he resembled a piglet. He even let out a grunt when Miss Camilla introduced him to us.

After the ladies had walked into the house, I politely inquired, "Where are you from?"

"Nowhere around here." Fenton kicked at an anthill.

"What you doing here then?" Lily May asked.

He bent down to brush ants off his shoes. "Staying with my aunt while Mom visits Dad in the hospital."

"Was your father wounded real bad?" I asked.

"Yeah."

"I'm so sorry to hear that. Where was he hurt, if you don't mind my asking?"

"Neck and shoulder."

"You know how it happened?"

"Artillery fire." Fenton pointed a finger at Lily May and me, and made noises like a machine gun being fired. "When the order came for the troops to withdraw, all the guys did but my dad. He stayed behind and held off the whole German army." Fenton puffed out his chest. "He got lots of medals for bravery. Bronze Star, Purple Heart—"

"You sure does talk funny," Lily May interrupted.

And, truly, he did. Fenton put "r" sounds into words where I'd never heard them before.

Even so, I wished Lily May hadn't commented on it.

"Would you like some Juicy Fruit?" I asked, pulling a fresh pack of gum from my pocket. I opened it and handed Fenton a stick. Then I gave one to Lily May and took one for myself.

"Thank you for the Juicy Fruit gum," Lily May said a little too loudly.

We quietly chewed for a moment or two. Then Fenton spat his gum onto the ground. "So, what's there to do around here?"

"Well, we can go walk amongst the trees and the flowers," I suggested. "The roses are blooming in the side yard."

Fenton scowled.

"Or we can sit on the porch and play Chinese

checkers."

He scowled harder.

"Or Rook or Monopoly. I've got lots of games."

"I'm going to go sit in the car." He started toward the limousine.

"No! Wait!" I cried.

"Let's go to the cow pond and hunt tadpoles," Lily May said.

Fenton stopped. "I don't mind," he said.

We climbed the stile over the fence and into the pasture. The cow pond was at the lower end, and in hot weather, the cows often stood in the water, chewing their cud. Today, though, they were lying in the shade of an oak tree nearby. Proud Beauty stood among them.

"Whose horse is that?" Fenton asked.

"My father's. We don't ride her much anymore because she's gotten old and mean."

"I've had riding lessons," Fenton said.

"You ain't riding that horse," Lily May said. "Lessons or no."

We walked on to the cow pond. There hadn't been any rain for a while, and the pond wasn't much more than a mud hole. We circled it a couple of times but found nothing of interest.

"Let's go see if any huckleberries are left in the patch behind Ida's house," I said.

"Naw, that's no fun." Fenton headed back toward the stile, Lily May and me trailing behind.

When we came near Proud Beauty, he stopped. "I took riding lessons at camp. I know all about horses."

"Let's go climb a tree," Lily May offered.

"Where's the tack?"

"Oh, I know what!" I clapped my hands. "Let's go to the kitchen and get Ida to give us some pound cake and lemonade!"

Fenton shook his head. "I'm riding the horse."

He started toward Proud Beauty. Lily May started toward him. "Boy, you can't ride the horse. Mr. Jim don't allow nobody to be fooling around her."

Fenton kept going.

"I say you can't ride that horse!" Lily May repeated loudly.

Fenton halted abruptly and faced her, his face twisted with rage. "Shut up, you ugly black bitch!" he shouted.

The world slammed to a halt.

I had to say something. I couldn't allow—

But before I could open my mouth, a brown hand shot out and delivered a slap to his face that sounded like the crack of a pistol.

Fenton stumbled backwards. His cheek turned white and then changed to red. His eye started twitching. Howling like a whipped hound, he ran for the house.

"Let's go climb a tree," Lily May said.

High in the branches of the old cedar, we waited, eyes strained toward the house.

Presently, the front door flew open and Miss Camilla marched out with Fenton affixed to her side with one arm. Behind them came Maggie, her small frame bending forward as though in supplication. Octavos had the limousine door open. Miss Camilla pushed Fenton in, crammed herself in beside him, and they were off, leaving Maggie in a roll of dust. She stood watching them leave and then walked back to the house. Lily May and I stayed where we were.

A few moments later, the back door slammed and Ida called, "Lily May! Margaret! Y'all come here right now!"

I tightened my grip on the branch.

"You! Margaret! Lily May! Get yourselves to the

house!"

Slowly, I climbed down the tree. When I reached the ground, I looked up. Lily May was still on her perch.

"I ain't coming," she said.

I walked around to the back steps, crossed the porch, and went into the kitchen. Ida was banging pots around in the sink. She didn't so much as glance at me as I passed.

Maggie stood in the parlor, hands gripping the top of a chair. "What happened?" she asked.

My throat was drawn into a knot, and I tried several times before the words stumbled out.

"Fenton said he was going to ride Proud Beauty, and Lily May told him he couldn't."

"Yes?"

"He kept saying he was going to ride, and Lily May kept saying he couldn't."

"And?"

"He got mad and—and he said, 'Shut up, you ugly black bitch.'"

Maggie's jaw dropped.

"So I slapped his face." My words came out in a whisper.

"You—you what?" Maggie's eyes widened and gradually assumed a hard, steely look. Then she nodded and said, "You did the right thing, Margaret. Yes, indeed. You did what was right."

For the next several days, Lily May stayed away from the house. I never did find out what she told her momma. But whatever it was must have satisfied Ida, because she acted as though everything was fine. Maggie did, too.

For a long time, I thought about what had happened. Why I'd taken the blame for something Lily May did. How surprised I was when I said what I did to Maggie. The words must have come from some place deep inside me that

I hadn't known even existed. It had to do with Lily May being colored and my being white—and Fenton being white.

But Maggie had said I did the right thing, and I thought so too, in some tangled-up way. Fenton deserved to be slapped. I hadn't the nerve to do it myself. Yet in the end, I'd done the right thing.

CHAPTER 17

The summer was nearly over, and my thoughts had turned to preparations for school, when out of the blue Betsy invited me to go with her to Tybee Beach. Earlier, Aunt May Belle had told Maggie that Betsy was feeling low and Uncle Ira thought she should get away for a while. Of course, Louisa had been invited first. But she begged off, claiming too many commitments—dates with boys that she could have easily broken.

But all that suited me fine. I was eager to go on vacation with Betsy.

We arrived at Tybee Beach in the late afternoon and drove around for an hour before finding our cottage at the end of an oyster shell road. A screened porch facing the ocean was set up with tables and chairs and two cots, and we decided to do our living out there. After unloading about half the stuff from the car, we slipped into pajamas, then made bologna sandwiches and took them along with Cokes to the porch, where we settled down in two rockers. Betsy set her food on a table and lit a cigarette. "Ahh," she sighed, exhaling the smoke. She sounded as though she were in pain.

"Are you feeling low, Betsy?" I asked.

"Everything's fine." Her face looked gaunt in the shadows.

The beach was deserted and the tide was coming in, each heavy wave struggling to crest higher than the last, to break farther up on the dry sand. Near the water's edge, sandpipers glided on invisible legs while above them, coral-tinted gulls shrieked and dove for the last catch of the day.

Betsy stumped out her cigarette in a clam shell. "Did you know my family used to come to Tybee every summer?

Sometimes your family came with us."

"My mother? Did she come, too?"

Betsy nodded. "I can just see her there on the beach. Once, she stayed out the whole morning, painting a seascape. She had on this wide-brimmed hat and a long-sleeved white dress. There was nothing around her but the sea and the sky."

"I have a picture of her like that on the beach!" I exclaimed. "It's my favorite one."

"I can understand why." Betsy took a sip of her Coke, leaving her sandwich untouched.

I leaned toward my cousin. "Betsy, you hardly ever talk about Mother. No one does. Why is that?"

She shrugged. "Nobody said much about her after she died. I was only nine at the time, and I assumed it was supposed to be that way."

"But other people talk about family members who die."

"Well, I *can* tell you that your mother was a beautiful woman and an artist. Father once said artists aren't like other people. They have a certain enigmatic quality about them. Weezie—beautiful, artistic, enigmatic.... Why don't you just think of your mother that way?"

"What did Uncle Ira mean by enigma—"

"I also remember Father once called her Jim Norman's phantom of delight, you know, from the poem. My mother never thought that was particularly clever."

"Were Aunt May Belle and my mother close?"

"Not especially. Mother said Aunt Weezie was restless. 'Weezie and Max, they're the restless ones.' Sometimes I wondered if she wasn't just a little jealous of them."

"There's a picture of Aunt May Belle and my mother with some other girl standing outside in tennis dresses," I said. "Aunt May Belle sure looked unhappy."

"Weezie and her little friend, arms around each other,

faces scratched out?" Betsy grinned. She must have guessed that during those long afternoons while I waited at her house for Papa, I'd poked through everything, including pictures in the attic.

"The girls' faces weren't scratched out in the picture we had at my house," I said, hoping Betsy would assume that was where I had seen it.

"Did you say *had* the picture?"

"Papa took— It got lost."

"Well, my mother didn't like Aunt Weezie's friend, that's for sure."

Betsy pushed her untouched sandwich toward me. "Why don't you eat it?"

I picked up the sandwich. "And what about Mother's friend in the picture?" I was hoping my cousin would reveal more about Mother.

But Betsy held her watch up to the moonlight. "My word, it's past ten! Time for bed."

I lay down on my cot, but I planned to sit back up in a few moments so I could watch the tide go out. I breathed deeply of the warm, salty air....

The sun's glare on my face woke me up. Betsy was sitting on the step outside the porch in her pajamas. I got up and joined her. "I wish you'd woken me. I wanted to see the sun rise over the ocean."

"I've only been up a few minutes."

Beyond the broad beach, tiny waves lapped the shore and slipped back, leaving lacy fringes behind. Betsy stood up and brushed off her backside "Let's get some breakfast and then go swimming."

"Shouldn't we bring in the rest of the stuff from the car?"

"I'll tend to that while you fix us something scrumptious to eat."

"Can I fix anything at all?"

"As long as it's scrumptious."

I set the porch table with mismatched china and silver from the kitchen cabinet, made coffee for Betsy, and squeezed orange juice for us both. Then I cut chunks of the angel food cake Aunt May Bell had sent with us into soup bowls, spooned canned peaches over them, and poured on condensed milk.

"Breakfast is ready!" I called.

Betsy came from the bedroom. "Why, you've served a meal fit for angels!" she exclaimed.

"And there's plenty more where that came from," I said.

I was on my second helping of cake when I noticed that Betsy had eaten only a few bites of a peach. "Don't you like what I fixed?" I asked.

"Oh, I do, Margaret. It's that I never have much appetite in the morning. I usually just tank up on coffee."

It could have been the way the sunlight struck her face that made the circles under her eyes look so dark. I was about to ask how she'd slept when she got up and took her dishes to the kitchen. I finished up quickly and cleared the rest of the table.

When I came from the kitchen, she was sitting in the rocker, staring out at the ocean.

She turned toward me. "Let's wash dishes later. Get into your bathing suit. Last one on the beach is a rotten egg."

She had hardly gotten into the bedroom to change before I slipped out of my pajamas and into my suit right there on the porch. I ran from the cottage down to the water and stood in the shallows, letting little waves dredge the sand from under my feet and wondering how deep I would sink before she came out.

I'd sunk past my ankles when she walked through the screen door. She was wearing a black bathing suit with a white towel flung over her shoulders. As she walked toward me, a breeze lifted the ends of the towel, turning them into wings. She looked like some stick-legged sea bird.

That night we roasted hot dogs over a fire on top of a sand dune. Betsy ate half of one and buried the other half in the sand. "Fertilizer for sea oats," she explained.

After we'd eaten, we settled down on our towels to watch the waves crashing in. The air smelled of sulfur and fish.

Betsy scooped up a handful of sand and let it drift through her fingers. "Is that picture of Max still hanging in your parlor?" she asked.

"The one Mother painted of him with the dog?"

She nodded. "Father wanted her to paint another one like it to give to my mother on her birthday."

"I never saw the picture at your house."

"Aunt Weezie never painted it." Betsy drew her knees up to her chest. "Her excuse was that Max didn't like posing. But Father would have been satisfied had she copied the one she'd already done. I sure wish she had. Max was so gorgeous. I secretly planned to marry him when I grew up."

"Louisa did too!"

"Really?" Betsy faced me in the dark. "Did she tell you that?"

"Well, no. I heard it somewhere." I coughed, trying to distract her. Doubtless she knew about Louisa's diaries. I didn't want her asking me if I'd read them.

But all she said was, "Well, it's past history now."

The waves drew ever closer. I edged farther back on my towel.

Betsy yawned. "Wonder if German subs are out there under those waves."

"You think there might be?"

"Submarines have been spotted off the Florida beaches."

I studied the swells beyond the breakers. A particularly large one was moving rapidly landward. It could well be a submarine. It could beach a few yards away, and German sailors could jump out with guns. Fortunately, the swell peaked and crashed into foam.

"You think any Germans are out there right now, spying on us through periscopes?" I asked.

"Now, that's really scary." Betsy gave an exaggerated shiver. "Let's go back to the cottage."

I lay on my cot, too tired to brush off the sand that was scratching my back and shoulders.

Germans with guns were chasing me down the beach while Alicia Patricia cried in my arms. I ran into the waves. She cried louder. Lifting her high, I plunged deeper into the waves. My head went under the water, but I still heard her cry. I forced myself upward.

Betsy lay on her cot, sobbing softly. She might have been crying in her sleep as I sometimes did. But then she sat up and lit a cigarette. I watched the tip glow and dim in the dark. She stumped out the cigarette, lay down, and began crying again. I got up and went to her.

"Betsy, what's wrong?"

"I just want to die; that's what's wrong." She turned onto her stomach and buried her face in the pillow.

I knelt beside her and stroked her hair. "Is it because you don't have a baby?"

She nodded.

Poor Betsy. Which was worse, not having a baby and wanting one badly or having one, losing it, and being left with remorse?

"But you haven't been married long, Betsy. Ida's sister

was married five years before she had Dexter. Ida said sometimes folks have to try a long time before they have a baby."

Betsy turned onto her back and wiped the tears from her eyes. "But you do have to try. Both of you at least have to try."

I didn't know much about how to start babies, but I did know it took a woman *and* a man. And it involved kissing. Probably in some special way.

"I bet Rodney feels bad, too. But there must be things you can do. Tell you what, when you get home, ask Aunt May Belle to have Uncle Ira talk to Rodney about doing his part. Uncle Ira won't mind. He's so sweet. He can tell Rodney without hurting his feelings."

Betsy sat up and started to laugh. "Oh, Margaret, you're really too much." She reached over and hugged me.

After she let me go, she lay back on the cot. "But you're right about one thing. There are things I can do."

I tried to stay awake to make sure she didn't cry anymore but wasn't successful. The next morning when I woke up, she was lying on her back, snoring softly. Quietly, I got up, dressed, ate a bowl of cornflakes, and went outside to play in the sand. Betsy slept until noon.

For the rest of the week, I kept a close eye on her. Although she never ate much, she seemed to feel better. And as far as I could tell, she didn't cry anymore.

After we got back home, I planned to call every day to make sure she was all right. And I did call her once. She said she was fine. But with school about to start and so much to do, I didn't get around to calling again.

CHAPTER 18

"Is this seat took yet?" Laverne Pruitt pointed to the desk beside mine. It was still twenty minutes before class would start, but the seventh grade room was already half filled.

"No, you can have it," I said. "Mrs. Keon doesn't care where we sit as long as we behave."

"It's them boys what cause all the trouble." Laverne sat down and put her notebook on the top of the desk. Last year, Gene Autry's picture was stuck to the cover with electrical tape. This year, it was Roy Roger's.

"Well, at least Jimmy Bunger won't be around to start any more fights," I said.

Jimmy, the boy whose seat I had taken my first day at Slocum, had dropped out last spring after his daddy barged into the classroom, cussing and yelling because Miss Lampley had said Jimmy behaved worse than an animal. Mr. Hudson was there in a flash to escort Jimmy and his daddy out of the school. Moments later, I saw them through the window headed down the highway, Mr. Bunger flailing his arms and no doubt still cussing and yelling.

"And we won't need to be worrying no more about Lola Jean Thrasher and her meanness," Laverne said.

"What happened to her?"

"Got herself hitched."

"Married? You're kidding! She's only a few years older than me."

I looked around to see who else was missing. "Where's Lester Timmons?"

"Aw, that runty snuff-dipper run off from home. His old man whupped him one too many times."

So my tormentors were gone, and in a way I was

grateful. Certainly, I was glad Lola Jean was no longer around, although I felt sorry for whoever married her. I also felt sorry for poor little Lester. How could he survive on his own?

Laverne's pencil fell to the floor, and when she bent down to retrieve it, I smelled the strong odor of stale sweat mixed with Evening in Paris perfume. I got up and stepped over to the window. The schoolyard was strewn with clumps of newly mowed grass, and the air bore the sweet scent of hay. I took a deep breath before sitting down.

"Notice how different folks look this year?" Laverne pointed to some boys standing near the blackboard. "Their legs grown long as stilts."

"And that fuzz over Clive Pinkard's lip," I said. "Looks like smudged charcoal."

Laverne giggled.

Pearl Hubert Norton appeared in the doorway and paused to survey the room. Her eyes fell on me. I smiled and she quickly glanced elsewhere.

"There's another one what looks different." Laverne nodded toward Pearl Hubert. "Tacky different. Tight blouse with her buddies poking out like two headlights."

"She works Saturdays at Stumpy's," I said. "Probably bought the blouse with money she'd earned and didn't realize it was too small."

Laverne sighed and drew back her shoulders, revealing two small mounds of her own. "Oh well, if you got 'em, you might as well show 'em."

I glanced around at the other girls in the room. All but two stuck out in front. Nonchalantly, I hunched over my desk.

I was almost flat chested. I checked every night but nothing was happening. If things didn't start to change soon, I was going to take an old bra of Louisa's and wear it to school stuffed with cotton. I would not go through life as a freak.

* * *

Ever since I started to Slocum, Papa had dropped me off in the morning and Sam had picked me up in the afternoon. Everyone else rode the school bus or walked. Since riding home in a car made me different, I had begged Papa to let me walk, but he said two miles was too far. This year, though, he said I could walk.

Maggie was not happy about it. "True, Jim, she's older," I'd heard her say, "but she's also maturing. You know what could happen."

Papa replied, "You told her to stay on the road. I told her to come straight home. She's already been everywhere, and nothing has happened."

They were both wrong. I was not maturing, as Maggie thought. And Papa had no idea what had already happened to me.

But regardless of what either of them believed, I was glad I could finally walk home from school.

After class on the first day, I started out across the clay ball field next to the school. The field was dusty, and by the time I reached Flowering Peach Road, my white socks were orange. Pausing, I took a chocolate kiss from my book bag and popped it into my mouth. Then I jumped the ditch and started toward home.

"Wait up, Margaret Norman!" someone called from behind.

I turned to see Myrtie Lou Millwood and the Comstock brothers, F.L., T.C. and W.B., hurrying across the field toward me.

"You can walk with us," Myrtie Lou said. "It's funner if

you got company."

Myrtie Lou was the same age as I but a year behind me in school. Her father was a garbage collector. He had once come to our house to see about picking up our trash, but Papa told him Sam buried ours in the woods.

"What 'cha eatin'?" F.L. asked.

I opened my book bag, took out four kisses, and passed them around.

The Comstock brothers weren't triplets, although they looked alike and were all in third grade. They lived on Flowering Peach Road past where Cardinal Hill Road joined it. Although they had less distance to walk than Myrtie Lou or I, they traveled much farther. When Myrtie Lou and I turned onto Cardinal Hill Road, F.L., T.C., and W.B. were galloping full tilt back toward the school, yelling and shooting each other with their fingers.

"Where is that little dog that used to ride on the top of your daddy's truck?" I asked as we approached Myrtie Lou's house.

"Little Yip? The dog Pa come across one day when he was fixing to chunk a sack of trash in the fill. He heard this little yip, and when he opened the sack, there she was, stuffed in with the papers."

We paused at the end of Myrtie Lou's drive. I took out my last two kisses and gave one to her. "So, what happened to her?"

"She got hold of some bad meat and died."

I shifted the kiss to the back of my mouth where it stuck. My throat felt closed up. "What's the matter?" Myrtie Lou asked.

I shook my head and tried to swallow the chocolate. But it wouldn't go down.

Myrtie Lou peered at me, eyes drawing close like big fish eyes. "Want some water?"

I nodded and she ran down her drive. I waited a moment. Then I walked past the wild privet hedge near the road and into her clean-swept dirt yard.

A path lined with whitewashed tires sunk halfway into the ground led from the drive to the bright orange door of the little green house. On one side of the door stood a wood-burning stove, its top crowded with potted nasturtiums. On the other side sat a bathtub painted purple with lily pads floating in water. Beyond the house was a row of rusty bedsprings propped upright and covered with grapevines.

I started toward the path lined with tires when I heard a sound coming from behind the house, where a shed scaled with car license plates stood. Someone back there was spying on me.

Myrtie Lou came out with the water. I took a gulp and washed the candy down.

"Thank you," I said, returning the glass. I nodded towards the shed. "Who's back there?"

Myrtie Lou turned to look. "Oh, that's just Claud. Claud, you come out from there!"

A moment later, a shaggy-haired boy appeared and shambled toward us. He wore patched overalls and a faded blue shirt. He held his head so low that I couldn't get a look at his face.

"Claud, this here's Margaret that lives up yonder on top of the hill. Margaret, this here's my brother, Claud."

"Hey, Claud," I said.

Without lifting his head, Claud mumbled something that sounded like, "Hey-yo."

"Claud, he's shy," explained Myrtie Lou. "He can't look nobody in the eye. He quit school in sixth grade on account of Miss Lampley was fixing to make him stand in front of the class."

141

"I know. She did it to us." I said. "We all had to stand up and tell about a book we had read."

"Claud helps Pa on his garbage route now. Only he won't never go to the door if the lady forgets to set out the trash. He won't even hardly go in a store."

While Myrtie Lou talked, Claud scraped the ground with his shoe. Once he did raise his head enough to peek over at me. His soft brown eyes were rimmed with thick lashes. He did not need to be shy about how he looked.

"Well, guess I better get on home," I said. "Pleased to meet you, Claud. Thanks for the water, Myrtie Lou."

"Stop by for a drink every day if you like," Myrtie Lou said.

Claud looked at me sideways.

I did stop by every day for a drink. No, I'll be honest, I stopped by to see Claud. And every day was the same. While Myrtie Lou went for my water, Claud wandered over, and I said, "Hey, Claud, what 'cha doing?" He said, "Not much," and scraped his shoe on the ground until I said something else.

Behind the house were some old car hoods, wired together to form an enclosure. One day I asked what they were for.

"Rabbit pen," said Claud.

"You have rabbits?"

"Come look."

I followed him to the car hoods. Penned inside were two rabbits. "Where did you get them?" I asked.

"Bought 'em."

"What for?"

"Raise rabbits."

"Where are the other rabbits?"

"Both of 'em male."

For some reason, my face grew uncomfortably hot.

Claud started giving me presents. One day while Myrtie Lou was gone for my water, he gave me a rhinestone pin with a stone missing. Another day, he gave me a hand mirror with a small crack near the edge. He gave me a jar of cold cream that had hardly been used, a vase with a chip on the lid... When I got home, I always hid the presents away; I didn't want to explain where they came from.

One afternoon toward the end of the school year, Claud was out by the mailbox when Myrtie Lou and I arrived at their house. As soon as she'd left for my water, he reached into the box and drew out a brown paper bag.

"For graduating from grammar school." He held out the bag.

"Thank you," I said. "Should I open it now or wait till I graduate?"

"Whichever suits."

But from the look on his face, I could tell it suited *him* now.

I reached into the bag and took out a wooden box with a barely visible crack running across its smooth top. I dropped the bag and lifted the lid. "The Blue Danube Waltz" started to play.

"Oh, Claud! That's my most favorite waltz. Thank you, thank you so much!"

"You like it?" His face glowed.

"Yes! Yes, I do!"

"The top was broke clean off. But I glued it back on and sanded it smooth and rubbed it all good with tung oil. The song weren't hurt a bit."

Those were the most words Claud had ever said to me at one time.

"It's the most beautiful music box I've ever seen," I said.

And then I, Margaret Norman, age twelve, did the

most appalling thing I had ever done in my life. Clutching the box to my chest, I stretched up on my toes and kissed Claud Millwood right smack on the mouth! For one delicious moment, my lips pressed against his, warm and soft and tasting slightly of salt.

I came down off my toes. Claud's face grew dark. He stumbled backwards, then turned and ran up the drive, passing so close to Myrtie Lou that she spilled half the water.

"What ails Claud?" Myrtie Lou's eyes were stretched wide. "He looks like a bear done took off after him."

"I don't know," I said.

I swallowed the water and gave back the glass. "I've got to get on home."

Maggie had cautioned me to stay on the road. I'd left it, and nothing bad happened. Papa had warned me to come straight home; I hadn't and suffered no ill. Then this, right there on Cardinal Hill Road where I had only paused for a moment. No one had warned me of this.

The next day, as we approached Myrtie Lou's house, I told her I couldn't stop anymore. Ida needed me to come straight home to help in the kitchen. Myrtie Lou looked disappointed, but she didn't ask questions.

There were only a few more days until summer vacation, and I rushed out of school to get a good start on Myrtie Lou. When I passed her drive, I could see Claud fooling around in the yard. I never looked at him directly but hurried on by with my eyes straight ahead.

* * *

I was with child. It had started the day I kissed Claud Millwood on the mouth. I had picked up the germ—or whatever it was—and it had worked its way down to my

144

stomach.

Now, I could never get married, for no man would have me. I could never have friends. What parent would allow a daughter to associate with someone like me? I couldn't even attend Garrett High School in the fall. Girls in my condition weren't allowed to enroll. And the worst thing of all, my family would be in disgrace.

There was no doubt in my mind that I was with child. A few weeks before I kissed Claud, I had become a bona fide woman. It happened while Sue Lee Wright and I were downtown at a Saturday matinee of *Mrs. Miniver*. Mrs. Miniver had just found the German pilot in her garden when I went the ladies' room and made the discovery. Maggie had warned me it might happen soon. She'd tried to explain what it was, but we both got embarrassed. That was all right, though. Sue Lee had already shared what her sister told her. Ginger had called it "the curse." The curse was due again the first week of June. But the first week of June came and went and nothing happened. The second week came and went. Then the third week...

I tried to stay calm. Papa noticed nothing, but Maggie and Ida seemed suspicious. Once Maggie asked if I was feeling all right, and, of course, I said I was. Thank goodness, Lily May was away visiting kinfolk; I could never have hidden my secret from her.

There was only one thing to do—kill myself. The problem was the best way to do it. It had to look like an accident. But if I threw myself under a car, I might still end up alive with broken bones to boot. If I swallowed all Maggie's blood pressure medicine, some people might think I did it on purpose. I could shoot myself with Papa's shotgun, but I wasn't sure he had any shells. The best way would be to fall out of Papa's sixth story office window. I'd pretend to reach for a piece of paper caught by the wind and lean out too far. Doreen Hoyt could explain how it happened. I'd do it soon.

But on the last Tuesday in June, the crisis came to an end. I woke up to find stains on my sheet and pajamas. In case I was dreaming, I blinked my eyes a few times. The stains were still there.

I felt lighter than air, a balloon wafting upward. I glided into my clothes, got a wet rag to scrub out glorious evidence, and floated out to the kitchen where I consumed two bowls of cornflakes with sliced bananas on top.

"Look like you done got your appetite back," Ida commented.

Maggie came in with a bunch of hydrangeas. One fell to the floor.

"Whoopsy daisy," she said, picking it up.

"But they aren't daisies. They're hydrangeas!" I started to laugh.

I couldn't stop. My eyes watered, my nose ran, I almost fell out of my chair.

Maggie and Ida stared at me and at each other. Then they laughed, too.

CHAPTER 19

"These are for you." I handed Lily May a paper cup half full of the malted milk balls that I'd saved from the bag Maggie brought me from town.

"'Preciate it." She took two balls from the cup and stuck one in each cheek. She looked like a chipmunk.

"Momma say you miss me," she garbled.

"Why did she say that?"

"You be moping around. Miss Maggie say so, too."

I didn't respond. So, Maggie and Ida thought Lily May's absence was the reason I had acted so strangely. Let them believe it.

"Papa's bringing home a watermelon to celebrate Fourth of July," I said.

"How big?"

"Big enough."

Lily May extended the cup. "Want one?" she asked.

I put a ball into my mouth and ran my tongue over its thin, waxy skin until it slid off and the soft, fragrant chocolate coated my mouth. "This is my most favorite candy," I said.

"I like Tootsie Roll best," Lily May said.

After supper, we took our slices of melon outside and sat on the carriage steps. Leaning over so juice wouldn't drip onto my skirt, I bit into the crisp, sweet flesh.

Lily May bumped my shoulder. "Bet I can spit my seeds farther than you."

"I doubt it," I said.

At first, I didn't half try, and my seeds landed far short of hers.

She bumped my shoulder again. "Told you I could."

I changed my technique. Holding the seed loosely

between my lips, I drew a deep breath and released it with a "plooff!" That seed and the others that followed shot out beyond hers, a fact I was quick to point out.

Lily May jumped to her feet. "Girl, you cheating!" she yelled.

"I most certainly am not!"

"You lean so far out your butt ain't even touching the seat."

"You lean out that far out yourself."

"I ain't playing with no cheater." Lily May sat back down and turned away from me. She took another bite of the melon and smacked as loud as she could, which she knew greatly annoyed me. We ate for a while without speaking.

Then she said, "How come the sun rising?"

"It's not, you stupid."

"What that over yonder then?"

I looked in the direction she pointed. An orange glow lit the horizon.

"Oh, my goodness!" I jumped up and ran toward the house. "Papa, looks like a fire down near the highway!"

In an instant, he was in the yard.

"It's around Stumpy's," he said and hurried to the house for his keys.

Lily May and I scrambled into the back seat of the car.

The road to Stumpy's was full of potholes and ridges, which Papa usually maneuvered around. This time, though, he drove straight down the middle, bouncing Lily May and me all over the place.

"Sure hope we ain't fixing to get ourselves killed," she muttered.

Papa turned. "Where did you two come from?" he asked.

We didn't answer and he seemed to forget us.

He had just brought the car to a stop when the shed next to the store collapsed into a mass of sparks and flames like fireworks gone berserk. Stumpy was running back and forth in front of the shed, little arms flapping like a stricken bird's wings.

"You two stay here!" Papa jumped out of the car.

He ran toward the shed and disappeared into the narrow passageway between it and the store. My insides jerked into a knot.

"Papa!" I screamed, tumbling from the car and running after him. "Come back! Come back!"

Lily May was beside me, yanking my arm. "Quit your hollering. He know what he doing!"

Immediately, he reappeared with a hose jetting water. He trained the hose on the roof of the store where burning debris had ignited some shingles.

Sobbing, I lurched forward toward him— I couldn't budge; Lily May held my arm in a vice.

"Let go!" I tried to pull free.

"You behave," she ordered, easing her grip.

There was an explosion. Lily May and I stumbled backwards as a fireball shot upward and vanished into the night.

"Must of been that kerosene Stumpy keep in the shed," she said.

The flames on the store's roof were out, and Papa began spraying the side nearest the shed.

I said, "Sure hope he can—"

The rest of my words were drowned out by the arrival of Clyde Craddock's Model A Ford with Clyde at the wheel, urgently tooting his horn. He was almost upon us before he slammed on the brakes. Springing from the car like a grasshopper, he shouted to Papa, "I done called the firehouse!"

"Well, where's the truck?" Lily May shouted back.

Clyde spun around. "Y'all get back from there now!" He started to shoo us like chickens.

Suddenly, Papa dropped the hose and sprinted to the front of the store. He got there just in time to grab Stumpy as he was about to go through the door.

"Turn me loose!" Stumpy cried, struggling to get free. "My babies! My babies! I've got to get to my babies!"

"You can't help those birds," Papa said. "There's too much smoke in there for you to do anything for them."

"But they'll all die if I don't save them!" Stumpy stopped struggling, slumped to his knees, and began to bawl like a calf.

The hose Papa had dropped was coiling around like a snake, shooting water in every direction. Clyde grabbed it and was about to turn it back on the store when he noticed some people gathered near the highway.

"Y'all move now! Get away from here!" he yelled at them while pointing the hose straight at us. Shrieking, Lily May and I ran behind his jalopy.

Siren blaring and lights flashing, the fire truck finally arrived. Two firemen jumped out, unwound hoses, and sprayed the store—roof, side, and front. Then they sprayed what was left of the shed. It was all over quickly.

While one fireman rewound the hoses, the other one talked with Papa, Stumpy, and Clyde. Lily May and I edged in closer to hear.

Noticing us, Papa ordered, "You girls go on to the car."

He hadn't said to get into the car, so we sat on the running board. My hands were shaking. In fact, my whole body was shaking. The kerosene explosion and Clyde's sousing were bad enough, but what had really distressed me was when I saw Papa run between the store and the shed. I thought he'd be burned to death.

Yet while I trembled over what I'd been through, I felt relieved. For during that time when I believed I was with child, I'd had troubling thoughts. I'd thought that if Papa were out of the way—if it were only Maggie and Ida and me—somehow I'd be all right. Thinking such thoughts must have meant I didn't love Papa.

Tonight, though, if Lily May hadn't held me back, I'd have thrown myself into the flames. I'd have sacrificed my life trying to save his. That proved I loved him deeply.

The firemen finished their job and drove off. The folks on the highway dispersed. Papa, Stumpy, and Clyde went into the store. Lily May and I followed them inside. Except for the strong smell of smoke, everything in the store seemed the same. With one bleak exception. There was no chirruping, no fluttering of wings. The canaries all lay dead in their cages.

The three men stood near the front counter while Papa explained insurance to Stumpy, who nodded and mopped his eyes with a handkerchief. Then Clyde got a grocery sack and, winking at Papa, said, "Why don't y'all go outside? I'm fixing to clean up a little."

We sat on the benches in front of the store. I tried not to look through the door, but I couldn't help it. I watched Clyde move from cage to cage, scooping out small yellow bodies and dropping them into the sack. Then he went out the back door to where the burn barrel was. I covered my ears; I couldn't stand the sound of the crackling and popping. A few minutes later, Clyde came around to the front of the store and sat on the bench next to Stumpy.

"Stumpy, want to tell us how all this came about?" Papa asked.

"Lester Bunger," said Stumpy.

Lester was the older brother of Jimmy, the boy whose father had cussed out Miss Lampley. Lester had begun hanging around Stumpy's as soon as Pearl Hubert Norton began working there. I'd see him strutting around, talking loudly.

"Lester gave Pearl Hubert this silver identification bracelet for her birthday," Stumpy said. "He had her name engraved on the front and his on the back. For a while after that, she treated him nice. Then she stopped wearing the bracelet. Claimed a link had come loose."

"I heard when she said it," Clyde butted in. "Told her I'd fix it, but she said never mind."

Stumpy shook his head. "Nothing was wrong with the bracelet, and Lester knew it. This afternoon, he came stomping in here, demanding to know where she was. I said I hadn't seen her all day. He yelled a few choice words and stomped out.

"Around eight, after I'd locked up for the night, he was back, yelling and banging on the front door. I let him in. He tore down the aisles, swearing he'd kill her. He stormed back to my room and upended the bed."

"You should of called the law on him right then and there," Clyde said.

"I sure wish I—" Stumpy's voice broke into a sob.

"Take your time, Stumpy," Papa said.

Stumpy blotted his eyes. "When Lester was satisfied Pearl Hubert wasn't in the store, he charged out, ranting something about the shed. I ran to my room for the key. I didn't want him breaking the door down. But by the time I got outside, he had this bucket of gas and was throwing it onto the shed. I yelled at him to stop, but he paid no attention. He lit a book of matches and threw it, and when the flames shot up, he took off running. That fool wanted to burn Pearl Hubert alive."

On the ride home, I asked Papa how would it have been if Pearl Hubert had died in the shed.

"Lester would be charged with first degree murder," he said.

"No, what I mean is, what I mean is how would it have been for *me* if I'd seen her die in the flames."

"Don't think about that," Papa said.

It was past midnight before I got to bed. I didn't expect to sleep, but I did. And I dreamed. I was standing in front of an old house, and Claud Millwood was with me. "Why did you put it in there?" he asked. I didn't know what he meant. Then, the house was on fire and Papa ran out, holding a baby. They were both on fire.

I must have screamed because when I woke up, Papa and Maggie were standing beside the bed. "Were you having a nightmare?" Papa asked.

"I guess so. I can't remember."

I slept with Maggie the rest of the night.

The next day, the police picked up Lester and took him to jail.

No one knew where Pearl Hubert was. Whenever I went to Stumpy's I asked about her. But not even her father knew where she was. Finally, one of the old men who hung around the store said he'd heard she was living with kinfolk in the North Georgia mountains.

After he got out of jail, Lester was back at the store, strutting around as though nothing had happened. As though it was no bother to him that he'd driven a girl from her home, killed twenty-three canaries, and broken a little man's heart.

CHAPTER 20

As I passed her in the hall on my way to return Maggie's scissors, Louisa glanced up from the phone.

"And, Mimi, there are so many people!" She was signaling her friend Mimi Fuller that she wasn't alone.

I ambled along, taking my own sweet time. Once inside Maggie's room, I closed the door and put my ear to the keyhole.

"Coast clear," said Louisa. "Now, back to F."

Even though it was wartime and most young men were away in the military, there was still no shortage of them around Louisa. She had taken to referring to them by their first initial, F, of course, being Frank Varnedoe. She probably thought I didn't know who she meant. But I knew them all, even the three Bills: B-one, B-two, and B-three. I also knew she wasn't serious about any of them and had dated one after another all summer long.

Currently, she was seeing a lot of Howard Murray, a flat-footed 4-F'er who worked in his father's textile mill. Louisa seemed especially interested in Howard. So I, naturally, was especially interested in doing all I could to promote the romance.

"But F will be here next week!" Louisa exclaimed. "What will I do?"

Frank had been stationed at Fort Belvoir, Virginia, where he was an instructor in the engineering school. He was coming home for a few days before shipping out.

"I do write to him regularly," she protested. "It's the patriotic thing to do."

Louisa write to Frank regularly? Ha. In more than one letter to me, he had complained that he had received no letters from her. He'd made a joke of it, inquiring if a tank had run over her hand or if she'd joined up with the Navy. But I could tell he was bothered.

I myself wrote him at least once a week and not just because it was patriotic. I didn't want Frank to forget me before I had a chance to grow up. In the margins of my letters, I drew little pictures that he might enjoy—a rooster in full crow, a wobbly calf, a sow with a litter of pigs. Frank wrote that the pictures reminded him of his farm, and someday he'd show it to me. I could tell that he liked me, maybe more than just liked. Once he had written for me not to get serious with any other men while he was gone. He could have been kidding. But he also could have been asking me to stay true to him. He signed all his letters with "Love."

My back started hurting from bending over the keyhole, and I was about to drop to my knees when I heard a car coming up the drive. Moments later, Howard Murray's yellow convertible pulled up in front of the house.

Quickly, Louisa said good-bye to Mimi, and I heard her bedroom door close.

I answered the bell. Howard stood at the front door, wearing gray slacks and an apple green sports shirt open enough at the neck to expose dark, curly chest hairs. He smelled of cigar and lime juice. I showed him into the parlor.

"Where are y'all going?" I politely inquired.

"Swimming party," said Howard.

"Out at Franklin's Pond?"

"No."

"Lake Rebecca is much nicer. Ever been there?"

Howard got up and began to pace back and forth.

I changed the subject. "Did you read in the paper about those men who got caught selling counterfeit gas coupons? Imagine people so low down they'd try to make profits off of the war!"

Howard scowled.

Then I remembered an article in last week's newspaper about the fat contract his father's mill had gotten to manufacture underwear for the Army. "I mean Louisa says—"

"Louisa? You said Louisa?" Howard walked over and sat beside me.

It was my chance. "Louisa says anybody who interferes with the war effort is worse than a skunk. She really admires people who give their all to the cause. Like your father and you. Working so hard to turn out all that stuff for the Army. She thinks it's so patriotic."

Howard smiled modestly. "We do what we can."

Louisa appeared at the door and he jumped to his feet. "Say, you look swell!" he exclaimed.

They left arm in arm, and I couldn't help feeling pleased with myself.

* * *

"Has Frank been out to see y'all yet?" Sue Lee Wright asked.

It was Saturday and I was spending the night at her house. The next day I would ride to church with her family and afterwards go with my family to Frank's house for dinner.

"He only came for a short visit," I said.

Sue Lee knew nothing of my feelings for Frank. How just hearing his name made me flutter inside. How the way he looked in his lieutenant's uniform, all tanned and hard muscled, interfered with my breathing. Had she known, she'd have blabbed how I felt to the world.

Her parents were out for the evening, and we were

having our supper in the kitchen. Francine had already set out our plates of spaghetti and was sitting in a chair in the corner, paring her fingernails.

"Bless this food to our bodies and us to Thy service, amen," Sue Lee muttered, not even closing her eyes.

I cut off some spaghetti, which was all glued together, and put it into my mouth. The sauce tasted like pencil shavings. I looked at Sue Lee, who was stirring the goop around with her fork.

"We'll eat later," she mouthed.

After a few minutes, she said, "All finished, Francine," and got up from the table.

Francine stepped over. "Y'all ain't ate worth nothing. Miss Julie sure going to hear about this."

Sue Lee took two RC Colas from the refrigerator, and before Francine could protest announced, "Mother said we could have them."

Outside the kitchen she whispered, "When my parents go out, Francine dumps the leftovers on me."

Except for white furniture, everything in Sue Lee's room was pink—pink walls, pink rug, pink curtains, pink bedspread and pillows. As soon as she had locked the door, she pulled a box from under her bed. Inside were a jar of cashews, a can of smoked oysters, a jar of olives, a tin of chocolate truffles, and two boxes of cookies.

"Mother's company hoard," she explained. "She'll never miss these few little things."

She spread a pink sheet over the rug and laid out the food. We ate until we were stuffed.

After cleaning up the mess and getting into pajamas, Sue Lee put "In the Mood" on the phonograph player. Ginger had taught her to jitterbug, and she had promised to teach me. I already knew how to waltz from practicing the foot positions that were printed out in a magazine. Frank loved to dance, and I wanted to be prepared in case the opportunity arose.

"Boo-pee-dupe, dupe, dupe!" Sue Lee sang along with the record.

Suddenly, she grabbed my hand and started to sling me around.

"Wait, Sue Lee! Stop! I don't know the steps. What do you do with your feet?" I was lurching around like a drunk marionette.

She lifted the phonograph needle, laughing so hard she could hardly stand up. "Oh, Margaret, you should see yourself. You look hilarious!"

"You're going too fast; I can't make out what you're doing. You've got to slow down."

"Okay, don't get your dandruff up. It's not all that hard. Just hang loose and jive."

But this time she took me through the steps slowly. Again and again until I could do them.

Finally, she turned off the light and we climbed into bed. Outside the window, a full moon lined a tree limb with silver. I thought about Frank. How glorious he looked in his lieutenant's uniform. How luscious it felt when he hugged me.

I also thought about Howard Murray and how cleverly I had gotten him steamed up over Louisa. Howard would take care of her. A sensation of power surged through my veins. It was exciting to fool around with other folk's lives.

"If you could go with any boy in the world, who would it be?" Sue Lee asked dreamily.

"Oh, I don't know," I lied. "Who would you choose?"

"Hmm, let me see...." She started way back in kindergarten and discussed every boy she had known since. She wanted to go with them all.

I closed my eyes and turned onto my side. Sue Lee

began snapping her fingers. I began snapping mine. We were out of bed and dancing again, this time in moonlight.

And this time it was Frank holding my hand, swinging me out, drawing me back—

Someone pounded the door. Sue Lee flipped off the record.

"You two settle down!" Mr. Wright thundered. "It's way after midnight."

We hadn't even known her parents were home.

The next morning I felt like a rag. Sue Lee begged her father to let us skip Sunday school and catch the bus downtown for church. He wouldn't hear of it.

The service seemed unusually long, and so did the drive to Frank's house with my family afterward. After we passed through Clearwater, South Carolina, Louisa directed Papa to turn onto a dirt road running between two cornfields.

"That's all part of the Varnedoe property," she said, waving her hand toward the fields.

"The peaches too?" I asked. We were approaching an orchard with thousands of trees planted in precise rows.

"All of it." There was a proprietary note in her voice.

We rode past a cotton field, another peach orchard, and four whitewashed houses. Louisa took out her compact and inspected her face. She licked one finger and straightened an eyebrow.

I smoothed my hair and breathed into my cupped hands, trying to get a whiff of my breath and wishing I'd remembered to bring my package of Sen Sen.

"Turn here!" cried Louisa.

Papa swung the car onto a drive, causing me to veer sideways. I barely touched Louisa, but a few grains of powder spilled from her compact onto her skirt, and she shoved me hard.

"Stay off me, idiot!" she hissed. "Look what you've done!"

"It's not my fault! You should have told Papa earlier he needed to turn, so he wouldn't have to jerk the car around."

"I don't want to hear any more fussing!" Papa said sharply.

Louisa brushed off the powder, almost hitting my face with her hand. I wished she *had* hit me. Then I could really complain.

The drive was straight and long. On either side were fenced pastures where Holsteins and Guernseys grazed on blue-green Bermuda grass. At the end of the drive stood a two-story white house with square columns across the veranda. Frank and his mother were outside on the steps. As we pulled to a stop, they started down toward us.

Wilfreda Varnedoe was a small, almost frail-looking woman, except for her eyes—black agates that snapped when she talked. "So this is the artist Frank has been telling me about," she said to me after introductions were made.

Louisa eyed me sharply, and I gave her a smug look.

As we started inside, Miss Wilfreda took my arm. "Invite me to your first art show and I'll buy a painting. Flowers, perhaps."

Frank, who was walking behind us, tapped my shoulder. I turned and he grinned. Louisa missed it. She was busy picking a thread off her sleeve.

The central hall of the house was shorter than ours and wider. Old portraits hung on the walls. Vases of wildflowers sat on side tables. Through a doorway on the left, I saw a room with tall shelves packed with books. Miss Wilfreda gestured toward the doorway on the right.

"Come sit in the parlor," she said.

The room was crowded with dark, shabby furniture. A large tapestry with a rip down one side hung on a wall.

Frank saw me stare at the tapestry and grinned. "Mater's a great preserver of things past," he whispered, "even when things past are in shreds."

After we sat down, a butler appeared with a tray of drinks in small crystal goblets. As he approached me, I glanced around. Papa, Miss Wilfreda, and Maggie were absorbed in conversation. Louisa was searching her purse. Frank had stepped from the room. The butler held the tray out to me; I picked up a goblet and gulped down the drink. My head exploded. Later, when we went into dinner, I still felt dizzy.

Ida always served big Sunday meals, but nothing compared with the meal Miss Wilfreda's cook served. There was baked ham *and* fried chicken, boiled okra, butter beans, rice and gravy, corn-on-the-cob, squash casserole, sweet potato soufflé, sliced tomatoes, pickled peaches, watermelon rind preserves, cornbread and biscuits. I took some of everything the first time around and a little of some things the second time around. When dessert, almond cake topped with peach ice cream arrived, my stomach was in danger of bursting. After coffee in the parlor, Miss Wilfreda said, "Would you all like to see those Guernsey calves Mr. Norman and I have been talking about? A stroll might do us all good."

"Splendid idea," Papa said "How about you, Maggie?"

"Yes, indeed!"

Louisa shot Frank a quick glance. "I'm so sorry I'll have to decline," she said, "but I have a blister on my heel and it hurts me to walk."

"If you don't mind, I'd like to look at some those books in the library," I said. I needed to stay behind to keep an eye on Louisa.

"Then I'll gallantly offer to remain with the young ladies," said Frank.

After the others had left, he asked, "Would you two like to sit on the veranda?"

Before I could answer, Louisa said, "Margaret, if you're going to look at books, you've got to keep them inside the house."

No law said that I did. But it was all right; I could see the veranda perfectly well through the library window. I took down an art book and settled into a chair. I had a perfect view of Frank and Louisa sitting on a porch swing. In a few minutes I'd go out and ask Frank some question or other. I opened the book and leaned back in the chair....

* * *

Maggie was shaking my shoulder. "Sister, it's time to leave."

I straightened and looked all around. "Where am I?" I asked. I had slept through the whole afternoon.

On the ride home, Louisa was unusually quiet. Even when I rolled down the window, causing her hair to blow wild, she didn't complain. Something was wrong.

The next afternoon, I was lying across my bed, reading *Jane Eyre*, when I happened to glance out the window and see Frank's car parked alongside Papa's. I got up, brushed my hair, and hurried out of the room.

Ida was at the kitchen sink, peeling potatoes.

"Isn't Louisa still in town with her girlfriends?" I asked.

"Mr. Frank be here to see Mr. Jim," Ida said.

I went down the hall to the parlor. The door was closed and the voices inside were too low to hear. I bent my ear to the keyhole.

"Aw, now, little Biscuit, come back from there."

Ida stood at the end of the hall. I shushed at her with my hand.

"Margaret, come here," Ida said louder.

I shushed at her again, more vigorously this time.

She started toward me. "Margaret, get yourself away—"

I straightened and walked out the front door. Once outside, I started to run. Away from the house, down to the woods. When I couldn't run anymore, I stumbled along till I was halfway to Flowering Peach Road.

A thicket of Carolina cherry trees lay to my right. I crawled inside it and sank into the carpet of leaves on the ground. I wished I could sink into the ground and never come up.

By the time I started back up the hill, saffron shreds in the sky were all that remained of the day. Cicadas crowded the air with their love calls. A cardinal perched in a crepe myrtle tree exchanged love notes with its mate.

In the kitchen, Ida was drying some saucers. "Where you been to? You done missed the excitement. Mr. Frank asked Mr. Jim for to marry Louisa. Mr. Jim he say yes. We been celebrating."

I sat at the table and Ida put a slice of pound cake before me. I watched the cake blur into the saucer and the saucer into the table.

So he would marry Louisa. Louisa, who never answered his letters, who carried on with every man she could find. Louisa, who never cared for anyone but herself. Didn't he know it was I who truly loved him? That I had loved him from the moment I saw him and would till the moment I died?

I got up from the table and went to the porch off my bedroom. Mother's little green car, which Louisa had driven to town, was parked beside Papa's big gray one. The spot where Frank's car had been was empty. As empty as my own heart.

CHAPTER 21

For three nights, I cried myself to sleep in despair over Louisa's engagement to Frank. Then I began to realize that all was not lost. Frank was overseas. I wrote to him regularly; Louisa did not. Howard Murray was still in the picture. He and Louisa often talked on the phone. Occasionally, he took her to parties. After all, Frank and Louisa were only engaged, not married. As Maggie would say, "There's many a slip between the cup and the lip."

Summer was nearly over, and in two weeks I'd start attending Garrett High School for girls, a two-story, yellow brick building near the bottom of Fredericks Hill. There was so much I needed to do: put my wardrobe together, and learn about classes and teachers, which necessitated phone conversations with Sue Lee, already informed by her sister Ginger. Most exciting of all, I had to buy art supplies! Papa was finally going to make good on his promise to let me take art lessons.

He planned to drive me to my first lesson, and the first Tuesday after school, he was waiting out front in his car.

"How was your day?" he asked after I'd settled into the front seat.

"Fine. I really like civics class. Sue Lee Wright is taking it, too."

We proceeded down the long drive to Washington Way, where he stopped at the traffic light.

"Have everything you need?" He nodded toward the back seat where, the night before, I'd placed a paper bag containing my art supplies.

"All except the Number 25 brush. The store still hasn't gotten it in."

"Your Latin class, how is it?"

I looked at Papa. He was sitting more rigid than usual, hands tightly gripping the steering wheel. And all these questions, when he usually just asked, "How was your day?"

"Latin's okay. Sue Lee's in that class, too."

The light changed and he turned onto Washington Way.

I glanced at the back seat. "Oh, my goodness, I forgot my paint shirt. It's on my dresser. Papa, could we go home and get it?"

"Your teacher will have something you can use this time."

But she might not, and if I came unprepared, she might think I wasn't a serious student. It was important to make a good first impression. Art was the link between my mother and me. I had to succeed, to show the connection. I slumped down in the seat.

Papa switched on the radio. The announcer was reading the day's cotton report with an urgency that suggested millions hung on his every word. I stared out the window. At the top of the hill, he turned onto a street paved with red bricks. The tires sounded a muffled tattoo as we rolled across them.

"Not far now." Papa extended and flexed his fingers.

My heart quickened. After yearning so long for this day, now that it had finally arrived, I was scared.

We passed two blocks of large houses set back on wide lots. In the middle of the third block, Papa slowed the car and nodded to his left. "Home of Tallulah Cassels. Largest house on the street. Probably the largest in the town."

From where I sat, I couldn't tell. All I saw were five brick chimneys rising above a green mass. The yard was a jungle. Camellia bushes crowded against magnolia trees three stories high. Azaleas clumped around dogwoods. In what spaces remained, forsythias, bridal wreaths, and rambling roses tangled together.

Papa turned into a tunnel of green that came out in front of a Victorian mansion badly in need of repair. A small balcony hung loose on one side off an upstairs window. Bees buzzed in and out of a hole near the top of a porch column. Everywhere, white paint had flaked off, exposing gray wood underneath.

"Built by the late John Joseph Cassels," Papa said. "In his day, one of the richest men in the state."

We rode past the house and stopped in front of a yellow cottage with white trim and green shutters. A brick walk bordered with boxwoods led from the drive to a porch that extended the length of the cottage. As we stepped from the car, one of the two evenly spaced doors painted in wild floral patterns opened, and a woman wearing a purple smock stepped onto the porch.

"Jim Norman!" she said, walking down the steps toward us. "It's been a long time." Her voice sounded detached.

In the sunlight, her hair, which was gathered into a bun near the top of her head, shone like new copper pennies.

She stopped a few feet away and looked Papa up and down with bold green eyes. "A little thicker around the middle, a lot grayer on top. Otherwise, much the same."

"How are you, Tallulah?" Papa bowed stiffly. "This is my daughter Margaret. As I mentioned to you on the phone, she seems to have inherited her mother's interest in art. I'd like you to see what you can do with her."

Miss Tallulah turned her bold eyes upon me and studied my face—every contour, freckle, and pore. "She doesn't resemble Weezie, except about the brow and the chin." She stepped back to examine the rest of me, which in the past year had become rather bony. "And she has your slender build."

Papa shifted from one foot to the other. "Except for the coloring, Louisa is the one who takes after her mother. In looks and in temperament."

"So I've heard," Miss Tallulah said dryly.

The scene played out before me made me feel wobbly right down to my toes. In the first place, I didn't like being stared at. In the second place, I didn't like seeing my father so ill at ease. In the third place, who was this woman who seemed to know so much about my family? When Papa first mentioned her name, I had a vague sense of having heard it before. But when I asked who she was, he said only that Uncle Ira—whose opinion he valued—had insisted that she was the best art teacher around.

Papa glanced at his watch. "I need to get back to work. Margaret, you know where to wait for the bus to ride downtown. I'll meet you at my office after your lesson."

As he turned to walk back to the car, I had an impulse to follow, to leave this odd woman with her unsettling ways.

But before I could move, she took hold of my arm. "Come with me," she said. "We'll see how much of your mother's considerable talent has been passed on to you."

The cottage consisted of one large room, airy and bright with windows across the back and side walls. The front wall was lined with shelves that held art supplies. Propped on the top shelf were copies of paintings, some of which I had seen before in Uncle Ira's art books.

Near a back window, easels were set around a small table. Miss Tallulah pointed to an easel that held an open sketchbook, a paint-smeared shirt draped over the top. A tray of art supplies rested on the camp stool nearby. "You can work there," she said.

I lifted my bag of art supplies. "I brought everything on your list, except the Number 25 brush."

She nodded toward the tray. "This time, use what's already out."

She took a vase of half-dead roses from a shelf and set it on the table. "Paint it," she said, and walked to a sink where she began washing brushes and paint pots.

I sketched out the roses and stepped back to examine my work. Something wasn't quite right, but I moved on to the paints. I mixed red and white pigment, adding water a drop at a time, and began painting the roses. The pink was too bright, so I mixed in a speck of black, redrew some petals, and put on more paint. It wasn't much better, but I didn't know how to improve it. I painted the leaves gray with a suggestion of green and paused again to look at my work. It still didn't look right.

I was applying a spot of white to a leaf when Miss Tallulah said, "Move aside. Let's see what you have."

Frowning, she studied the painting, tilted her head one way, then the other. She leaned close to examine a smudge on one side of the vase.

"What's that?" she asked.

"A shadow. It's supposed to look like a shadow." I felt myself growing hot.

She splayed her fingers over the smudge. "Then be a shadow."

With her thumb, she followed the lines of the vase and stopped at its center. "Something's flat here."

She lifted her thumb. "And the tint of the leaves, certainly not citron. More the color of— of bilge water?"

I wanted to jerk up the picture and run from the cottage.

"But now here," she traced two fingers along some petals and stems, "look what you've caught—the dried look of the flowers, the sad curve of their stems. And this pale, fragile pink. A hint that color will soon fade completely."

Stepping back from the painting, she turned toward me, unsmiling. "You do have promise, Margaret Norman," she said. "Considerable promise."

Something within me cut loose, and I blinked a few times. "Thank you," I said hoarsely.

Her eyes probed my own. "Is your father right? Do you have your mother's deep love of art?"

"I didn't know my mother like that. In fact, I didn't know her at all."

Gesturing toward the easel and paints, she said, "Clean up your mess and take off that shirt. I'm putting you in a class with four other girls, all older than you, all having studied with me for some time. You'll have to work hard. You are planning to work hard on your art, aren't you?"

"Yes, ma'am, I am."

And I did. At school, during dull general science, I sketched profiles of classmates. In the afternoons while waiting at Papa's office, I copied drawings from books I'd brought with me. On weekends, I went to the woods and drew whatever I could find. Louisa may have inherited my mother's disposition and beauty, but I had inherited her talent in art. I wanted there to be no doubt about that.

* * *

"You've got to sit down!" Sue Lee said over the telephone. "Sit down, Margaret. Are you sitting down?"

I dropped into the chair next to the phone table and shifted the receiver to my other ear. "I am now. What's the matter?"

"Just the most terrible thing in the world!"

I gripped the edge of the table. "What is it, Sue Lee? For goodness sakes, tell me!"

She blew her nose hard. "Well, last night, I went to

youth council meeting at church."

"Yeah, you told me you were going."

"And afterwards I was supposed to ride home with Mary Nicolette Law 'cause her father was there at the deacons' meeting. But you know it's really out of the way for Mr. Law to take me home, and Mr. Harper passes almost in front of my house."

"You didn't ask the *minister* for a ride?"

Sue Lee still had a crush on Mr. Harper, badgering her mother to invite him for dinner and sending cards on his birthday. Once she even sent an anonymous valentine.

"I didn't exactly ask him," she said. "I just went to his car and—"

"And?"

"I don't know what made me do it, but I got in the back seat and scrunched down."

"Sue Lee, you didn't!"

"He came out and got in the car and we were a couple of blocks from the church and he started singing, 'When the roll is called up yonder,' and I giggled or something. Anyway, he jerked the steering wheel and the car jumped the curb and hit a telephone pole. It broke out a headlight and bent the front fender."

I clapped a hand to my heart. "Oh, Sue Lee, how awful!"

"I know! And the police called my parents, and I explained I was trying to save gas for the war by getting Mr. Harper to take me home instead of Mr. Law, but they still about killed me. They won't let me go anywhere or have any more fun for the rest of my life!"

It was all too much for my friend. Her weeping was piteous to hear.

When her sobs finally subsided, I said, "Everything will work out all right, Sue Lee. Your parents will let you do things again."

"No, they won't. They'll never give in. I can't listen to the radio. I can't spend the night out. We can't sit together in church—" She grew too distraught to continue.

I waited a moment and said, "But we will still see each other at Sunday school and regular school. We can still talk on the phone."

The next Sunday, I was back with Papa and Maggie in the family pew. A few rows ahead of me on the other side of the aisle, Sue Lee sat between her parents. During the prelude, she looked back at me, her face drawn and forlorn.

Directly in front of my family, Miss Clarissa Hoadly sat alone in her pew. For as long as I could remember, Miss Clarissa and her crippled daughter, Laura, had always sat in front of us at church, even after the time Papa moved us to a pew nearer the pulpit. The next Sunday, those two were in front of us again.

When the congregation stood to sing the Doxology, Miss Clarissa turned and stared at me. I looked down at the floor. When we stood to sing "A Mighty Fortress," she turned again and stared. In fact, every time the congregation stood during the service, Miss Clarissa stared at me. I felt most uncomfortable.

On the way to the car after the service, I asked Maggie why Laura Hoadly wasn't in church with her mother.

"The poor thing has become too incapacitated to attend," Maggie said.

Laura, a thin, sallow-faced woman, had eyes that reminded me of those of a kitten I had once seen that had been stomped by a cow. My earliest memories of Laura were of her walking down the aisle in an odd, lurching manner. Later, she'd started using a cane.

"But she's always been incapacitated," I said.

Maggie said nothing.

The next Sunday, as soon as I slid into the pew, Miss Clarissa turned and nodded. I managed to smile. She nodded several more times during the service. The Sunday after that, before the service began, she said to me, "What a lovely dress you are wearing." I thanked her. While the offering was being collected, she turned and said, "Your hair is so pretty." I squirmed and Maggie patted my knee.

"It's so embarrassing," I complained on the ride home from church. "Why is she talking to me?"

"Next Sunday, you sit on the aisle," Papa said. "That will put more distance between you."

But putting more distance between us didn't help; Miss Clarissa only spoke louder. While we recited the Apostle's Creed, she called to me, "Remember, dear, mind your mother." While Mr. Harper pronounced the benediction, she leaned back and pleaded, "Please, Laura, be careful!"

"Perhaps we should change pews," Maggie suggested as we rode home.

"Doubtless she would change, too," Papa said.

"Did you hear her call me Laura?" I asked. "What did she mean?"

"Her behavior grows more bizarre all the time," Papa said.

"But what did she mean calling me Laura?"

Papa switched on the radio to a news station, and we rode the rest of the way home without speaking. During dinner, I brought up the subject again. "Why did Miss Clarissa call me Laura?"

Papa paused and looked thoughtful. Then he said, "Perhaps in some way you remind her of her daughter."

That pitiful, dull-eyed creature? "But how—?" I began.

Papa's frown silenced me.

After dinner, I went to my room and lay on my bed.

Maggie came back and sat beside me.

"Child," she said, "your father thought I might—" She nibbled her lips. "Clarissa Hoadly is a confused person. In her state of mind, she could imagine any young girl is her daughter."

"But I don't look like Laura. I have brown eyes and straight hair."

"Of course, you don't look like her. But Laura didn't always look the way she looks now. She was once a lovely young lady."

"Did you know her back then?"

"I've only heard."

"What happened to her?"

"She was in an automobile accident."

"Was Miss Clarissa in the accident, too?"

"No."

"Then why does she act so peculiar?"

Maggie pulled her handkerchief from her sleeve and blotted her lips. "Unresolved grief, perhaps. Anger over what happened to her child. Your father thinks it's best if you put the whole thing out of your mind."

When I was small, Papa wouldn't tell me about my mother when I asked him to. I thought I understood that. It hurt too much to talk about her. But why wouldn't he answer questions about Laura Hoadly? Why wouldn't he allow Maggie to? Did he think I'd stop being curious? That I'd forget?

Unanswered questions are never forgotten.

CHAPTER 22

As I passed Maggie's room on my way to the kitchen, I heard her say, "...sometimes all one can do is love and endure."

Backing up a few steps, I peered through the door. She and Ida were on the other side of the room near the window.

Maggie looked over and saw me. "You want something, child?"

"No ma'am, I'm just on my way to get something to eat. Anything wrong?"

"We're having a conversation. Nothing that concerns you."

I continued on to the kitchen. Everything that went on in our house concerned me. Sooner or later I'd find out what they were talking about.

It concerned Ida, that much I knew. And not just because of what I'd overheard. The day before, I had stepped onto the back porch where she was ironing to ask if she'd seen a book I'd misplaced.

"Naw." She ran the iron over my blouse. The rising steam smelled of warm breezes and sunshine.

I was about to go back inside when it struck me that Ida hadn't been singing. Ida always sang when she ironed. She claimed it made her work easy.

"Anything wrong?"

"Naw," she said again. But she held her head in way that I couldn't look into her eyes.

Months passed and I'd almost forgotten Ida's conversation with Maggie. Then one rainy November morning, as I lay in bed, listening to a crepe myrtle branch scrape against the outside of my window, Maggie came back to tell me it was time to get up for school. I told her my throat felt itchy and I hadn't slept well. She put her hand on my cheek.

"You have a fever," she said. "You'll stay home today."

Later, she brought back a tray with a glass of orange juice and a bowl of hot oatmeal covered with cream and brown sugar. It tasted so good, but each swallow cut my throat like a knife. I set the tray to one side, slid under the covers, and fell asleep. When I woke, I felt better. I got up, put on my slippers and robe, and went to the kitchen, expecting to find Ida or Maggie. Instead, there sat Lily May on a stool, eating an apple.

"What are you doing home from school?" I asked. "You sick too?"

Since starting to high school, I didn't see Lily May often. She was now a sophomore at Rainey Institute. Horace, Junie's husband, who worked downtown, drove her back and forth every day.

Lily May took the last bite of her apple and threw the core into the slop bucket. "I ain't sick," she said.

"Then why aren't you at school?"

"I don't go no more."

"What? But you've got to get an education if you want to be a teacher."

"I ain't studying about being no teacher."

"Why not? Teachers get lots of respect."

"Teachers get nothing but hard work and misery. They don't make no money, neither."

"But what if you decide to be a nurse or a secretary? You've got to get an education for them."

"I don't want to do none of that stuff, so ain't no use wasting my time in school."

I pulled my robe closer, but it didn't warm the chill in my heart. "Lily May, don't drop out of school. You need to get your education."

"I done made up my mind, and ain't nobody can change it."

She stared past me through the window; her chin trembled a little. Then she slid off the stool and started toward the back door. Her skirt bulged out in front.

"Lily May! What's th—"

"What's the what?" She peered at me sideways.

"You're not— Are you going to have a baby?"

She widened her eyes as though surprised by my question. "How come you to say that?"

"You're poked out in front!"

She looked down at her tummy. "Aw, that ain't nothing but the sausage and grits I ate for breakfast."

"You're teasing. You're having a baby."

My knees felt weak and I sat down in a chair. It seemed only a short time ago that I thought I was having a baby because I'd kissed a boy on the lips. I knew better now; Sue Lee had shared all Ginger told her.

"Oh, Lily May, you shouldn't be doing that. You aren't even married." My throat felt as though it had been scraped with a cheese grater.

She smoothed her skirt over the bulge. "Don't just married folks can have babies. Or is you so dumb you still don't know that?"

"I do know. But you were going to get your education. You were going to be a teacher. Papa was going to help you go to college and everything. I don't understand."

Lily May gave me a look that was as hard as a skillet. "No, you sure don't understand, Margaret. You don't understand nothing." She turned and walked from the kitchen.

I felt dizzy and weak. What did she mean saying I didn't understand? I understood she had surrendered a

176

dream.

I went back to bed. Later, Maggie came to my room, took my temperature, and gave me two aspirins, which helped ease the pain in my throat. I tried not to sleep because when I did, I had troubling dreams. Sometimes, I couldn't tell whether I was asleep or awake.

Lily May and Margaret, closer than sisters. Ida would tell of the time when we were babies, and Lily May climbed into my playpen and took my rag doll. When my screams brought Maggie and her to the room, they found Lily May hugging both doll and me, trying to comfort.

Maggie had made us identical topsy-turvy dolls. At one end was pink-skinned, blue-eyed, yellow-haired Topsy. At the other end was brown-skinned, brown-eyed, black-haired Turvy. For years, we'd played with those dolls. Sometimes we switched roles. I would be Turvy, all bossy and quick-tempered like Lily May, and she would be Topsy, all whiny and stubborn like me.

I'd made up stories about Lily May and me. After she slapped Fenton Lupton and I took the blame, I imagined we were downtown when a redneck cracker made an ugly remark about a white girl and a colored girl being together. Without hesitation, I'd stepped up to that cracker and told him he should be ashamed of himself. Everyone around admired how I'd stood up to the man. Another story was about her high school graduation. The principal announced she was the most outstanding student in the class, and Lily May said, "I wouldn't be so outstanding if it weren't for my good friend, Margaret Norman." The whole audience stood and applauded while I sat with my head humbly bowed.

Lily May and I had grown up together; we were the closest of friends. True, we had recently drifted apart, but the bond was still there. She had no right to leapfrog over me into the middle of life. I felt betrayed. Without my even being aware, she had taken away something precious.

* * *

While I lay across Maggie's bed, still weak from my bout with strep throat, she sat near the window, tatting, knobby fingers flicking the needle over and through loops of thread that formed into a long, lacy pattern.

"Who's the father?" I asked.

Maggie pressed her lips together.

I repeated the question. "Who's the father?"

She sighed and laid down her work. "Lily May won't say, but Ida thinks it's James Roy Curtis."

"James Roy Curtis, who's that?"

"Horace's cousin."

"That man from Detroit who visited at Hazel and Odell's last summer? He's way too old for Lily May."

Maggie said nothing.

"Why does Ida think it's James Roy?"

Maggie shook her head. "It's an unfortunate situation all around."

I'd get no more information from her.

I had met James Roy Curtis. One Sunday afternoon when I was in the back yard, this shiny black car pulled up behind the house. Ida, Junie, and Dexter got out. They'd stopped by to show Maggie how much Dexter had grown. We went to the kitchen where Maggie gave Dexter a cookie. As soon as he'd eaten it, he wanted to go back outside to his daddy. I said I'd take him.

Horace was propped against the fender of the black car, and Dexter ran to him. I walked to the car and leaned down. Lily May was crowded up against the man behind the wheel.

"How you doing, Lily May?" I said.

"Hey." She didn't look at me.

The man leaned over and stared past her at me. His eyes were like snake eyes, constant and cold. I straightened and went to sit on the carriage steps to watch Horace gallop around with Dexter on his shoulders.

Maggie, Ida, and Junie came outside.

"James Roy," Ida said, "get yourself out from that car so Miss Maggie can meet you."

The man didn't budge. Then after a moment he opened the door and slid out.

He was short with yellowish skin. His black suit had wide, padded shoulders and a yellow handkerchief folded in the coat pocket. He was old enough to be Lily May's father.

"Miss Maggie, this here's James Roy Curtis from up there in Detroit," Ida said. "He make them big Army trucks like what's out at Camp Walker."

"Nice to meet you, James Roy," Maggie said.

"How-to-do, ma'am," said James Roy.

Not long after that meeting, James Roy and his car went back to Detroit, and I never saw him again, at least not up close.

For the next several months, Lily May stayed away from our house. Occasionally, I'd see her taking in firewood or sitting in the sun on her doorstep. By spring, she looked as though there was a giant balloon under her skirt.

On the second Sunday in April, I woke up at first light to the noise of two sparrows arguing on the porch railing outside my screen door. Rolling onto my side, I coughed just to watch the birds fly away. I slipped out of bed and went out on the porch. Beyond the dew-silvered pasture, smoke rose from Ida's chimney. She was fixing Lily May's breakfast. I took a deep breath of the spring-sweetened air, held it a moment, and let it out with a rush. Tingles charged through my body.

The door to Ida's house opened and she came out with a suitcase. She walked down the steps, set the suitcase on the ground, and went back inside. When she came out again, she was holding Lily May's arm. Slowly, they walked down the steps. Ida picked up the suitcase, and they started toward my house. I ran inside to the kitchen. Papa and Maggie were at the table, drinking coffee, Maggie in her church dress and Papa in shirtsleeves.

"Papa, Lily May and Ida are coming over with the suitcase," I said.

He swallowed the rest of his coffee and stood. "I'll put on my coat and tie and be ready to take them to the hospital."

I hurried back to my room for my slippers and robe. By the time I got outside, Ida and Lily May were in the back of the car, the suitcase propped up between them.

"I sure hope you get along all right, Lily May," I said through the half-opened window.

Lily May, lips tight, stared straight ahead.

I reached through the window and touched Ida's shoulder. "Can I do anything while you're gone?"

"Huh-uh," Ida answered without turning toward me.

Papa came out and got into the car. I watched while it disappeared around the side of the house.

* * *

"Do that bottle be warm yet?" Lily May came into the kitchen, Tamisa in the crook of her arm.

Ida stood at the sink, washing dishes, and did not turn around to look at her daughter. "The bottle be warm, but it ain't what that baby need. That baby need nursing."

"I ain't no cow," Lily May said.

I got up from the table where I had been sketching a

bowl of yellow squash and green peppers. I went to the stove, lifted the bottle out of the pot of warm water, and dried it on a towel.

"Here, let me feed Tamisa," I held out my arms.

"'Preciate it." Lily May gave me the baby and headed toward the door. "I got stuff to do at the house."

Tamisa, a plump, pretty baby with skin the color of a caramel apple, reached for the bottle. I sat in the chair and covered her front with a diaper. Through the window, I saw Lily May hurrying home. Whatever "stuff" it was she had to do must have been very important.

Tamisa made urgent sounds and wiggled all over. I put the nipple into her mouth. She sucked hard, pushing the bottle with her hands.

How different now from the first time I'd held her. The first time, a tiny wraith had interposed itself between her and me, and I'd felt I might cry. But that didn't last long. My poor Alicia Patricia was no match for lively Tamisa, and she soon disappeared.

Maggie came in from the yard with roses she'd picked, and Ida, turning to look at them, banged a frying pan on the sink, causing Tamisa to jump. "Lord 'a mercy!" cried Ida. "I's sorry to make such a racket. But my nerves is so bad with that old bugger back, and Lily May acting so mulish."

"I thought James Roy was to be here only a week," Maggie said, taking a vase from the cabinet.

"That what he said, but look like he staying forever," Ida said. "Lily May say she ain't messing around. Sure hope she telling the truth."

Lily May was *not* telling the truth, but I kept my mouth shut. The last time I'd gone to Stumpy's with Papa, I saw the black car with James Roy behind the wheel parked next to Clyde Craddock's Model A. Inside the store, Lily May, her back to me, was getting two drinks out of the drink box. I went to the candy counter, and when I looked around, she was gone. A few days later when I walked to the mailbox, I noticed someone standing behind a pine tree. "Who's there?" I called, even though I knew who it was. Lily May stepped out from the tree. She had on a new dress and her hair was pomaded. "You sure fixed yourself up to go stand in back of a tree," I said, trying to be funny. "Mind your own business," she said. I got the mail and had started for home when I heard a vehicle stop on the road. I turned to see the black car speed away.

Tamisa had finished her bottle, and I lifted her to my shoulder to burp her. Sooner or later, I'd have to tell Ida what I knew, but I wanted to put it off as long as I could. It was hard changing loyalties.

Maggie sat at the table and began arranging the roses in the vase. "Ida, why couldn't Lily May stay with your aunt while James Roy is here?" she asked.

"I say don't she want to visit Lucy soon as I hear he back around. She say Lucy got too many gnats at her place. I tell her Cousin Otis and Cousin Rubylee wants her to come down and see them. She say they always be arguing. Truth is she don't want to leave."

Three pats and Tamisa rewarded me with a loud burp. I got up and put her into the clothes basket, the same basket Lily May and I had slept in when we were babies. Tamisa drew her legs up under her tummy and closed her eyes. I went back to my chair.

Ida emptied the dishwater into the sink and dried her hands on her apron. "Reckon I'll get them diapers off the line before I starts fixing supper," she said.

After she'd left, I said to Maggie, "Couldn't Papa find some legal way to keep James Roy away from Lily May?"

"I'm not sure. But I am sure the police wouldn't waste their time interfering in a situation like this."

Maggie picked up the vase of roses. "I'll put these on the dining room table. Why don't you go ahead and set it for supper?"

I had just put the glasses around when I heard a commotion and hurried back to the kitchen. Ida stood there, her face looking wild.

"Lord have mercy!" she cried. "You don't know what she done!"

Maggie pulled a chair out from the table. "Sit down, Ida. Tell us what's happened."

But she stayed where she was, her face squeezed up tight. "While I in here carrying on about what Lily May might be fixing to do, she be out there a'doing it!"

"Doing what?" I asked.

"Packing that suitcase. Crawling out that back window. Lord, help me, my baby done run off with that man!"

Ida opened her fist. Inside was a crumpled paper. Maggie took it and read the message aloud:

Mama, I done gone to Detroit with James Roy. I'm going to get me a good job and make me some money. Don't worry about nothing. Take care of my baby.

Lily May

CHAPTER 23

With barely a change in weather, the summer of 1944 slipped into fall, which soon gave way to winter with blustery days and gray skies. The gloom in our family echoed the unpleasant weather. Papa and Maggie were concerned over the grim war news from the Pacific and Europe. I'd made a D on an algebra test and was afraid I might fail the course. Ida stayed churned up over Lily May. Then Tamisa, our one little bright spot, started to cry all the time. Papa drove Ida and the baby into town to see Dr. Girardeau, who found she had an ear infection. He wrote a prescription for a new drug called penicillin and recommended paregoric for pain. What a relief. I was afraid Tamisa was pining for her mother, a problem neither the doctor nor the grandmother could have fixed.

"How is she feeling?" I asked Ida. I'd just arrived from school and found Tamisa sitting in the clothes basket in the kitchen, chewing her rattle.

"Ain't cried all day, thank the good Lord," Ida said. "Now, if I just knowed her mama be all right up in that cold place by herself."

"Lily May is doing fine, Ida." I picked up Tamisa and took her to the table where Ida was grating carrots. "She's going on seventeen. She knows how to take care of herself."

"I sure pray she do."

I ran my finger across Tamisa's soft cheek. She smiled and leaned back against me. Moments later, she was asleep.

I put her back into the basket and walked toward the door. "Better get a start on my homework before supper," I said.

I was working on the Latin account of Caesar's second invasion of Britain and didn't hear the telephone ring.

When I looked up, Papa and Maggie were standing in my room.

"Frank has been wounded," Papa said.

I jumped up from my desk, knocking papers and books to the floor.

"Hit in the thigh in the Ardennes Forest near Bastogne, Belgium," he said. "It happened two weeks ago, but his mother just received word today. Today, she also got a letter from Frank. An Army nurse wrote it for him. He's in an Army hospital in England but will soon return to the States. He said not to worry."

I was having trouble breathing.

"Child, could I get you some water?" Maggie asked.

I shook my head.

"I'll be in my study if you need me," Papa said as he walked out the door.

"Why don't you come to my room?" Maggie said.

"I'll be there directly."

After she had gone, I picked up the papers and books off the floor and sat again at my desk. I concentrated hard on Frank's getting well. No need to worry, he said in his letter. He was alive and would soon be back in the States. No need to worry; he was alive. I got up and started toward Maggie's room. When I entered the hall, the telephone rang. I picked up the receiver.

"Let me speak to Papa." Louisa was calling from college.

"Miss Wilfreda has already phoned—"

"I want to speak to Papa. Now!"

A hot rage flashed through me. "Go stick your head in a bucket," I snarled. But first I covered the receiver.

I called Papa to the phone and sat on the settee opposite him.

"Yes," he said to Louisa. "But you don't have to rush

home. You can't do any— Yes, his mother received her letter. It was equally short."

So Frank had sent letters to both Louisa and Miss Wilfreda. Why didn't he have the nurse drop me a line as well? Tears sprang into my eyes. I brushed them away as Papa hung up.

"Why don't you and Maggie come to my study?" he asked. "I'll show you on the map where Frank's platoon was located when he was hit."

During the early days of the war, Papa had pinned a map of Europe on his office wall, and every day he followed the battle lines. After the Normandy invasion, he began to stick red pins in the names of towns as they fell to the Allies—except the names of towns that fell to Third Army. He stuck yellow pins in those names. Frank was in General Patton's Third Army.

"It must have been about here." He pointed to a pin in a town near the German border. "There was fierce combat in this area."

Maggie and I leaned closer to see the small yellow ball protruding from a green space. So benign on the map. But I had seen newsreels and knew it wasn't benign—bomb craters, ragged tree stumps, soldiers sprawled in the snow. Had Frank lain in the snow? Red staining white? My stomach hardened into a knot.

I had gotten a letter he must have written shortly before he was wounded. Enclosed in the envelope was a perfectly dreadful sketch of a tent labeled "Third Army Headquarters." Next to the tent stood three stick men with huge captain bars on their shoulders. One man held a sign that read "ME." I'd taped the sketch to my mirror and giggled each time I saw it. In my next letter to him, I had offered free art lessons when he got home.

"Notice me at HQ of Old Blood and Guts," Frank had

written. "Now, there's a general who knows how to make the best use of his men. Take me, for example. The moment he saw me, he knew I was sharp. He started calling me to HQ every night. He'd say, 'Frankie old boy, what you reckon we ought to do tomorrow?' I'd whip out a battle plan. He'd look it over, ask a few questions, and say, 'Looks like we're set to go.'"

Of course, Frank was kidding. He'd never even met General Patton, although he mentioned in a letter to Maggie that he'd seen him pass by in his jeep.

Frank remained in a hospital in England for almost two months before being transferred to Walter Reed Army Hospital in Washington, D.C. Louisa, who was between quarters at Converse, rode up with Miss Wilfreda to see him. The night she returned home was rainy and cold.

"He's a very sick man," she said as we walked down the hall, Papa carrying her suitcase.

"Tell us about him at supper," Maggie said.

Louisa shook her head. "No supper. All I want to do is to lie down."

She did look exhausted. Her shoulders sagged; her eyes were puffy and red.

"I'll put a plate back for you," Maggie said.

After supper, I went to my room to finish an algebra assignment. When I arrived in the parlor, I found Louisa, Papa, and Maggie pulled up close to the fire. I brought over a footstool and sat behind them.

"...wrapped in bandages from his waist to his toes," Louisa was saying. "His doctors say he could still lose his leg."

I pressed my fingers against my mouth to hold in a cry.

"His mother must have been distressed to see him so badly hurt," Maggie said.

"I was distressed, too." Louisa's chest heaved. Papa

offered his handkerchief. Maggie patted her arm. I reached out to touch her, then drew back my hand. She wouldn't appreciate sympathy from me.

Louisa blew her nose and continued, "He'll have a limp for the rest of his life."

"Frank is a hero," said Maggie. "His wound is a badge of honor. We're all proud of him."

"Miss Wilfreda said he was awarded a Bronze Star even before he was wounded. He hadn't told anyone." Louisa looked down at Papa's handkerchief, which she had twisted into a cord.

Without looking up, she said, "He offered to release me from our engagement. Said it wouldn't be right for me to go through life with a cripple."

"But he won't lose his leg!" I blurted out.

All three turned to stare. They hadn't realized I was in the room.

"He'll be all right," I said more softly. "I just know it."

And I did know it. After word came that Frank had been wounded, I had asked Maggie, "If you pray real hard for something, won't God give it to you?" And she said, "God hears and answers your prayers for good, according to His will." I wasn't exactly sure what she meant. But I did know that once I had not prayed for a baby to live because I had assumed that she would. But she died, and I learned that things badly wanted should never be assumed as certain. So I prayed hard for Frank, that God in His mercy would heal him. I had come to believe that He would.

There was another prayer I wanted to pray but could not bring myself to do it. It was that Frank would not marry Louisa. She did not love him; she would not make him happy.

I decided to let God do what He thought was best— although I greatly hoped His conclusion was the same as mine.

Louisa returned Papa's handkerchief and stood. "I need sleep," she said.

She started toward the door and then paused. Without looking back, she said, "I'll marry Frank no matter what."

Later in bed, I went over all that had been said. Louisa was set on marrying Frank, even if he ended up with one leg. Was she doing it because she was noble, or was there some other motive? I slid out from my covers and knelt on the floor.

"Dear God," I began. "Dear God…"

But what could I ask for? He wasn't going to arrange special favors for me. The ache in my heart crept through my whole body.

* * *

The door to Louisa's room was slightly ajar. I pushed on it gently and peeked inside. She sat on the edge of her bed, her body convulsing with sobs that were no louder than sharp intakes of breath.

I hesitated and then stepped into the room. "Can I help you, Louisa?"

Instead of the emphatic "No!" I expected, she merely shook her head.

And since she hadn't told me to leave, I stayed where I was. Gradually, the sobbing subsided.

Patting the bed beside her, she said, "Sit here and be quiet."

I did as ordered. In her desolation and pain, it would seem that any warm-blooded creature, even I, could bring a measure of comfort.

She stared dull-eyed at the floor for a while. Then she said, "I'm all right. Thank you."

I got up and left.

* * *

Louisa did not return to college. Some days she helped in Papa's office; most days she stayed home. Frank called every night, and I was told to stay out of the hall while they talked.

One Saturday morning, I came into the kitchen to find her and Papa sitting at the table, talking over cups of coffee. Neither acknowledged my presence.

"...no reason for you to ride the train with me," Louisa was saying. "I can manage perfectly well by myself."

"That's not the issue, Louisa. The issue is why you insist upon marrying so quickly. Why can't you wait until he is better? Or at least until he's dismissed from the hospital?"

Louisa stiffened her mouth. "Papa, Frank said we could marry whenever I choose, and I choose to marry as soon as I can."

A week later, an Army chaplain performed the wedding in Frank's hospital room. Papa and Miss Wilfreda, who had ridden up on the train with Louisa, witnessed the ceremony.

Back at home, I stayed to myself as much as I could. My heart was shattered, and I couldn't let anyone know.

CHAPTER 24

"Did you already know about Betsy and Rodney's divorce?" I asked.

Maggie and I sat at the kitchen table, preparing Sunday night supper. I peeled hardboiled eggs while she broke chunks of tuna into a bowl, her foot propped on a stool. She had stumbled over a root in the yard two days earlier and sprained her ankle.

"I heard the news the same time as you," she said, "Thursday night, when your papa told us."

The eggs were too fresh, and the whites stuck to the inside of the shells. I scraped out what I could with my fingernail and pushed the saucer over to Maggie so she could chop the eggs into the salad.

"Looks like Papa would have said something earlier. He's Betsy's lawyer. He must have known about this for months," I said.

"I need mayonnaise and pickles," Maggie said.

I brought them to her from the refrigerator and went to the sink to wash lettuce leaves. "Sorry you missed Uncle Ira's lunch at the country club yesterday. He had Betsy arrive a few minutes late, so he could tell us that the reason for this get-together was to cheer up Betsy, and that if we wanted to eat, we'd better give her a hug."

"Your uncle is a kind, thoughtful man." Maggie speared a pickle from the jar and diced it over the salad bowl.

"He's funny, too. Kept saying things to make us laugh. Well, Aunt May Belle didn't laugh. She was mad because Papa posted a legal notice about the divorce in the newspaper. He said it was the law, but she said she didn't care. People read that stuff just to have something to gossip about."

"How was your cousin?"

"Betsy claimed she was happy the whole thing was over, but she looked awfully sad."

Maggie stirred mayonnaise into the salad. "She has looked sad for a very long time."

"Which reminds me of something. At the debutante ball, I saw Rodney and Bannister James out in the parking lot, wrestling in the back seat of a car. You remember Bannister? He got killed in the war. Anyway, the whole thing looked peculiar, but I never told Betsy about it. You think maybe I should, even now?"

Maggie nibbled her lower lip. "I don't know, Margaret. I...." She picked up a spoon and scooped the salad onto the lettuce leaves I had arranged on a platter. "It's over now. Over and done. Would you fetch saltines from the pantry?"

The next time I saw Betsy was at our Saturday lunch at Thelma's Cafe around the corner from Goldsmith's Stationers. I chose not tell her about Rodney and Bannister.

"Please, Betsy, you've got to eat more," I urged. I'd already finished half of my chicken salad sandwich while she, as far as I could tell, had only nibbled a few potato chips.

"All right, little momma." She picked up her sandwich and took a small bite.

Even before the divorce, she did not eat much. Now she ate even less. She had also quit wearing makeup and allowed her crinkly hair to go wild.

"Aunt May Belle says you'll get sick if you don't start taking care of yourself." I warned.

"I'm just fine," she replied.

But Aunt May Belle was right. The next week, Betsy was put in the hospital. Dr. Girardeau said her condition was the result of poor nutrition and nerves and that she would get well only when she made up her mind to get well.

One evening during her second week in the hospital, Papa, Maggie, and I arrived at her room to find her sitting on the side of the bed, wearing lipstick and a new floral robe. Her hair was brushed and tied back with a ribbon.

"You're looking so much better tonight," Maggie said.

"I'm cured," Betsy beamed. "Positively, undoubtedly, unquestionably cured."

"When will the hospital dismiss you?" Papa asked.

"As soon as I put on two more pounds. I feel like a calf being fattened for slaughter."

A sound from the hall made us turn. Mr. Moon, manager of Goldsmith's Stationers, stood in the doorway.

"Oh, my!" he exclaimed.

Milton Moon had a bald head, a round face, and full lips. At work, he acted officious and pompous. But there in the doorway, hat held over his broad middle, uncertain smile on his face, he appeared downright demure.

"Come in, Mr. Moon," Betsy said. "Meet Margaret's family."

Tentatively, he stepped through the doorway, and Betsy introduced him to Papa and Maggie.

"How-do-you-do. How-do-you-do."

Mr. Moon bobbed his head like one of those glass birds that bobs endlessly over water. I bit my lip to stifle a giggle.

"Mr. Moon is my most faithful caller," Betsy said. "He drops by every night to insist I get well. Claims customers threaten to take their business elsewhere if I don't hurry back."

Mr. Moon's face turned Christmas ball red, and my giggle exploded. I tried to turn it into a cough, but no one was fooled.

* * *

"Does Louisa know we're coming?" Although I forced my voice to sound normal, I was taut with excitement. Papa and Maggie had picked me up after school, and we were on our way to visit Frank for the first time since he returned home from England.

"She knows," Papa said. "Frank's physical therapy should be over soon after we arrive at the hospital. We'll visit him in the lobby until she drives him home."

Frank and Louisa were staying with Miss Wilfreda in South Carolina. Twice a week, she drove him to Mell General Hospital on top of Fredericks Hill. In the back seat, I shifted my position so Papa couldn't see me through his rearview mirror putting on lipstick. It wasn't the first time I'd worn it in public. Maggie had noticed, but Papa had not. I surely didn't want him to now.

The afternoon was sunny and crisp. We rode up Washington Way between rows of ginkgoes, their fall leaves fluttering like a million canaries, past block after block of stately homes until we finally turned onto the hospital grounds. It was the first time I'd been to Mell General, although I'd viewed it many times from the old cedar when it was still George Walton Hotel, a resort for Yankees who came south for mild winters and golf.

Papa let us out at the entrance and drove off to park. While we waited, a young man walked through the door, one sleeve hanging empty. I gasped without meaning to, and Maggie put her hand on my arm.

Papa arrived and we entered the lobby. Louisa, who was sitting near the back, didn't get up as we approached. She looked tired and pale.

"How is he?" Papa asked after we had sat down.

"Better. The first week was awful. He was in such pain, I didn't think I could stand it. He still has a long way to go."

All about us, family members or friends were visiting with patients, many on crutches or in wheelchairs. Across from us sat a couple about Papa's age talking to a man in a white jacket. The woman started to cry. A young man—a boy, really—his hand in a bandage the size of a football, passed us and gave a low wolf whistle. Absently, Louisa put her hand to her hair. But the boy was staring at me.

A nurse appeared at the end of a corridor, pushing a man in a wheelchair. He had on the same gray plaid shirt and dark trousers he often wore when he came out to visit. His hair had grown back to its prewar length. Any moment, he would spring from that chair and stride toward us with his familiar heavy-heeled gait.

"Sit down, Margaret," Louisa said.

I dropped to my seat. I hadn't realized I was standing.

"Is it Frank?" Maggie asked, peering down the hall.

"I believe it is," Papa said.

He and Maggie got up and started toward him. Louisa took out her mirror to examine her face. The nurse wheeled him to us and I stood again.

"Well, if it isn't Meg-o-my-Heart all grown up and gorgeous," he said.

His skin was gray; his eyes were sunk in their sockets. I bent down to hug him and felt nothing but bones. As I straightened, I turned my head away. But Louisa still saw the tears and looked disgusted.

So much to say, yet so little was spoken. Maggie asked about his therapy. He said it was helping. Papa mentioned that with the current high demand for beef, he might consider putting more of his land into pasture. He said he'd give it some thought. I told him Ida sent greetings. He thanked me.

No one asked, "Were you scared when the shells whizzed about you?" "How does it feel to get hit?" "What is it like almost to die?"

A young woman with a little boy came in and sat down on a nearby sofa. I heard her instructing the child to stay put. Then she got up and went to an office. As soon as the door closed behind her, the little boy got up and walked over to Frank.

"You a soldier?" he asked.

"Yes, *sir*," Frank said, saluting smartly.

The boy returned the salute. "Where'd you get it, soldier?"

Louisa leaned forward as though to protest. Frank put up his hand to stop her.

"Right about here, general." He pointed to his hip.

"Well, I don't see no bandages."

"I don't have to wear them anymore, sir."

The boy's mother came out of the office and beckoned to him. He ignored her. "Well, soldier, my dad got hurt worser than you. He got both legs blowed off at the knee."

Frank reached over and tousled the little boy's hair. "I'm sorry to hear that, son," he said softly.

"Cecil, come here and leave that man alone," Cecil's mother said sternly.

"It's all right, ma'am," Frank said. "He's telling me about his dad. I wish him the best."

Louisa stood and gripped the bars on the wheelchair. "We need to get Frank home. He's missing his afternoon nap."

His afternoon nap? Was Frank so helpless he had to be driven home for a nap? He should protest. Instead, he reached back and patted Louisa's hand.

* * *

It was too chilly for a party outdoors, but Betsy was having one anyway, a family welcome-home party for Frank. And her back yard did look glorious with its lush winter rye grass, flaming azaleas, and tree branches tipped with chartreuse and gold. A table stood in the center of the yard with a bowl of hyacinths surrounded by platters of food. Card tables and chairs were set up around it.

Moments before Frank was to arrive, we gathered in the front yard, and when his car pulled into the drive with Louisa behind the wheel and Miss Wilfreda in the back seat, we broke into "For He's a Jolly Good Fellow." Grinning broadly, Frank emerged and made a grand bow. He had put on weight since I last saw him and had acquired a tan. The only signs of his ordeal were his cane and considerable limp.

"What's Milton Moon doing here?" hissed Louisa as she, Maggie, and I filled our plates at the food table. "He's not family. And look how he's dressed."

While the other men were casually dressed, Milton had on a dark suit, matching vest, and gray tie. He looked like an undertaker.

"Likely he's here to help Betsy," Maggie suggested.

He certainly did try to help her. He hovered over her like a bee over clover. If she so much as wiggled a finger, he buzzed into action.

Maggie and I took our plates to a table near the one where Aunt May Belle and Uncle Ira sat with his sisters. Aunt May Belle, eyes fixed on Milton, was scowling fiercely. Earlier, Betsy had told me that her mother was not happy with his attentions to her. I thought I knew why. Milton had grown up in Pitch Creek, which was not exactly Fredericksboro's silk stocking district. "But," Betsy had said, "Father says he's smart and has a bright future. And oh, Margaret, he's so sweet, I can't help but adore him."

Betsy appeared at our table. "Excuse me, Miss Maggie, may I borrow Margaret?" She pointed to a large safety pin holding together the waistband of her pink flowered skirt. "Mother has spoken. I need to remedy this situation."

When we reached her bedroom, I said, "Slip off your skirt, and I'll sew on the button."

"I don't have the button. Anyway, my motto is never to sew when a pin will do. Just fasten it to the underside of the band."

The job wasn't easy, and Betsy wouldn't hold still.

"When are Frank and Louisa starting their family?" she asked suddenly.

I jerked and the pin jabbed my finger. "Frank's not—I mean, he's not strong." I wiped the ooze from my finger onto the underside of my skirt.

"That shouldn't hold the man back." Betsy giggled. "Oh, well, I always wanted to have the first offspring in the family. Maybe I'll still manage to do it."

"But you just got divorced." My finger ached dully.

"Dear child, time's a-fleeting. When a girl reaches the ripe old age of twenty-four, she doesn't have many good years left."

The pin was finally in place. "Are you saying you and Milton might marry?"

Betsy giggled again. "Let's get back to the party."

* * *

Saturday, I was late arriving at Goldsmith's Stationers because Papa had to drop off papers at his secretary's house. Miss Doreen's husband was sick and she'd stayed home all week to nurse him. The store was empty when I walked in, but moments later, Betsy emerged from the stock stockroom, flushed and disheveled. "I was helping Milton

198

sort through some cartons," she explained.

I laid my package on top of the counter, removed the brown paper, and held up a watercolor of a camellia with large pink and white petals surrounding a cluster of small ruffled ones.

"It's kind of early to give you a wedding present," I said, "but I had this all done."

Betsy widened her eyes. "Why, Margaret, this is perfectly beautiful. And it's not early at all." She leaned closer to the painting. "This flower is unusually pretty. Where did you find it?'

"Miss Tallulah's yard. It's a new variety of camellia called Louis Law. Some friend brought it to her from Brunswick."

"Whose yard did you say?"

"Tallulah Cassels. You know, my art teacher." I'd mentioned her name to Betsy several times, but apparently it hadn't sunk in.

"Tallulah teaches you art?"

"Yes. I had the impression you knew her."

"Oh, I do. She and your mother were best friends. They once took a trip to New York and—Oh, do you remember that picture? With the scratched-out faces? That was Weezie and Tallulah. Father thinks Tallulah is marvelous. Mother doesn't agree."

"I can understand Aunt May Belle's feelings. Those big eyes always staring at you."

"The staring is the artist in her. Like sizing you up for a portrait. Artists must see not only the surface but also what lies beneath it."

I shook my head. "There's plenty to see right there on the surface. I sure don't need to see beneath it to know she's letting her house fall down around her."

"But beneath the surface is the the reason. Tallulah

hasn't money for repairs. Her grandfather may have amassed a huge fortune, but it was spent by her father, who left his daughter with nothing but the house and its taxes."

"You mean Miss Tallulah's only income is what she gets from giving art lessons?"

"That and the occasional painting she sells. Father's bought several."

"Really? Which ones?"

"The beggar and his monkey that hangs in the library. Mother thinks it's the ugliest thing she ever saw. The still life of fruit in the dining room, which she likes. She thinks Father bought it in Italy and he lets her believe it."

Milton came from the stock room with a carton of clipboards. Betsy called, "Darling, come and see our first wedding gift!" She held up the painting.

He walked over and studied the picture. "Well executed," he declared solemnly. "Very well executed."

I couldn't help it. I laughed. Milton Moon might well have been complimenting a jailor on his skill in dispatching a killer.

CHAPTER 25

Just because I'd gotten soaked a few times waiting for the bus after art class, Maggie took it upon herself to arrange for me to stay at Miss Tallulah's until Papa picked me up after work. I was not pleased.

"But I'll disturb her, hanging around all that time," I protested.

"No, it will be fine," Maggie said. "You'll have extra time for your painting. And"—she put her hand on my arm—"you may learn things you've always wanted to know."

I thought she meant learn things about art. Later, I wondered if she didn't mean something else.

Occasionally during class, Miss Tallulah turned us art students loose in her yard with instructions to find something interesting to paint, and I'd spend so much time looking around that I wouldn't get done with my picture. On those days I didn't mind staying late. One afternoon I was touching up some lichen on a tree branch I'd painted when Miss Tallulah said, "Sweep the floor while I wash these jars. Then we'll go to the house and have tea."

Tea with my art teacher? Why would I want to do that?

"I really should finish this branch," I said.

"Suit yourself," she replied.

The branch was already finished, and so was the frog that sat nearby on a stone. I painted a dirt rim at the base of the stone; I lengthened the rim; I added crumbles of dirt.

Miss Tallulah looked over my shoulder. "Any more dirt and that frog will kick it right out of your picture."

I added more crumbles anyway. Then I cleaned my brushes and swept the floor. Moments later, we were crossing the yard to her porch, which at one time had been painted dark green but was now more of a weathered-wood gray.

"Look out!" She pointed to a step that was splintered and warped. "That board is rotten."

I avoided the step and followed her into the kitchen.

The room was enormous. Along two walls were glass-fronted cabinets crammed with dishes and silver. A table and chairs were set up in front of a huge bay window with a view of the tangled jungle that was the side yard.

She pointed to one of the chairs. "Have a seat."

"Can I help you?"

She shook her head. "I assume you like jessamine tea?"

"Yes, ma'am." I'd never tasted jessamine tea.

She set a kettle of water on the stove and took a yellow tea set decorated with dragons from a cabinet.

"China from China," she said, bringing the set to the table. "My father brought it back years ago."

"It's very pretty," was all I could think to say.

She spooned loose tea into the pot and poured in boiling water. The aroma was straight out of Paradise.

Pointing to the pot, she said, "You know the tea has real flowers in it."

"Yes, ma'am," I lied. The white flakes mixed with the tea leaves looked nothing like the yellow jessamine that grew on Cardinal Hill.

Miss Tallulah sat down and opened a small drawer on the underside of the table. She took out a can of tobacco, cigarette paper and matches, and a little gadget with a rolling band. She placed the paper on the band, sprinkled tobacco across it, and pushed a lever. Out rolled a cigarette as perfect as any that came from a pack.

"In deference to penury," she said, holding up the cigarette.

I had no idea what she was talking about.

While the tea steeped, she smoked. Then she filled our cups.

"One lump or two?" She lifted the lid off a large silver sugar bowl.

"Two, please."

"Milk?"

I'd never had milk in my tea, but I said yes, and she poured in a dollop. I stirred and sipped. The tea tasted like the essence of flowers.

After returning the cigarette gear to the drawer, she drew out an old postcard. "This brings back memories." She held up the card. "Greenwich Village. Ever heard of it?"

"Yes, ma'am. It's part of New York."

She laid the card on the table and began sipping her tea, eyes half closed.

Abruptly, she stopped sipping and turned her eyes upon me. "What do you know about your mother?"

Tea sloshed in my cup as I set it back on the saucer. I'd been taking art for over two years and, except for that first day, Miss Tallulah had never mentioned my mother.

"Anne Louisa Norman. What do you know about that astonishing creature?"

I pushed back my chair and bent down to retie a shoelace. I retied the other shoelace. I straightened a sock.

"You're fourteen now— Fifteen? Yet you know next to nothing about your own mother."

I looked up at her sideways. Was she being sarcastic? Was she angry because she thought I didn't care? Perhaps she was mad at Papa for not talking to me. I straightened in my chair but kept my eyes lowered.

She shook her head and then picked up the teapot. "Here, let me refill your cup."

* * *

I never knew which afternoons Miss Tallulah would invite me to her kitchen for tea. Each time she did, she served a different kind of tea and used a different tea set. It had been almost a month since my last visit, and the aroma of the tea rising from my chartreuse cup scattered with violets was that of a deep forest after rain. I dropped in two lumps of sugar.

"You may need more sugar," she said. "This green tea is strong."

"Two lumps will be fine." I stirred, sipped, and grimaced. The tea tasted like bitter leaves.

She smiled at my involuntary expression.

"You're right," I said and stirred in two more lumps.

Not much better. But I drank the tea resolutely and kept my face steady.

Holding her cup close under her chin, Miss Tallulah let the rising steam bathe her face. Her eyes were fixed on a crystal vase with purple and yellow irises that sat in the center of the table.

"Not right," she said after a moment, and set down her cup. "Would you get that malachite vase from the bottom shelf?" She nodded toward a cabinet.

I found the green vase and brought it to her. She set it next to the crystal one and, with a quick motion, transferred the irises into it. Then she poured in the water and shifted the flowers, making them look more haphazard yet somehow more interesting.

"Ever seen this before?" she asked.

"Not irises that exact shade of purple."

"I mean the vase. I thought you might recognize it from a picture. Weezie once painted it full of white roses."

Weezie? My breath caught. I felt the way I had the first time I got on a Ferris wheel—eager yet fearful.

My teacher kept her eyes on the vase, hands running

over its surface. "Curious why someone who never knew her, mother would have no interest in learning about her."

"Oh, but I do have an interest, Miss Tallulah. A very strong interest."

From bits I had picked up over the years—what Papa and others had said, what was engraved on her tombstone—I envisioned my mother as an ethereal beauty. Gifted, sensitive, mysterious. But there was so much more about her that I yearned to know.

"No one will tell me anything," I said quietly.

Miss Tallulah looked at me now, eyes stretched wide, lids barely showing. My fingers started to twitch and I hid them in my lap. If only I could hide my face as well with all the apprehension and yearning that must show there.

"Hasn't May Belle told you anything?"

"No, ma'am. Aunt May Belle doesn't like to bring up the past."

Miss Tallulah chuckled. "So she's never told you about the time Weezie and I played Robin Hood and got her to be Sheriff of Nottingham?"

I shook my head.

"We tied her to a tree and went off and forgot her. After she'd hollered an hour or so, the maid came out and undid her."

"Aunt May Belle never mentioned it." I thought of the mutilated picture at Aunt May Belle's house. "She has a picture of y'all three girls standing outside together," I said.

"In tennis dresses? May Belle scowling? Weezie and I were about to head for the courts when she showed up, wanting to play. Of course, we couldn't let her. We hadn't a fourth."

"She sure looked unhappy."

"Poor May Belle." Miss Tallulah shook her head slowly. "We didn't always treat her with kindness. And she wasn't one to forgive. Not me, at any rate. I apologized once. It was after Max died. Said I was sorry for being mean when we were children. She would have none of it."

I leaned forward. "Max? My uncle Max, was he—"

But Miss Tallulah waved her hand as though shooing a fly and turned to point out the window. "This morning, I saw a bluebird on that forsythia there. Its feathers were the most amazing indigo shade."

* * *

On most occasions of tea with Miss Tallulah, the talk was of art—painters, their works and their lives. Sometimes she brought up my family. Sometimes, heart pounding, I asked a question about them, which she might answer or completely ignore.

One afternoon while she poured Earl Grey tea into turquoise-blue cups with silver rims, I ventured a question. "Were you and my mother close friends?"

She nodded. "We played together, worked together, got into mischief together."

"And you both loved to paint."

"We had an excellent teacher, Glascock Renault. His works hang in museums."

"Didn't you two once take a trip to New York?" I tried to sound casual.

She narrowed her eyes. "Who told you that?"

"Well, your postcard from Greenwich Village...." No need bringing up Betsy's name.

Miss Tallulah raised an eyebrow.

"We did take a trip to New York. Afterwards we referred to it as our Yankee fiasco, and not all in jest. Weezie had just gotten her car, and nothing would do but we load up our canvases and head for the big city. We

206

needed a dealer, she said, and should have no trouble finding one. We were, after all, two of the South's most promising young artists."

I could visualize the two: the brunette and the redhead destined for greatness in a little green car stacked with paintings. "Did you find a dealer?"

"No, but Weezie—" Miss Tallulah's face darkened. "We ended up hawking our wares on a Greenwich Village sidewalk. She sold a painting to a man who said the dog in the picture looked like one he'd once owned. I sold a sunset to a woman who claimed the colors went with her wallpaper."

"But y'all really were good artists. Seems like someone would have appreciated your work."

Miss Tallulah shrugged. "Neither of us tried to find a dealer again."

She took two yellow roses from the alabaster vase on the table and laid them across the turquoise-blue saucer before her. "Nice, don't you think? The texture, the colors together?"

* * *

The April day was perfect, and I should have felt happy. I'd made a B on the algebra test I thought I had failed, and Miss Tallulah had praised my sketch of two robins. But as I sat at her table, drinking spiced orange tea from a lemon cup traced with green vines, I felt depressed. The night before, I had dreamed I was standing naked in a room full of strangers. Looking for somewhere to hide, I ran to the next room. But it was just like the first, and I woke up crying and couldn't get back to sleep.

"Whatever happened to that portrait Weezie did of Max?" Miss Tallulah asked, fishing a shred of tea from her cup with a finger.

"The one of him with his arm over a dog? It's in our parlor."

"This time of year always reminds me of Max."

"Did he like spring?"

"I wouldn't know about that. But it was on an April day that Weezie and I turned him into an Easter rabbit. We tied cardboard ears to his head and set him in a box with papier-mâché eggs. He tried to eat one of the eggs, and we grabbed it away, which started him howling."

"In the painting, Max looks like my mother," I said. "Were they much alike?"

"He was as handsome as Weezie was beautiful. Also like her, he was impulsive and reckless."

"Reckless? Is that why he got himself killed?"

"Surely you know?"

"Only that it was all very sad."

"And all very unnecessary. It was right after his fiancé broke their engagement. That night, Max was at the club and, according to friends, deep in his cups. Then he made a phone call and left. And the next thing anyone knew—BAM! Into the tree."

When Miss Tallulah said, "BAM!" I almost jumped out of my seat. But she didn't seem to notice; she was staring out the window.

"Poor Weezie. Poor girl, to be waked up at three in the morning to hear your brother is laid out on a slab. News flash to the world: 'Besotted Young Man Loses Control of His Car.' So banal. So pathetic."

She ran a finger around the rim of her cup. Around and around, creating a high squeaking sound. "But was it an accident? Weezie wasn't so sure. She took it badly."

"Are you saying Max meant to—"

Miss Tallulah shrugged. "I went to the junk yard. The

front end of the car, the engine, all pushed toward the back. The wonder wasn't that Max was killed but that Laura was not, jammed as she was under the dashboard with those dreadful head injuries. And the irony was that Clarissa didn't even know Laura was gone from the house."

"Laura? Clarissa Hoadly?" I asked.

Miss Tallulah nodded. "It was Clarissa who had forced Laura to break her engagement to Max. But that night, she'd sneaked out the window to join him."

Laura Hoadly from our church was the person in the car with my uncle! Poor, pitiful Laura who couldn't even walk anymore.

"Miss Clarissa and Laura always sat in front of us in church," I said. "If we changed our pew, they changed theirs."

"Sounds like Clarissa. Never let Max's family forget." Miss Tallulah tightened her lips.

Then she gave her head a quick shake. "But what good does it do to dwell on the past? One must accept and move on. So I keep telling myself."

That afternoon as I got into the car, Papa frowned. "What's she been telling you?"

"I don't know what you mean."

"Oh really? Well, it doesn't matter. You'll stop these lessons right now."

"No, Papa, please, I'm learning so much. I just stayed up late last night, studying for an algebra test. I'm tired."

"Why must you go in her house? Why can't you stay in the studio and paint?"

"I do stay in the studio most of the time. When I go to the house, we just have tea in the kitchen and talk about artists and stuff. I like to know things."

"Know things?"

"About art."

209

A pained expression crossed my father's face. "Margaret, you realize she isn't family."

"Yes, I know."

He started the engine. I put my books on the floorboard and stared out the window. We were quiet the rest of the way home.

* * *

My sixteenth birthday fell on a Tuesday. There would be no celebration. Papa was out of town and had already presented me with a ten-dollar bill.

I'd even forgotten it was my birthday until I walked into the kitchen that morning and found that Ida had fixed my favorite breakfast: cheese omelet with sausage and grits. When I sat down to eat, I noticed a small box by my plate.

"Happy birthday!" Maggie said, coming into the kitchen.

"Thank you," I said.

I unwrapped the box and took off the lid. Inside was Maggie's breast pin, the one she wore on special occasions. It was a pendant hanging from a gold bar. Etched on the front of the pendant was a peacock perched on a rail fence. On the back, the side nearest the heart, was a picture of Benjamin Cay, Maggie's sweetheart. The pin was to have been his gift to his bride. But he died before they were married and his mother gave the pin to Maggie after the funeral.

"Oh, Maggie." I jumped up and hugged her so hard that we both nearly lost our balance.

"Mercy, child," she said when I let her go. "It's not of great value; it's not solid gold."

"Who cares? You could have left it to me in your will. I could have waited."

"You take it now. I don't want to miss the pleasure of seeing you wear it."

I laughed. "Also, I'd be past middle age before it was mine." Maggie was eighty-seven, but she wouldn't die any time soon. I'd recently read of a woman who celebrated her one hundred and fifth birthday. Maggie would live to at least one hundred.

The next day as we sat sipping tea after art class, Miss Tallulah said, "I understand yesterday was your birthday. As soon as we finish our tea, I have something to show you."

I lifted the pale coral cup to my lips and quickly downed the rest of my herbal tea.

She led me from the kitchen, through a large dining room papered with pink cabbage roses, a wood-paneled foyer, and up a broad flight of stairs. At the end of a hall, she paused at a door.

"Father's room," she said, opening the door.

It smelled of mildew and dust. Over a four-poster bed dangled a section of loose ceiling plaster. We crossed the room and she opened a narrow door, revealing a circular staircase.

"Up there," she said.

The room at the top of the stairs was small and encircled with windows. A paint-spattered table cluttered with old art supplies stood near the wall.

"Used to work here," she said. "Wonderful light."

She began to sort through stacks of paintings until she came to one that she pulled out from the rest. "I'd meant to give it to her, if she wanted it."

She turned the canvas around, and I gasped.

It was a life-size portrait of a young woman with dark, flowing hair and dark eyes. She wore a gypsy costume with bright-colored beads and dangling earrings. Her head was turned slightly, but her eyes, flashing mischief, looked straight out of the painting.

"Mother!" I cried. "It's her, isn't it?"

Miss Tallulah shifted the portrait so she could see it. "Oh, it's Weezie all right. She didn't particularly like it. Said it exposed too much of her soul."

"How old was she when you painted it?"

"Around eighteen when I started. I worked on it off and on for a year." She held out the portrait. "It's yours if you want it."

I was stunned. I couldn't even open my mouth. How could I thank her? What should I say? She seemed bored with my efforts.

Downstairs, she wrapped the portrait in newspaper, tied it with string, and set it near the back door. I tried to thank her again.

"You said you want to know your mother. This picture is one more way that you can."

When I went out to the car, I laid the painting on the back seat.

"Finished another picture?" Papa asked as I settled beside him on the front seat.

"No, sir. This is one Miss Tallulah gave me."

"Nice."

He didn't ask any more questions; I didn't volunteer any more information. He'd find out soon enough what was portrayed on that canvas.

And what would he think if the painting truly did expose my mother's soul? I couldn't imagine he had ever seen it.

After reaching home, I asked Maggie to come to my room and showed her the painting.

"What a beautiful girl your mother was," she exclaimed. "She looks so high-spirited, so full of life."

She turned from the portrait and put her arms around

me. "Oh, my dear child," she said.

I hung it on the wall opposite my bed, and her eyes followed me wherever I went.

I imagined being raised by this magnificent woman instead of plain, gentle Maggie. The thought was exciting, yet oddly disturbing.

CHAPTER 26

According to Aunt May Belle, Betsy and Milton's wedding was handled with "as much taste as possible under the circumstances." While a large contingent of Moons attended the service, only family and intimate friends of the Goldsmiths were present. Betsy wore a blue chiffon gown with a pearl necklace; Milton wore a tuxedo with a cutaway coat. No write-up appeared in the newspaper.

Two months passed before I saw Betsy again. Then one Saturday, we met for lunch at Thelma's Café.

As soon as her French fries arrived, she began to poke them around with her finger. "Bee, go on and bring more of these," she said. Then, grinning at me, she added, "Can't get enough to eat these days."

When Bee left our table, Betsy leaned close. "Now, this is top secret. Don't tell a soul, but I'm expecting a baby."

"Oh, Betsy!" I cried. "I'm so happy for you." I didn't mention that I wasn't surprised by her news. The radiance on her face had already made the announcement.

She shook a puddle of ketchup onto her plate. "It's due in December, a safe nine months past our wedding. But we're not telling anyone yet. Milton's mother worked herself into such a tizzy worrying that we'd hankypanked before we got hitched that I say now let her wonder and wait."

I had met Gertrude Moon at the luncheon Aunt May Belle gave before the wedding. It had been a lively affair. While Betsy's kin required only a handful of seats at the dining table, Milton's multitude necessitated that tables be set up in every downstairs room but the bathroom. Besides Miss Gertrude, there were her five daughters, their husbands, and, as nearly as I could count, nineteen nieces and nephews—all chubby, full lipped, and round faced. All miniature Miltons, except they had hair. After lunch, Betsy and I were headed upstairs so she could show me her going-away suit, when someone called out, "Look-a-here, now!"

We turned to see Miss Gertrude at the foot of the stairs.

"It's all set," she told Betsy. "Preacher Ronny's conducting the service. Y'all understand that's how it'll be?"

"Yes ma'am, Mother understands," Betsy said.

"I'm letting my boy marry in the Whiskeypal church. I sure don't want no man with his collar turned backwards leading the vows."

Betsy seemed to have trouble clearing her throat. "Yes, ma'am," she finally got out.

"Just making sure." Miss Gertrude sauntered off, ample hips undulating beneath her red flowered skirt.

"The Whiskeypal church?" I asked Betsy when we were in her room with the door closed. "Does she think Episcopalians are heavy drinkers?"

"No telling. But I shouldn't have laughed. It's hard enough having her boy marry 'used merchandise,' so to speak, but in high church as well? The compromise was either Preacher Ronny McCoy at St. Matthews Episcopal or the Right Reverend Daniel Mallard at Pitch Creek Church of the Spirit. Mother decided Preacher Ronny was preferable."

The second order of French fries arrived. Betsy rolled two thick ones in ketchup and stuffed them into her mouth. "One for me, one for my little new Moon," she garbled.

"And what will you name your new Moon?" I asked.

"If it's a boy, Milton says he'll be Junior, even though I told him the first son should bear the name of the maternal grandfather. Ira Goldsmith Moon. Now, that sounds presidential."

"If it's girl, will you name her Elizabeth for you?"

"No. Nor May Belle nor Gertrude. Something romantic like Natasha or Mahalia. Mahalia Moon, isn't that lovely? Mahalia means tenderness in Hebrew, you know. A tribute to Father's Jewish heritage."

"Oh, Betsy, Uncle Ira would love it."

She picked up her Coke and sucked on the straw, producing a loud, raucous sound. "Wonder should I order another?" she mused. "No, I'll just pick up a candy bar on the way out."

As we walked to the cash register, she nudged my shoulder. "Remember, not a word to a soul."

* * *

Frank and Louisa had stayed at his mother's home until they could buy their own nearby. The house had belonged to Frank's cousin, and Louisa planned to furnish it with antiques. Miss Wilfreda had already promised an antique dining suite and a sofa.

I was pleased to learn about the new place, because it meant Louisa would move her things out of her bedroom and I could move my things in. Her room was much prettier than mine, which was originally built for a live-in servant. Louisa's was airy and light with a view of Fredericksboro out the front windows.

At supper one evening about a month later, Maggie said, "Louisa was here this afternoon with a truck and a helper to pick up some of her things."

"Finally," I said, "I can start moving in."

As soon as the meal was over, I hurried to Louisa's room. But when I opened the door, I stopped with a jerk. "Maggie, come here!" I cried.

The room was stripped almost bare. Louisa had not

216

only taken her personal things but had also made off with the vanity and stool, the two chairs by the fireplace, the gold-frame mirror over the mantle, *and* the full-length mirror. She'd even taken the crochet spread off the bed.

Maggie came alongside me. "I'll make an organdy skirt to go around my sewing table and you can use it as a vanity," she said. "We'll buy a new stool and mirror and spread."

I went to the dresser and opened a drawer. Louisa's summer clothes were still folded inside. I opened the wardrobe and saw that her summer dresses still hung on the rack. "She took things that aren't hers and left behind things that are."

"We'll pack her belongings in boxes so you can move in," Maggie said.

"Well, at least she didn't haul off the bedroom suite," I said.

The bedroom suite with its warm walnut tones and carved bunches of flowers was the prettiest furniture in the whole house. I couldn't wait to start using it.

By the next Saturday, we had all of Louisa's belongings ready to move. I was in my new room, arranging sweaters in a dresser drawer, when I happened to glance out the window. A truck was rounding the corner of the house. I left my room and went out to the backyard. This time Louisa had *two* helpers with her.

"We didn't expect you," I said. "We might have been gone."

"The door wouldn't have been locked. I could have gotten my things," she replied.

I followed her into the house. "You didn't need to bring workmen. I could have helped carry out the boxes."

Louisa reached the door to my room and stopped. "What's this?" She was staring at the painting of Mother, which I'd gotten Sam to hang over the mantle where the mirror had been.

"A picture of Mother."

"I know that. Where did it come from?"

"My art teacher gave it to me."

"Tallulah Cassels? Why should she give you something like that? I mean, it must be quite valuable."

"It was a birthday present." Did I ever feel smug!

Papa and Maggie came to the door, and Louisa pointed to the portrait. "Papa, what do you know about this?"

He barely glanced at the painting. "It doesn't resemble the Anne Louisa I knew."

"Why don't we go sit in the parlor?" Maggie suggested.

"But why would Tallulah Cassels—"

"We want to hear about the work on your house," Papa said.

"I can't stay but a minute."

We crossed the hall to the parlor, where Louisa took a seat near the door. "Papering bedrooms is my most recent project," she said. "I did the guest room in yellow roses to set off my bedroom furniture. I'm out here today to collect it."

"The furniture in Margaret's room?" Maggie said. "It must weigh a ton."

"That's why I've brought two men to move it," Louisa said.

"I'm using it now," I said.

Louisa shrugged. "Sam can bring up the furniture from your room in the back."

Papa cleared his throat. "Louisa, that walnut suite has been in the front bedroom for more than a century. It is not to be moved."

Louisa opened her mouth, then closed it. Pink

splotches appeared on her neck.

Maggie got up from her chair. "I'll ask Ida to make us some lemonade."

"No, sit down, Maggie," Papa said. "Margaret won't mind seeing to it."

He was right. I would not mind at all. I needed to be out of the room. Papa had turned down Louisa, and I wanted to laugh.

"What you snorting about?" Ida said when I got to the kitchen.

"Must be the pollen," I told her.

"This time of year? I doubts it."

She took down the cake box and told me to cut slices of pound cake while she made the lemonade. Through the window, I saw Louisa standing on the back steps, calling the workmen into the house. I watched as they carried out boxes.

Ida put the refreshments on a tray, and I took them to the parlor and passed them around.

Louisa nibbled her cake, sipped a little lemonade, and stood up. "There are still a few things I need from my room," she said. "Then I'll be going."

As soon as she left the parlor, I slid her barely touched cake onto my plate. No sense in wasting it.

A crash jarred the whole house. We sat frozen. Then, as one body, we rushed to the bedroom. Louisa lay on her back, eyes closed, diaries and ballet shoeboxes scattered about. The wardrobe lay backside up on the floor. At first, I thought she had cleared it. Then I saw one foot pinned underneath. Papa shifted the wardrobe as though it were made of balsa wood. He scooped up Louisa and started down the hall. I ran ahead, opening doors. Somewhere along the way, Ida joined us and "Lord-have-mercied!" us out to the car.

"Phone Frank, will you, Ida?" Papa said, laying Louisa on the back seat. "Tell him to meet us at the hospital."

Maggie got in beside Louisa and cradled her head in her lap. I hopped into the front seat beside Papa. On the way into town, he ran two stop signs and took four curves on the wrong side of the road. I held on to the dashboard. Louisa moaned a few times. Maggie said, "There, there, precious girl."

"Please, God, don't let her die," I silently prayed. "And please, God, forgive me." Only moments ago I had exulted because Papa turned down Louisa. If he hadn't, the workmen would have been the ones removing the diaries from the top of the wardrobe, and Louisa would never have been hurt. I glanced at Papa, trying to read what he was thinking. But his face was rigid.

At the emergency room entrance, two men in white coats lifted my sister onto a stretcher and rushed her away.

Papa turned to Maggie and me. "Go sit in the waiting room while I ring Ida to see if she was able to reach Frank."

He joined us a few minutes later. "He's on his way."

Frank had forgotten his cane and was limping so badly as he rushed into the room that I was afraid he might fall.

"Where is she?" he shouted. "I've got to be with her."

"She's in surgery, Frank," Papa said. "The doctor will let us know when it's over."

Frank wheeled on his good leg and started out the door. Then he paused, turned back, and sank into a chair.

Eons passed before Dr. Christian Screven, the surgeon, appeared. "She's had a concussion, but it doesn't appear serious. The ankle is another matter. The bones are shattered. I've set them the best I could, but they may never be right. To be perfectly honest, Louisa may not be able to walk on that foot again."

Frank stiffened. "If the girl's foot is still hitched to her leg, she will walk." He sounded so confident, so much in command. But his hand shook when he brushed the hair from his forehead.

An eternity later, we caught the elevator to Louisa's room on the third floor. She was asleep, her face pale as marble, her bandaged foot propped in a sling that hung from a brace attached to the bed. Frank kissed her forehead and pulled a chair close. Papa, Maggie, and I sat nearby. No one spoke. The only sound in the room was Louisa's heavy breathing.

Until my stomach rumbled like thunder.

Papa looked at me and then glanced at his watch. "We've missed lunch and now supper, but we still may be able to get something in the hospital cafeteria," he said. "Frank, you especially need to eat if you plan to stay here tonight."

"I'm not hungry, sir, but you all go on."

"We'll bring you back something," Maggie said.

The lettuce and tomato in my sandwich were mushy and the bacon was burnt. But I ate it all, hoping to ward off more stomach noises.

By the time we got back to the room, visiting hours were over. Louisa was still sleeping. Maggie handed Frank the pimiento cheese sandwich and Coke she had brought from the cafeteria. She gently kissed Louisa goodnight. Papa kissed her too, and patted her shoulder. And then I kissed her, surprised by a rush of tenderness that swept through me. It was the first time I remembered ever kissing my sister.

"I'm so sorry this happened," Papa told Frank as we walked to the door.

Frank drew a sharp breath, and I hurried into the hall; I couldn't have stood it if he'd cried.

Riding home, Maggie said, "I wonder what she did to

cause the wardrobe to topple."

Papa speculated. I remained quiet.

But I knew exactly what had happened. Louisa was trying to reach the diaries, which she had put on top of the wardrobe the summer after her freshman year in college. She'd used the bottom drawer as a step and, gripping the top ledge with one hand, strained with the other to reach the ballet shoeboxes. I'd done the same thing, only, when I felt the wardrobe beginning to tilt, I'd stepped down and brought over a chair.

The next day, Papa and Sam set the wardrobe upright. I gathered the diaries into a paper bag and brought them with me to the hospital that afternoon. Louisa greeted us weakly.

"This morning was rough," Frank told us, "but the nurse gave her something for pain and she's comfortable now."

While the others talked, I showed Louisa the diaries. "Where do you want them?" I asked.

"Oh, anywhere." She closed her eyes.

I put them in the little closet alongside her clothes.

"The doctor says healing could take a long time, and Lulu better make up her mind to be patient," Frank said. "And when she does start getting about, she can expect quite a limp."

Louisa snorted. "I'll get rid of my limp before you get rid of yours."

"And in the meantime, we'll make do with one pair of walkers between us," Frank said.

The low afternoon sun fell across his face, creating shadows, deepening lines. His hair was thinning on top. He looked almost as old as my father. I took a deep breath and slowly released it. I wasn't in love with Frank anymore.

* * *

Municipal Hospital was one block off the bus route from Garrett High School and Papa's law office. On days when I had lots of homework, I visited Louisa in the afternoons rather than ride back in the evenings with Papa and Maggie. The afternoon before my big Latin test, I walked into her room to find her sitting in bed, flipping through a magazine.

"I thought Betsy might be here today," I said. "She told me she was going to stop by."

"She came in earlier." Louisa laid the magazine on the table. She looked tired. Her foot was out of the sling, but her ankle was still in a cast. "Betsy has gotten so tedious. All she talks about is having that baby."

"She says she wants a dozen of them."

"So why didn't she marry a man half-decent looking? I can't imagine anything worse than a pack of fat-faced brats like that horde of Milton's nieces and nephews." Louisa shifted her leg and grimaced.

"If you ha—" I caught myself. I'd almost said, "If you have an ugly baby, I'll take it."

I started again. "Uncle Ira's family are all good looking. The baby might take after them."

"Not likely." Louisa rubbed her leg above the cast.

I went to the window to pull dead leaves off a flower arrangement. I could feel my sister's eyes on me. When I was done, I sat in the chair where Frank usually sat and picked up the magazine.

"Want me to read to you?" I asked.

With narrowed eyes, Louisa studied my face. "You know something, Margaret, I never have liked you."

I concentrated hard on putting the magazine back on the table.

Of course, I knew she had never liked me. I'd seen how other girls treated their younger sisters. Ginger Wright might sometimes be cross with Sue Lee, but there was no doubt that she liked—that she loved her. And Ida had never been mean to Junie. I'd always known how Louisa felt about me. Yet hearing the words—

"You were always in the way. Into my things. Your table manners were atrocious. Such a slob. You and Lily May running around in the dirt. And if it weren't for you, my mother . . ." She turned her face to the wall.

I opened my mouth, but no words would come out. Deep inside, they were all tangled up with sorrow and pain. My sister blamed me for our mother's death. She wished I had never been born.

Usually, Papa came to Louisa's room to get me when it was time to go home. This afternoon, though, I was waiting for him in front of the hospital.

"I'd have been glad to come up for you," he said as I got into the car.

"Louisa wanted to sleep," I said. "There was no point in my hanging around."

CHAPTER 27

Everyone said it was too soon after her accident for Louisa to be having a housewarming party, but she wouldn't hear of it. Miss Wilfreda's cook had already prepared most of the food, but at Maggie's suggestion, I offered to help with last-minute tasks.

Louisa seemed grateful. She sat at the kitchen table cutting wedges of cheese. "I didn't mean what I said that day in the hospital. I hadn't slept well the night before, and my ankle was giving me fits."

"I knew you didn't mean it," I said. I stood at the counter arranging parsley sprigs on a platter of stuffed mushrooms. "I didn't pay any attention to it."

Each of us knew the other was lying.

Louisa picked up the cheese tray. "When you're finished, set your platter on the dining table and get something to eat." She walked from the kitchen, right foot dragging behind her.

Moments later, I was in the parlor sitting beside Maggie with a plateful of food. I bit into a cucumber sandwich.

"Hmm, this is scrumptious," I said.

Maggie didn't respond.

I had just put the rest of my sandwich into my mouth when Papa, who was standing nearby, lunged straight at me. At the same time, Maggie's head struck my knee.

"Maggie? Maggie, are you ill?" Papa lifted her to a sitting position.

She looked around, dazed. "Did I doze off?"

"Margaret, get her things. We're going home."

When I got back downstairs with our wraps, Frank had our car pulled up to the front entrance, and Papa and

Uncle Ira were helping Maggie down the porch steps.

"I don't understand what this fuss is about," she said. "I'm perfectly fine."

Frank opened the car door. "Of course, you are, Miss Maggie. You were just trying to attract a little attention."

"Pshaw," Maggie said.

The next morning, I was waiting in the backyard when Papa and Maggie returned from the doctor's office. "What did he say?" I asked.

"Not much." Papa helped Maggie from the car. "He changed her blood pressure medicine and told her to rest a few days."

"All this to-do," Maggie said. "It's nothing but old age catching up with me."

"But you'll be all right, won't you?"

"Of course, child. I'll just take my medicine and stop gallivanting around to parties."

"And rest for a few days," Papa added.

Maggie did spend the remainder of that day in bed, but the next morning, she was up and about as though nothing had happened.

* * *

I was about to head up the steps into church when Sue Lee Wright rushed up and sank her talons into my arm.

"Did you see him?" she cried.

"Who? Mr. Axon?"

A few yards away, the church greeter stood in the vestibule, sporting a new toupee that looked like a beaver pelt.

"No, silly, Hines Stewart. Oh, Margaret, he's gorgeous. Absolutely, totally gorgeous."

Since at one time or another, Sue Lee Wright had

thought every male over age ten was gorgeous, I managed to keep my composure at this latest pronouncement. Back in eighth grade, Sue Lee had carried on a whole week over how gorgeous Hines was when actually he looked like a bean pole with a huge Adam's apple and a chin blooming with pimples. Once, he'd invited me to sit next to him on a church hayride, and I had politely declined.

"I haven't seen Hines since he went off to Davidson College," I said. "That was when? Two years ago? Probably wouldn't even recognize him now." I turned to go up the steps.

"No, wait." Sue Lee dug her daggers deeper into my flesh. "He's still in the educational building. He'll be out any second."

"I need to go, Sue Lee. Papa gets irritated when I'm late for church."

"Just one little sec— There, see he's coming out now." She let go of my arm and sashayed toward him. "Hines Stewart! I declare it's just been forever."

"Nice to see you, Sue Lee."

He looked beyond her to me. "Well, Margaret, we keep missing each other. Every time I'm here, you're somewhere else."

I stared; I couldn't help it. For once in her life Sue Lee had not exaggerated. His pimples were gone and he had grown into his Adam's apple. His eyebrows were thick, his jaw was squared out, he was heavier by at least twenty-five pounds—all muscle. Gregory Peck might not be the most ravishing creature to tread God's green earth after all.

I must have said hello, nice to see you, or something like that. The tumult raging inside me blocked any attempt at clear thinking. During the service, I heard not one hymn that was sung, not one word that was preached. For two rows behind me, breathing the same air that I breathed,

Hines Stewart sat with his parents.

The telephone rang at 2:07 p.m.

"It was good to see you this morning," Hines said when I answered.

"It was good to see you." My lungs had barely enough power to force out the last word.

"I'm leaving in a few minutes to drive back to college, but I'll be home in a month. Maybe we could go see a movie or something?"

"That would be nice."

"Great. I'll call you when I get back."

It took me a while to sit and recover. Then I went to the kitchen where Maggie and Ida were finishing up after dinner. Tamisa sat in my old high chair, eating cornflakes, one at a time. I went to her and rubbed my finger across her soft cheek. She offered a cornflake and I accepted, swallowing it whole like a Communion wafer, a token of grace.

"Hines Stewart called," I announced casually. "He wants me to go out with him next time he's home."

"Hines Stewart?" Maggie said. "I taught him in Sunday school. Such a bright little fellow. How nice he's inviting you out."

"You mind yourself," Ida growled.

* * *

It was our last Saturday lunch at Thelma's Café before Betsy quit work to await the birth of her baby. Since the doctor had told her to stop gaining weight, she'd ordered buttermilk instead of a milkshake to go with her chicken salad sandwich. That way she wouldn't feel guilty having lemon icebox pie for dessert.

"And so," I said, after excitedly telling her about Hines,

"this will be my first real date, and I need advice."

"Advice?" Betsy wiped her mouth on the back of her wrist. "I have plenty of that and all of it free."

"Well, what if he should try to hold my hand on our first date? Should I let him?"

"What do you think?"

"Maybe. Just briefly. Nothing prolonged like sitting through an entire movie in a clench."

"Sounds safe to me."

"But some boys try to kiss you on the first date. What should you do?"

Betsy grinned. "Now, we're getting into heavy stuff. Have you ever been kissed, Margaret?"

I took a long sip of Coke. She'd asked if I had ever *been* kissed. Technically, that ruled out the time on Cardinal Hill Road when *I* kissed Claud Millwood. "We've played spin-the-bottle over at Sue Lee's. Everybody acts silly. It hardly counts as kissing."

"What about prom parties? Been to any of those?"

"Sue Lee had one for her fourteenth birthday."

"You kissed at the prom party, didn't you?"

"Well, at a prom party, you can either dance or get refreshments or go—"

"I know how it works."

"I did let a few boys walk me around the block, and two of them kissed me. The first one got spit on my mouth and the second one cut my lip on his braces."

"So those kisses don't count?"

I shook my head. "This is different, Betsy. This will be the first time I'm out with a boy the whole evening, just him and me. And he's somebody I really do like."

"That does make it different."

I brushed some crumbs off the table. "Oh, well, I shouldn't worry. Hines isn't going to try to kiss me anyway."

"How do you know?"

"He's real religious."

"You'd be surprised at what some 'real religious' boys do."

Bee brought Betsy her lemon icebox pie, and she began eating eagerly.

"Well, if Hines does try to kiss me, I won't let him. I wouldn't want him to think I was fast."

"No, indeed!" Betsy said sternly. "That would not do."

"You're teasing. Seriously, though, you've got to help me. Sue Lee said Ginger told her you're supposed to have three dates before you let a boy kiss you. Is that right?"

"It sounds fine. But I wouldn't be honest if I said that's how it worked out for me."

"What do you mean?"

"Froggie Williams kissed me on the first date. I struggled, of course, but not very hard. Hugh Dowsey waited until the fourth date, and then asked my permission. Now Rodney, we had nine or ten dates before I finally kissed *him*. That should have told me something right there. But I was too dumb to pick up on it."

"Then you can't make a rule about when to start kissing."

"Margaret, you do know there are things beyond kissing? Things that could—"

"Oh, I know all about that stuff. You don't have to worry." I tried to sound well informed.

Betsy put her hand on mine. "You're sixteen now, dear. I believe you can trust your conscience to guide you."

* * *

I had on my dark green skirt with my pale green sweater, which Sue Lee had said made me look sexy. My eyebrows and lips were made up to look exactly like Elizabeth

Taylor's, whose picture was taped to my mirror. I'd been ready an hour when the doorbell rang.

Louisa had always made her dates wait and so I stayed in my room, letting Maggie welcome Hines and show him into the parlor.

Ten long minutes passed before I went to greet him. He sat with his back to the door.

"There you are," Maggie said, and Hines turned and stood up. "I was telling your guest what a sweet young lady you are."

My face felt instantly hot.

He smiled. "Good to see you, Margaret. Ready to go?"

On the way into town, Hines gave a play-by-play account of a football game he'd heard on the radio between Georgia Tech and The Citadel. I didn't have to open my mouth. The movie, *Sarge Goes to College*, was unusually silly, and he made no attempt to hold my hand. Afterwards, at the Brown's Drive-in, he pulled into the first empty spot he came to, near the front, under the lights.

The carhop arrived.

"What would you like?" Hines asked.

"I—I— Whatever you're having will be fine with me."

He ordered two chocolate shakes and two hamburgers, no onions.

No onions?

In the car next to ours, Dinah Shore sang, "I Wish I Didn't Love You So."

While we waited, Hines turned toward me. "What subjects are you taking in school?"

"Oh, English and algebra and chemistry and Spanish and Latin."

"Sounds like a heavy load."

"I do have to study."

In the next car, the boy draped his arm over the back of

the seat and fingered the girl's hair.

"Did you do anything interesting last summer?"

"Just worked some at my uncle's stationery store. Did you do anything interesting?"

"As a matter of fact, I did. My roommate's dad has an oil-drilling company in Texas, and Russ and I worked in the field. Hot, dirty business, but I got used to it."

The hot, dirty business might account for the muscles. "Are you going to work in Texas next summer?" I cleverly asked.

"I don't think so. Dad wants me to get experience at the bank. But I'd rather try for a job on a shrimp boat around St. Simons Island. Desert one summer, ocean the next."

"That would be nice."

"Where are you going to college next year?"

"Agnes Scott, if I can get in. My algebra grades aren't very good."

I cringed as soon as I said that. He already knew I couldn't carry on a conversation. Now, he knew I was stupid. I fumbled in my purse for a tissue to wipe an imaginary speck from my eye.

The carhop arrived and attached the tray of food to the open window. Hines passed me my order. My hamburger had a rubbery texture. I took a few bites and swallowed them whole. When I drew on my straw, nothing came up. The milkshake was frozen. Meanwhile, Hines wolfed down his food as though it was the first he'd had in a week.

"Take your time," he said, after returning his napkin and empty glass to the tray. "I'm a fast eater."

"Oh, no, I'm all done." I wrapped my napkin around the hamburger and handed it and my frozen shake to him.

As we backed out of the parking space, I noticed the couple in the next car embracing.

Riding home, Hines talked about a hike he and friends had taken along the Appalachian Trail, and I exclaimed, "Oh, my!" and "How scary!" in appropriate places. When we reached Flowering Peach Road, he turned on the radio. Dick Haymes crooned, "…just the thought of you, the ve-ry thought of you…." Hines hummed along with the music.

"I like Vaughn Monroe's instrumental version better," he said when the song ended.

"Vaughn Monroe's always good," I affirmed.

On the way up Cardinal Hill, we listened to Harry James's trumpet whine, "You Made Me Love You." In front of the house, he switched off the engine and lowered his window a crack. I lowered mine. A breeze with the tingle of fall stirred through the car. The night sky was clear; the city lights glittered.

Hines turned the radio down and leaned toward me. "Those lights are spectacular," he said.

"I never get tired of looking at them," I said.

He leaned closer. "Where is downtown? Where those red lights are blinking off and on?"

"A little more to the east." I bent my head toward him.

"And to the west, that string of lights that looks like a necklace?" His breath was warm on my ear.

"They're the lights going up Washington Way," I murmured, my cheek almost touching his lips.

He straightened. "Think of all the kilowatts being consumed."

He did not take my arm as we walked up the front steps. At the door, I thanked him and said I'd had a good time. He said it had been fun and opened the door.

Through a crack, I watched as he returned to his car, opened the door, got in, and drove out of my life.

Later in bed, I stared at the lights. They were multiplied now through my tears.

CHAPTER 28

Doreen Hoyt had worked for Papa as long as I could remember. And during all that time, she'd never changed how she looked: rouged cheeks; blond, shoulder-length hair; jiggly hips. She smelled strongly of tea roses.

Miss Doreen liked to do nice things for people. She baked caramel cakes for Papa's birthday, brought flowers to brighten the office, made divinity candy to share with the staff. Miss Doreen herself was like divinity candy—frothy and light and a little too sweet.

Clarence Hoyt, her husband, had a bad heart and spent his days in a recliner, listening to the radio. One evening in September, she came home from work to find he'd passed away in his chair. Papa, Maggie, and I attended the funeral. The next day, Miss Doreen was back at work, wearing the same black dress with white beadwork that she had worn to the funeral. Barely a month later as we rode home after work, Papa said, "I've invited Miss Doreen to church next Sunday and afterwards home to have dinner with us."

"But she has her own church," I quickly reminded him. Miss Doreen sang in the choir at True Light Baptist Church not far from far her house. "I wouldn't imagine they'd want her to miss."

"She's been lonely since her husband died," Papa said, "and Sunday is the loneliest day of all."

"Well, if she's so lonely, why doesn't she go whip up some divinity candy?" I muttered, my face toward the window.

The next Sunday between Sunday school and church, Papa left to pick up Miss Doreen.

During the doxology, I turned to see her, outfitted in a pink suit and white hat with pink feathers, jiggling down the aisle by his side. As they slipped into the pew, the odor of tea roses almost overcame me.

Clarissa Hoadly still sat in the pew directly in front of ours. But now, her brother, Judge Thomas Henry, sat with her, and she no longer paid special attention to me. Not that Miss Clarissa had stopped acting peculiar; she was still pulling hairpins out of her hair and waving at people on the other side of the church. That morning, as soon as Miss Doreen arrived at our pew, Miss Clarissa began sniffing the air. Then she turned around and stared at Miss Doreen. Judge Henry whispered to her, and she turned back around.

The next time Miss Clarissa turned, though, the judge left her alone. It was when the congregation stood to sing "Blessed Assurance, Jesus Is Mine!" Such wailing as came from Doreen. Such sliding of one note into the other. Papa's base remained steady, but Maggie's alto wavered, and I dared not catch her eye.

After the service, I hurried from church, hoping no one would stop me to talk. I'd almost reached the car when Sue Lee Wright clattered up on her heels. "Who was that lady sitting with y'all?"

"Just Papa's secretary. Her husband died, and we're trying to cheer her up."

"Have they had any dates?"

"Of course not!" I got quickly into the car, slamming the door shut behind me.

"Let me know how things develop," Sue Lee called through the window.

We arrived home to find that Ida had dinner all ready. The table was set with my mother's best linens, along with her fine china, silver, and crystal. Papa said grace and thanked the Lord not only for the "food that nourishes our bodies" but also for the "lovely guest who favors us with her presence." I squirmed in my seat.

After our plates were served, the lovely guest carried on about how warm and friendly the people were at our church. Papa, feigning surprise, exclaimed, "Presbyterians? Warm and friendly? Haven't you heard that we're God's *frozen* people?" Then, lips twitching, he added, "Although some of us might thaw a bit in the warmth of Baptist geniality."

Miss Doreen fanned herself and tee-heed while I gagged on my peas.

I was glad when dinner was over.

* * *

I didn't want to accept Miss Doreen's invitation to dinner the following Saturday evening, but Maggie said Papa would be disappointed if I stayed home. So I went.

She greeted us at the door in a floor-length green gown. Her living room had changed since the last time I saw it. The walls were still pink and hung with pictures of swans on lakes and close-standing couples on foot bridges, but Mr. Clarence's recliner and radio were nowhere in sight. And a new aqua rug covered the floor.

"May I offer you some blackberry wine?" she asked after we sat down.

Papa's eyes widened. "What? I had no idea a *Baptist* would keep spirits in the house."

"Go on with you, Jim," Maggie said. "Yes, Doreen, a little wine would be nice."

Tee-heeing and fanning her face with her hand, Miss Doreen left the room. I stared at the rug. It was embarrassing to watch my father acting so silly.

Miss Doreen had gone to considerable pains over her table. Glasses sparkled, silver plate gleamed. According to Papa and Maggie, the meal—chicken and dressing, green beans with bacon, mashed potatoes and gravy, devil's food cake—was delicious. To me it all tasted like paste.

Afterwards, in the parlor, Miss Doreen handed Maggie a dish of toasted pecans and insisted she try them. Maggie thanked her and took one nut. Then, as she leaned over to set the dish on an end table, her hand shook and a few nuts scattered onto the rug.

"Oh, I'm so sorry." She bent to pick up the nuts.

"Now, don't you do that, Miss Maggie," said Miss Doreen. "Don't you worry about nothing. I'll sweep these up in a jiff."

Papa sprang from his chair. "No, let me do it." He was out of the room and back in an instant with dustpan and broom.

It didn't occur to me until I got home, but how did my father know where that woman kept her cleaning equipment?

The next afternoon, I went to Maggie's room to get an aspirin for my headache and found her sitting at her table, writing a letter.

"Miss Doreen acts so silly," I said. "She makes Papa act silly, too."

"She does make him laugh, though," Maggie said. "I haven't seen him so lively in years."

I shook an aspirin from the bottle she kept in her dresser. "She wears such tacky clothes. And when she's not careful, she uses bad English. What will people say about their being together?"

Maggie frowned. "Margaret, Doreen Hoyt may not be your choice for your father, but she is a good woman."

I went to the bathroom for water to swallow the aspirin. Surely, Maggie felt as I did about Doreen. She just wouldn't admit it. Maggie, usually supportive of things that mattered deeply to me, was letting me down.

Back in her room, I said, "That woman would never fit in with our family."

"How do you know, child?"

"I just do."

"Margaret, neither of us knows where this friendship may lead. But you need to realize that as you grow older and become more independent, you and your father will be less connected. Let him find happiness wherever he can."

"I'm not trying to keep him from happiness. Good grief, it's not that at all. I'm going to go read a book."

Back in my room, I plopped down on the bed and propped pillows under my head. I had been reading *Jane Eyre* for the one thousandth time and was coming to one of my favorite parts where Rochester, disguised as a "gipsy," tells Jane her fortune. I began reading but couldn't concentrate on the words. I laid the open book on my lap.

Surely, Maggie didn't mean I would keep my father from being happy. I'd never been opposed to his having lady friends. When single women smiled at him, I often wondered what they might be like as stepmothers. I wouldn't have minded if he remarried someday. But that stale dumpling as my mother's successor? I looked across the room at Mother's portrait. If Papa wanted a lady friend, Aunt May Belle could arrange for him to meet someone suitable. Or—

I straightened, causing my book to fall to the floor.

Tallulah Cassels had been my mother's best friend. With her thick auburn hair and green eyes, she could be quite attractive. I should get Betsy have her father say nice things to Papa about Miss Tallulah. And at the same time, I could arouse Miss Tallulah's interest in Papa. Problem solved.

Leaning down, I picked up my book and began to read where I had left off: *The library looked tranquil enough as I entered it, and the Sybil—if Sybil she were....*

CHAPTER 29

"I've been thinking about painting a picture of my father," I said. I was sitting at Miss Tallulah's kitchen table, watching her pour orange pekoe tea into cobalt blue cups with gold handles.

She raised her eyebrows. "But you're not ready for portraiture."

"I know. But maybe if you could help me sketch out Papa's best features now—I mean, capture his personality on paper—then, when I am ready, I'll have those sketches to work from."

She poured milk into her tea and stirred it. "What might his best features be?"

"His... Well, I know he has gray hair and wrinkles and all, but I could leave off those things."

"You want me to help recapture your father as a young man?"

"Yes, yes, that's it. So his picture will match Mother's. And when I've finished, I'll hang it alongside hers."

"I didn't know your father when he was the age your mother was in her portrait."

"Then how he looked the first time you met him."

Miss Tallulah smiled faintly. "Well, let me see...I first met Jim Norman during a summer dance at the country club. Halfway through the evening, somebody showed up with this intense-looking man, and Weezie asked him to dance. She could be audacious like that. So lively. So sure of herself. The next thing I knew, he was escorting her everywhere."

"He must have been really handsome back then if my mother was attracted to him."

"Oh, he hasn't changed much. Not homely exactly, just

rather plain."

I stiffened a little, surprised by her bluntness. She seemed not to notice.

"It had been a while since Weezie and I made our debuts, and the ranks of eligible bachelors were thinning. I'd wasted my time looking for someone to measure up to my inestimable father. Weezie had just wasted her time.

"Then, out of the blue, she fixed her sights on Jim Norman. Amazing to me, really, what the attraction could be. I wondered if it weren't that air of reluctance about him, that way he had of drawing back as though playing with fire—which, in a way, he was.

"Before long, though, 'La Belle Dame sans Merci' had him in thrall. You know Keats's poem from school, don't you? You remember what happened?"

"The knight falls in love with the beautiful lady and dies or something?"

"The knight does fall in love. But in this version it was the lady who was broken. Not that the knight caused it. Weezie managed that all by herself." Miss Tallulah paused to study her hands. Then she continued. "One of those unfortunate things. No one's fault, really. Certainly not Jim's. Poor fellow, he hadn't a clue as to what was going on.

"During those final years, she often came here to paint. She wasn't the same as in earlier years. No longer exuberant and fun-loving. She seemed unhappy and it showed in her work. I imagine she destroyed them, those last paintings, I mean?" Miss Tallulah looked at me questioningly.

I shrugged as though I didn't know. But I did. My mother had not destroyed all the paintings. There was one in the lockup, a winter garden dated 1928. The sky was gray; the bushes were bare; a few withered blossoms sagged on their stems. The first time I saw it, I felt so sad that I turned it to face the wall.

Miss Tallulah refilled our cups, and I sat quietly watching the steam coil above mine.

This was to have been the day that I aroused my art teacher's interest in Papa. That I initiated the romance that would stand as a buffer between his vulnerability and Doreen Hoyt's tawdry allures.

But I realized that there would never be warm feelings between him and my art teacher. How could I have forgotten that first time I saw them together, how coolly they behaved toward each other, how obvious that neither one cared for the other? Nothing had changed. And nothing ever would.

I picked my cup and sipped the tea. Miss Tallulah's eyes were fixed on the table.

"There were things that happened while Weezie and I were in Greenwich Village," she said without looking up. "The story's well known, and sooner or later you're bound to hear versions of it, some rather ugly."

I leaned forward in my chair.

"I'd have thought your father would have already told you what happened or maybe your aunt. Apparently, they haven't."

She looked up at me now, eyes boring into my face. "Maybe because they thought you wouldn't understand?"

I shook my head. "Please, Miss Tallulah, I'll understand. You can tell me."

She sat very still. I held my breath.

Then she said, "All right, I'll tell you. It's right that you know the truth."

She rested her elbows on the table. "Now, you must put this into perspective. You must realize how things were back then. The Great War was over. The country was changing. Weezie and I thought we had to be up to date. We were flappers, you see, disdaining the old, embracing

241

the new—or so we thought.

"One evening in Greenwich Village, we were having dinner at a cafe where artists were known to gather, when this scruffy young man approached Weezie and said, 'I want to paint you.' He scribbled his address on a scrap of paper, gave it to her, and told her to be at his place the next morning.

"After he left, we asked the waiter who the man was, and he said Laing Mingledorff. Now, I knew of Laing Mingledorff; he'd recently won a prestigious award for a painting. So the next morning, we showed up at his studio. He wanted Weezie to pose as a nymph in a woodland scene done in an art nouveau style. And he wanted her to pose in the nude."

I gasped. "With no clothes on?"

"Oh, yes, we were shocked, too. She and I had talked boldly enough about embracing the Bohemian life. But when it came right down to it, with our conservative upbringing, posing nude was out of the question. At first, that is. Then she decided she would. After all, we were up in New York, and who was to know?

"The painting took months to finish, and I always went with her to the studio. It wasn't a sacrifice for me; I loved watching Mingledorff work. He was a master colorist and a meticulous observer of detail. But I also was there because my friend wanted me there.

"I had thought Mingledorff might portray Weezie as that free, untamed spirit I'd tried to reveal in my painting. Instead, he painted her as an innocent, an ingénue—which, when you think about it, was appropriate to the work's Edenic setting."

"I wish I could see the painting."

"That isn't likely. Although"—Miss Tallulah pushed back her chair and stood up—"I could show you photos. I hesitate, though, because they're so very inadequate. But at least they'll give you some idea of the overall composition."

She left the kitchen and returned moments later waving a manila envelope. "Now, these were obtained under subversive conditions—'No cameras allowed.' The quality is poor, but it was the best that could be managed under the circumstances." She opened the envelope, withdrew two photographs, and handed them to me.

The top one was of a thick forest with a young woman, obviously my mother, seated on a fallen tree trunk, one hand resting on the trunk, the other holding a flower unlike any I'd ever seen. A robe the same light tone as her skin lay on the ground near her feet, as though carelessly shrugged from her shoulders. The thought had earlier crossed my mind that seeing my mother nude might make me uncomfortable, but it did not. I was simply looking at a beautiful woman in a fantasy woodland. And even though the photo lacked color and detail, it was charming.

The second photo was of my mother's face, lips slightly parted, dark eyes searching for something outside the canvas. Her expression was not one I'd seen, and to me it didn't seem naive or innocent. The expression seemed to be one more of yearning.

I returned the pictures and thanked my teacher.

"Because of what happened later," Miss Tallulah said, slipping the photos back into the envelope, "I need to mention that Mingledorff's studio was also his home. And the home of the fair Leona, his fetching young paramour, who was always present making sure her lover's models remained models, nothing more." Miss Tallulah looked at me hard. "Weezie was never anything more than a model."

"I'm not sure what you mean—"

She cut me off with a shake of her head. "After the painting was finished, we packed up and came home, since

243

it was unlikely either of us could have earned enough money to live in New York. Weezie married and started a family. I began giving art lessons. The whole Greenwich adventure became a thing of the past.

"Sometime later I learned that Laing Mingledorff had died and there would be an exhibit of his work in New York. Immediately, I felt uneasy. Weezie's painting had been snatched up by a collector not known for letting his acquisitions be put on public display. I sincerely hoped it would be true in this case. But it wasn't. The painting was shown, and she was recognized by one of this city's fine, upright citizens—who couldn't wait to get home and start rumors.

"Now, I'd told you that Clarissa Hoadly had forced Laura to break off her engagement to Max. Clarissa used those ugly rumors, among other things, to bring an end to the engagement. Of course, it hurt Max. It hurt Weezie more."

"What about Papa? Was he upset?"

"Your father was gracious and handled the situation like a true gentleman would. Soon, everything settled down. Then Max and Laura were in that awful car wreck. Weezie felt it was her fault and she was devastated."

"Couldn't Papa help her?"

"I'm sure he tried. She closed herself off from her friends. I never saw her nor did anyone else. I heard she was expecting a second baby. A baby, a new life—I hope she'd find joy in the anticipation."

I said nothing. But I could have told Miss Tallulah that from having read Louisa's diary, I knew my mother had found no joy in that.

"It was a shock to hear that Weezie had died. She was my cherished friend, and losing her caused me great pain."

"Do you know what caused Mother's death?"

244

"There was talk of hemorrhage, infection...." Miss Tallulah shook her head.

"Did she love my father?"

Miss Tallulah looked surprised by my question. "I really don't know"—she studied my face—"but I do know that some questions are best left unasked."

She picked up the envelope with the pictures and stood. "While I put this away, would you mind clearing the table?"

I watched my teacher walk from the room, wondering if I would ever be able to sort through all I'd heard.

CHAPTER 30

It had been two years since Lily May left home for Detroit, and Ida had mailed her a round-trip bus ticket to come home for a family reunion on Thanksgiving Day. Tuesday before the big day, Horace took off early from work to drive Ida and Tamisa to the bus station to meet her.

Great preparations were underway. Odell was barbecuing two hogs over an open-pit fire in his yard, Hazel was making a wash pot of Brunswick stew, Junie was cooking vegetable dishes, and Ida was baking cakes and pies of all kinds. As for me, I couldn't wait to see Lily May and hear about life in the North.

After I got home from school Wednesday, I went to the kitchen and found Ida at the sink, peeling apples, while Tamisa zooming around like a crazed bee, waving a graham cracker over her head.

"Come here, squirt blossom," I said, grabbing her up as she tried to rush past.

"How you doing, Margaret?"

Lily May stood near the window. She was wearing a pumpkin-colored suit and a black hat with black feathers.

"Lily May! It's so good to see you!"

She looked me up and down. "You done growed some. My baby growed too." She reached out to Tamisa, who pushed her head into my shoulder. I squeezed the baby's plump little leg, and for a long moment, Lily May and I looked at each other. Her eyes seemed sad to me, and I groped for words to bridge all the time that had passed between us. I couldn't find any.

Finally, I said, "You going somewhere?"

"Horace fixing to take me to town to visit friends."

"How long will you be home? We need time to catch

up on things."

"I leaves Saturday morning. Two long days and nights riding that Greyhound. But I got to be on my job Monday morning."

"She ain't staying long enough to get the cramps out her legs," Ida said.

"Coming all this way, you ought to stay at least through Christmas." I shifted Tamisa to my hip. "But I guess Will Roy can't do without you."

"I ain't studying about that old man."

Ida said, "She have herself a new boyfriend. Young and good looking. He want to get married."

"Will you marry him, Lily May?"

"I ain't made up my mind."

Tamisa dropped her cracker on the floor and began pulling at my barrette.

"Ouch! Quit that, Tamisa." I tried to untangle my hair from her fingers.

"If you do get married and all," I said, "you won't take Tamisa to Detroit, will you?"

"She ain't taking that baby nowhere when she be working all day in a car plant," Ida said.

Lily May thrust back her shoulders. "I takes my child when I gets good and ready."

"Now, you know Tamisa can't be living no place where it snow half the year and mosquitos big as fists bites you the other half."

"Aw, Momma, you being foolish. Maybe not now, but someday I get my baby. You can't hold her forever."

I pressed my cheek into Tamisa's soft, spongy hair, and when I lifted it, I felt tears on my face.

Lily May poked the tears with her thumb. "That's the way to kill doodle bugs," she said, and rubbed her eyebrow.

I rubbed my eyebrow, our old secret signal. We

laughed.

Holding her hands out to Tamisa, she said, "Child, come here to me."

Tamisa squirmed to get down. But when I set her on the floor, she ran past her momma to Ida, who was still at the sink. Ida scooped her up and gave her a chunk of apple, which Tamisa pushed against her nose while staring at Lily May.

A wave of pity swept through me. I tried to embrace my old friend. But her face was closed tight, and I let my arms drop.

A few moments later, Horace drove into the back yard and tooted his horn. Lily May said goodbye and walked out the door. I did not see her again.

* * *

All our family, except Louisa and Frank who would be with his kinfolk in Charleston, planned to celebrate Thanksgiving at Aunt May Belle's house. Then, on the day before Thanksgiving, Uncle Ira phoned to say Milton had taken Betsy to the hospital. Since the baby wasn't due for another two weeks, I assumed it was a false alarm.

Thanksgiving morning, I awoke to find my room as cold as an icebox. Extending one arm out from the covers, I grabbed my robe off the floor, bundled it around my head and shoulders, and snuggled down to dream of Aunt May Belle's warm house and all the good things we'd have for Thanksgiving dinner.

The telephone rang in the hall.

"Who was it, Maggie?" I called after she had hung up.

"Your uncle. He and your aunt were at the hospital all night. No news yet from Betsy."

"Did he say they'd be home in time for dinner? I

imagine Nellie has everything fixed."

"I doubt if they leave the hospital any time soon."

I sat up, my robe falling off me. "I can't believe it. Betsy's little production has consumed everything for the last eight and a half months. Now, it's going to gobble up Thanksgiving, too."

"Did you say something?" Maggie asked.

I raised my voice. "Just wondering what we'll do for our dinner. We don't have a turkey or anything. Ida will be at her family reunion."

"We'll scrounge up something." Maggie's footsteps grew faint down the hall.

I shivered into my clothes and went to the kitchen to find her searching the refrigerator.

I peered over her shoulder. "Nothing here to scrounge up except those two apple pies we were going to take to Aunt May Belle's."

Maggie took out a covered bowl. "Stew from last night," she said. "I'll cut up more carrots and potatoes to stretch it. We'll make do just fine."

We would *not* make do just fine. Beef stew that was mostly vegetables was no substitute for turkey and dressing.

The morning dragged by with no further calls from the hospital. Papa made a fire in the parlor, and the three of us drew our chairs close to the hearth.

"This cold reminds me of a Thanksgiving when I was a boy in Savannah," he said. "I woke to find icicles hanging from trees. I'd never seen icicles, and I went outside to break off some to have with our dinner. Of course, they had melted by the time we were ready to eat."

"You should have run out for more," Maggie said.

"I did. But the day had turned warm and the icicles were gone. I came crying into the house. My father said, 'Son, be a man.'"

Papa stared into the flames, reliving his little boy hurt. For some reason, I felt annoyed.

The hall clock struck eleven. Maggie got up. "Come, Margaret, we'd better finish preparing our meal."

Thinking of all the good food going to waste at Aunt May Belle's house, I followed her out to the hall. We would eat in the kitchen since it was warmer than the dining room. I set the table with the first things I came across— mismatched plates, napkins with holes.

"Wouldn't you prefer to use the nice things?" Maggie asked as I took jelly glasses out of the cabinet.

"It won't make any difference what we use today," I said.

Just as Papa finished saying grace, the telephone rang again. I got up to answer it.

"Attention, please. Important announcement." It was Uncle Ira. "Milton Marcus Moon, Junior, arrived at 11:58 this Thanksgiving day. Seven pounds, nine and one-half ounces. Mother and baby are fine. And so are we all!"

I giggled all the way back to the kitchen.

The stew wasn't half bad, and Maggie had made my favorite salad, canned pears with grated cheese and red cherries on top. She'd warmed one of the pies and served it with lots of whipped cream. I only wished I had put a fresh cloth on the table and set it with good china and silver. We had something to celebrate after all.

It was late afternoon by the time we arrived at Betsy's hospital room. Aunt May Belle, Uncle Ira, and Miss Gertrude were slumped in their chairs, looking half dead. Milton was strutting about, puffed up like a gobbler.

"That boy's something else!" he declared before I was halfway through the door. "Doctor says he's never seen such a grip on a newborn. He's something else, that boy is." Milton smacked a fat fist on his palm.

Betsy lay in bed with her eyes closed. Maggie and I went to her.

"How are you, my dear?" Maggie asked.

Betsy opened her eyes. "They put me to sleep. I missed the whole thing."

"You ought to be grateful," Miss Gertrude said. "Wish they'd knocked me out when I was having my young'uns."

Milton gestured toward the door. "Please follow me. I'll escort you to the nursery."

Uncle Ira pushed himself to his feet. "I'd better go, too. Need to check how much my grandson has grown in the past hour."

"The boy has all the makings of a good athlete," Milton informed us as we walked down the hall. "Probably play college football."

I rolled my eyes at Maggie. She smiled.

I knew exactly how the baby would look—bald-headed, moon-faced, full-lipped. A new little Moon. I was prepared to say how handsome he was.

Milton tapped on the nursery window, and the nurse at the desk raised her hand without looking up. Milton rocked on his heels and jiggled change in his pocket. Finally, the nurse got up and went to a bassinette, where she picked up a bundle. She brought it to the window and pushed the blanket aside.

He had lots of black hair, a long face, and a scowl. It was all I could do to keep from laughing out loud. Milton Marcus Moon, Jr., looked for all the world like his grandmother May Belle.

CHAPTER 31

It was Saturday and unusually warm for a day in late November. I was at Ida's house, sitting across the table from her while she rinsed out clothes in a washbasin. Hazel and Odell had just left with Tamisa, who was spending the weekend with them.

"Ida," I said, "I'm a senior in high school. Before long, I'll go off to college, and no telling where after that. I want you to tell me how things were before I was born."

Ida sighed. "Lord, Biscuit, it be so long ago, I done forgot most everything."

"There are things you remember."

She squeezed out Tamisa's little red dress and dropped it into a basket on the floor. "The first time I laid eyes on your momma I be in the yard hanging out sheets and this green car come a-flying up the road and stop alongside me, dust chasing all over my clean wash."

"And Mother hopped out like a little canary in her yellow dress. She said Sam had told her about you, and would you come work for her, and the next day Woodrow loaded your things into Odell's wagon, and you and Woodrow rode over to Cardinal Hill. I like that story."

"Them was happy times. Miss Weezie a bride. Me and her cleaning out that old house, going through junk Mr. Jim's folks keep from the dawn of creation. Hauling stuff to the lockup, Sam dumping trash in the woods."

"And when you and Mother finished the house, you started on the yard and worked till right up before Louisa was born. I know all that, Ida. It's afterwards I don't know about."

Ida rubbed her arm across her forehead. "What I going to say, Biscuit? Don't nobody never talk about your momma. They may be things ain't my business to tell."

"Please, Ida, do tell."

She dropped the last of the wash into the basket and pushed the water basin aside. "It be after Louisa born that the misery commence."

"What misery?"

Ida closed her eyes and made a low humming sound. Then she stared at me hard. "You wants to know? I tell you. Set still. Don't ask no questions."

I nodded that I would.

Ida drew a deep breath. "Louisa the prettiest white baby ever be born. But she colicky, fussy. Miss Weezie want to tend her all by herself. Don't want no help, like she got to show what a good momma she be. But when Louisa turn three, Miss Weezsie give her over to me and commence to do other things, paint pictures, go places."

"So Mother ignored Louisa?"

Ida frowned, and I put a finger over my lips.

"Many's the morning she drive off in her car, and don't come home till supper. After Mr. Max move in with the family, she stay home more. Mr. Max make folks laugh. Well, not Mr. Jim; he keep his face straight. But Miss Weezie and Louisa they laugh. Miss Weezie act happy when Mr. Max be around. Then here come that mess about a picture somebody paint of her up in New York. Folks commenced talking and she get upset. But nothing like how upset she get when Mr. Max kill hisself in that car wreck. Miss Weezie say it be all her fault. I tell her it ain't, but she don't pay me no mind. After he die, look like she just close up.

"Oh, she try to act right when other folks be around. But when they gone, she let it out. Sam seen her crying down in the woods. I seen her too, setting on a pine stump, a-moaning and rocking.

"About then, Lily May come along. Strong, healthy baby. Sharp, too. Sure let me know loud and clear when something don't suit." Ida chuckled. "And as if I ain't busy enough with my baby and all that other, Woodrow decide to take hisself off. Don't say nothing to me, just pick up and leave."

"Oh, Ida, I'm so—"

"Uh huh." Ida shook her head hard. "I ain't wasting my time worrying over no cheating man. Woodrow can do what he please."

She got up from the table and filled two glasses with water from the pitcher she kept on a shelf. She sat back down and gave me one.

"Miss Weezie ain't doing well. Not eating, not sleeping at night, moping around all the time. Mr. Jim worried. He tell her go see the doctor. She do and come home with a bottle of pills. She take them and they help her to sleep. Mr. Jim think that fix the problem. When Miss Weezie finish that bottle, she get her another and keep it behind Louisa's picture on her dresser. Mr. Jim don't know it be there.

"One day Miss Weezie tell me you is on the way and she not going to take no more pills. I reckoned the doctor told her to stop. She stay in her room all the time. I hear her crying in there."

The question popped out of my mouth like cork under pressure. "Was Mother sad because she was going to have me?"

For a long moment Ida said nothing. Then she said, "Aw, no, Biscuit, Miss Weezie glad to have you. She say the reason she eat what she do—which ain't hardly nothing—is on account of she want her baby healthy."

I knew Ida was lying.

"One night about the time you due to come, I gets a knock on my door. I puts my shawl 'round my gown and goes open it up. Mr. Jim standing there and he say, 'Can you come?' I say, 'Soon as I grab up my baby.' After he leave I hurry so bad I puts my dress on wrong side out and don't know it till noon. I wrap Lily May in a blanket and we head for the big house. When we gets there, Mr. Jim be helping Miss Weezie in the car. Poor little thing, so heavy and slow. I leans in the window and say, 'Now, don't worry about nothing around here. You just mind after yourself.' She say, 'Ida, dear friend, look after things.' I always remember them words. They was the last I hear from her mouth.

"Next afternoon, Mr. Jim call from the hospital to report you born fine and healthy. Miss Weezie fine, too, excepting she weak. I glad to hear things is going good at the hospital 'cause they sure ain't going good at the house. Lily May come down the trots and whine day and night. Louisa sassy and won't mind what I say. Mr. Jim ain't sleeping when he do come home at night. The light in his room don't never go off. And all that go on for six days.

"Then come the seventh. Lord Jesus, have mercy!" Ida slapped her hands on the table, and I jumped as though I'd been shot. "It start up after supper. I gets Lily May settled in bed and takes my mending to set by the door where some good light still left. Directly, I see Mr. Jim come cross the field, staggering like he be drunk. I jumps up, pins and needles spilling ever-which-way, and I hollers, 'Mr. Jim, is you sick?' He don't say nothing, just keep a-coming.

"I runs down the steps. 'Mr. Jim, what's wrong with you?' "He sway like he fixing to fall. 'Anne Louisa... The hospital called....' 'Dear Lord God, don't tell me that! Not Miss Weezie. Not that sweet lady.'

"'Round about then, Lily May show up at the door. She look at me. She look at Mr. Jim. And she sets up to hollering and jumping around. I run up the steps to grab her before she fall down. 'Hush up, Lily May,' I say. 'Mr. Jim,

255

you go on to the hospital. I'm coming to look after Louisa. Go on now, Mr. Jim. Hush, Lily May.' Great God A'mighty, have mercy!"

Ida stopped speaking. I slumped in my chair as though I had taken a beating. She reached over and patted my shoulder.

"The night Miss Weezie die, I lie in bed, Lily May curled at my side. She wake up and fuss. I change her and she fall back asleep. I go set in the chair near the window. No moon in the sky, just a litter of stars. And below them, the gray field and the big house all dark and still.

"I sets where I is till the stars fade away. Then I gets up and dress and goes to the coop for a hen. I wring its neck and come back to pluck it and dress it. I leaves for the big house, hen in a pan under one arm, Lily May in her blanket under the other. The rim of the sky just turning to gold.

"I done made up my mind to fix a good breakfast. I gets everything ready and sets the table with Miss Weezie's nice china and a vase of roses, fresh picked. Then I set down to wait. Lily May wake up in her basket and commences to fuss. I feeds her a bottle and lays her back down.

"There's racket down at the end of the hall, and directly Louisa come in, dragging her suitcase. 'Where you think you going?' I say. 'Aunt May Belle's coming to take me to her house,' she say. 'Well, you better eat your breakfast now, so she don't have to wait.' 'I'm not hungry,' she say.

"I tells her, 'Look-a-here, Louisa, I done got you a cheese omelet what's your favorite thing. And chocolate milk all stirred in the icebox.' 'Leave me alone,' she say and climb up on the stool near the window.

"I dry the pots and puts them away, Lily May's big eyes following me all what I do. Miss May Belle drive up, and Louisa start dragging that suitcase to the door. I say, 'Here, let me tote it,' and takes it from her. 'Now, remember be sweet like your momma—' 'Shut up, Ida!' she scream and run out the house, me coming after, toting the suitcase.

"By the time Louisa get off, it too late for breakfast. I start on my chicken and dumpling what Mr. Jim say are the best in the world. I be spooning the last dumpling into the broth when he come to the door, face all pale and shrunk. 'Help me, Ida,' he say. 'I need a dress to take to the funeral home, and I don't know which one to choose.'

"I goes to the bedroom. Miss Weezie's dresses laid all over the bed, but ain't none of them right. I goes to the wardrobe and pull out a dress the color of the blue cornflowers what grows alongside the drive. 'This one,' I say. 'This one her favorite.' He say, 'All right.' I irons the dress and folds it with tissue in a box what I put by the door in the kitchen. He come in, holding his hat. I takes his hat and sets it on top of the box.

"'Now, don't leave here till you ate, Mr. Jim. I done fixed you chicken and dumplings what you like so much.'

"He say, 'Thank you, Ida. All I want is coffee, if it's not too much trouble.'

"I say, 'No trouble. You go set in the dining room. I'll bring it in there.' He don't move. I points and I say, 'I serve you in there.' He go to the dining room.

"Two times I ask if he want more coffee, and he say he don't. He come back to the kitchen, pick up his hat, and goes out the door. He about to drive off when I see he don't have the box. I run out and give it to him. He leave with me just a-praying, 'Please, Lord, help that poor man make it to town.'

"The funeral set for Saturday afternoon. I wear the black dress what I wore to my aunt Fanny's funeral and the black hat Miss Weezie give me on account of a lady at church got one just like it. Mr. Jim and me ride to town and stop in front of the big gray church Miss Weezie show me one time she taking me to the doctor on account of my cough.

"Mr. Jim don't get out of the car. I say, 'Ain't you got business to tend to before the funeral commence?' He say, 'I need to talk with Dr. Burnley. You wait in the church. It's cooler in there.' He get out and go to that brick building alongside the church, walking bent like an old man, hair in bad need of a trim.

"I goes inside the church and sets on the back pew. Directly, two men come in at the front, toting flowers. They set them down and goes out for more. Soon the church front look like a garden. The men wheel in the coffin. They open the lid and leave.

"An organ commence and folks be coming in. Some set in the pews. Some walk up to the coffin. Soon there a line at the coffin. I gets up and goes to the end of the line.

"A big man block me from seeing. Then he move on and there be Miss Weezie in her blue dress. I walks up to her head, but my feet won't take me no farther. Folks start going around. Seem like she sleeping, like if I say something, she wake up. I rubs her cheek. It feel cold and hard.

"Lord, I don't know how it get out, but that cry sound all through the church. Quick, I covers my mouth with my hand and hurries back to my pew."

Tears coursed down Ida's cheeks. Mine too. My nose flowed like a cracked water pipe, and I wiped it on my sleeve.

"Lord, you a mess, Biscuit." Ida reached into a box of rags, pulled one out, and gave it to me. I blew my nose hard.

After a moment, she said, "There be more to tell, if you wants it."

"I want it all."

"The day after the funeral, I be picking up in the parlor, Lily May on the floor, playing with blocks, and the phone ring. I answer and it be Miss May Belle wanting to talk to Mr. Jim. I gets him to the phone and goes back to the parlor. But I don't shut the door all the way.

"Seem like Miss May Belle wanting to raise you. She'll get Betsy's old nurse to help. Mr. Jim say he want to do what is best. He know the baby need a mother and May Belle the logical one. He think about it.

"By the time he hang up, I's a-shaking all over. I picks up Lily May and goes to the kitchen to fix lunch. I scorches the soup and steps back on my baby what sets up a howl. I gives her a cookie to hush her and start down the hall, just a-praying, 'Lord Jesus, give me strength to say what need to be said.' I knocks on the door and Mr. Jim say, 'Come in.'

"I say, 'Mr. Jim, I got to talk to you.' He say, 'All right, Ida. What is it?' I say, 'It be about Miss Weezie's baby.' He lift up an eyebrow but don't open his mouth.

"I say, 'It ain't right for Miss May Belle to be raising that child. Not that she won't do a good job and all, but Miss Weezie's baby belong here with us. She part of this family.' He say, 'But how can I do it? How can I manage?' I say, 'Us'uns can do it. Us'uns can give that baby all it need right here in this house.'

"He study the floor. I starts feeling itchy. Then he say, 'Ida, you're right. I believe I can work it out. We'll manage somehow.'

"Lord, I forgets about lunch. Mr. Jim gone to the hospital to fetch you, and we needs to be ready. Sam move the crib to Mr. Max's old room. I takes back the diapers and such. Sam sets me up a cot. I fix a drawer for Lily May to sleep in.

"When Mr. Jim get back home with this little bundle tucked in one arm, I at the kitchen sink, peeling potatoes. I

259

steps over to look. 'Aw, what you got there?' I say. Mr. Jim don't say nothing. I moves the blanket aside, and you looks up at me through dark little slits. I say, 'Ain't that the sweetest sight you ever seen? She an angel girl, that's what she be.'

"He nod his head, serious like. Then he pushes the baby right in my arms. 'Here, Ida,' he say, 'look after this child.' And he get hisself quick out of the room.

"I takes Lily May's hand and we goes to the parlor and sets in the rocker. Lily May crawl up in my lap. I rocks and I sings to both my babies. Mr. Jim don't show hisself no more that day."

Ida leaned back in her chair. "Reckon that's all there be to report," she said after a moment.

I didn't say anything.

"What?" Ida said.

"You know how Mother died, don't you?"

She reached down and picked up the basket of laundry. "I got to get these out to dry."

"I'll help you."

"You stay where you is."

I watched from the door as she pinned the clothes on the line.

When she came back in, I said, "Tell me how Mother died."

Ida frowned. "But I don't know how. I just got my suspicions."

"What are your suspicions?"

Ida drew her lips in and frowned. "I ain't saying they right. They just be my suspicions. One day before Miss Weezie leave for the hospital, I come in her room and she be packing her suitcase. I ask could I help, and she say she about done. I see her pick some little thing off the bed and tucked it deep in with her clothes, like she don't want me to see it. I don't think no more about it till the day after she die and Mr. Jim in the hall on the phone, and he say something about no cutting on her. Then he say, 'All right, I suppose we'll never know.'

"After he go out, I looks for that bottle Miss Weezie kept behind Louisa's picture. It ain't there. It ain't anywhere. That bottle was what I seen her put in the suitcase to go to the hospital. That poor little lady she want to die. She wait to make sure her baby all right, then she swallow them pills."

I felt as though I'd been dunked with ice water. "But why, Ida? Why?"

Ida shook her head slowly. "I sorry, Biscuit, I wish I could tell you. But I don't have no answer for that."

I folded my arms on the table and laid my head on them. "My poor mother," I said. "And my father. My poor, heart-broken father."

CHAPTER 32

The wind had whipped the cold rain into a frenzy, and Miss Tallulah and I got thoroughly soaked dashing under her umbrella from the studio to the kitchen. Now, we sat at the table, waiting for the peppermint tea to steep in its pale aqua pot sprinkled with violets.

Miss Tallulah shivered and hugged her shoulders. "This dampness penetrates to the marrow of my bones," she said. "I'm getting old."

"You're not old. You're younger than Papa, and Maggie says he's in his prime."

"A man in his prime is a woman in her decline. Not that it matters." She gave a short, mirthless laugh. "In the end, we all shrivel and die."

"Huh?"

"Don't mind me." She poured tea into our cups. "Days like this make me gloomy."

"It's the kind of day I like to snuggle down with a book—say, *Wuthering Heights*. I can just hear Cathy calling to Heathcliff across the stormy moors." I took a cautious sip of the tea. It burned my tongue.

Miss Tallulah ran her hand down the sleeve of her argyle cardigan and stopped at a moth hole. "Suppose I'll get another twenty years wear out of this sweater?" she asked, poking her finger into the hole.

"It's real pretty. I doubt if anyone will even notice that little spot."

"Aren't you the tactful one." She picked up a spoon and began stirring her tea.

A crack of lightning immediately followed by thunder startled us both. Seconds later, there came a crash from upstairs.

Thinking lightning had struck the house, I jumped up from my chair. "Shall I quick call the fire department?"

"Don't bother. It's just more ceiling falling in Father's room."

I sat back down. "You probably have a leak in the roof. One time plaster fell in our hall, and Papa got a man out to fix the roof right away. Letting it go can cause lots of damage."

"Fixing just one leak won't help this house. The whole roof needs replacing and should have been done years ago on Father's watch. That and other repairs."

She sighed. "Dear profligate Father. Always the means for elegance and style, but nary a farthing for anything as mundane as keeping a roof over our heads. I should have sold the place right after he died when I had an offer to buy. Then I'd have been free to live life as I chose."

She rubbed a spot of green paint on her wrist. "Ironic, isn't it? I married a house that's kept me in shackles, while Weezie..."

I waited, but she didn't go on.

"If you had been free, Miss Tallulah, what life would you have chosen to live?"

"Oh, I don't know.... Wandering through forgotten castles in Spain, painting Greek temple ruins, sipping champagne at midnight in some dingy Paris café."

"Then why didn't you sell?"

"Vanity. Surely, that must have been part of it. I liked living in the biggest house in the town, being the granddaughter of a very rich man.

"But there was more. I truly did love this audacious old place with its turrets and nooks and ornations. My roots were here—parents, grandparents. Even today their shadows hover in forgotten closets, in dark, closed-up rooms. I imagine someday we'll all go down together—

house, ghosts, and I.”

I shifted uneasily.

She laughed. “You remember in ‘The Fall of the House of Usher,’ how one stormy night the house sank into a tarn? On a day like this, it’s not hard to imagine this one collapsing into some giant puddle.”

“Aw, Miss Tallulah, you’re teasing. Things could still change. You could still sell your house and sip champagne in Paris.”

She shook her head. “Some decisions are amendable. Others are binding. And the sad thing is that at the moment one often doesn’t realize what she’s bound herself to.”

She stared through the rain-lashed window at a pine swaying stiffly in the wind. Was she thinking of the choice she had made not to sell her house? Or perhaps of my mother’s choice of a husband?

Once, I had made a decision. But it did not have to be binding.

As my words tumbled out, she stared in amazement. And when I had finished, she asked, “What now, Margaret?”

“I don’t know,” I said.

But, of course, I did know.

* * *

Maggie was at her dresser, folding handkerchiefs into the drawer. I sat on her bed and repeated my story. How, when I was eight, I found an abandoned baby in the woods and chose to raise it myself. How, when it died, I did not tell anyone.

When I finished, she came around and sat next to me. “Oh, my dear child,” she said.

264

I didn't respond; my eyes remained fixed on an old water stain on the floor. It looked like a teardrop.

"Can you locate the spot where the baby is buried?"

"I found it once several years back, but I don't think I could find it again." I didn't want to find it again.

I turned to face her. "Will you tell Papa for me?"

She shook her head. "He'll want to hear it from you."

"No, Maggie, you tell him." My courage was spent.

She put her arm around my shoulder and tried to draw me against her as she had when I was small and afraid. Back then, I'd have laid my head in her lap. Now, I sat rigid.

* * *

There was a year in my childhood when Stumpy had a calendar on his wall with a picture of a deer encircled by wolves. Whenever I went into the store, I stared at that picture.

One day, I asked, "Stumpy, what's going to happen to that deer?"

He said, "The wolves will kill it and eat it."

I felt queasy, and it must have shown on my face.

"Aw, now, don't you know about animals?" he said. "Whenever one gets in a fix, it goes all blank inside. Its spirit kind of moves out of its body, and it doesn't feel pain or anything else."

Then, I hadn't believed him. Now, as I rode to Hope Forest with Papa, I wondered if there wasn't truth in what Stumpy had said. I felt no dread or fear, only numb.

"...legal procedures must be worked through one at a time," Papa was saying. "Dr. Andrew Steele, the school's superintendent, is prepared for our visit."

Dr. Steele met us in his office and showed us a file. One summer day in 1938, two boys and a girl had run off

265

from Hope Forest. Six hours later, one boy turned up at a filling station, begging for food. The second boy was never located. The girl, Etta Lou Holt, age seventeen, was picked up three days later, after a farmer notified police he had found her lying on a pile of straw in his barn.

The door to Dr. Steele's office opened, and a woman motioned for him to step into the hall. While we waited, I stared through the window at the empty, gray campus with its few scraggly trees.

Etta Lou Holt. I pictured her asleep on the hay, her knees drawn up under the plain blue skirt, her matted red hair half covering her face. Then she was no longer asleep. She was awake and lying on the hard, sandy ground, writhing in torment and screaming in pain.

Papa reached toward me. "All this will be over soon, daughter," he said.

Dr. Steele reentered the office and continued with his report. The police had returned Etta Lou to Hope Forest, where she was placed in the infirmary and later released to her cottage. In August 1940, she had been withdrawn from the school. Her subsequent whereabouts was unknown.

Dr. Steele led us to the cottage where Etta Lou had lived. The housemother remembered her well. At the time she ran off, she was thought to be pregnant, having been discovered earlier behind a silo with a male resident. Willful and stubborn, she was not an easy girl to control. She had to be watched.

As we rode away from Hope Forest, Papa said, "The next step is to visit Will Tippit, the District Attorney. He will determine whether or not to prosecute. He may decide the case should come before a Grand Jury. He may decide something else."

"Something else?" Would they send me directly to jail?

We met with Will Tippit later that day in his office. I

answered his questions, and he said he'd get back with us. We did not have to wait long. A few afternoons later, as soon as I stepped into Papa's office to wait for my ride home after school, Miss Doreen said, "Mr. Norman would like to see you."

He sat behind the big desk, his face a mask. "Will Tippit called with his findings. He said he'd made every effort to contact Etta Lou Holt or a family member but wasn't successful. That means he has no complaining witness. Nor has he found any evidence of criminal intent. He has determined not to pursue the case further."

A smile broke across Papa's face. "I felt all along it would turn out this way. So now it's over. Over and done."

"I'm glad," I said lamely. But I didn't feel glad. I didn't feel anything.

After supper, I went to the front porch and sat on a step. The air was chilled. Clouds hovered low over the city, and no lights shone through.

"Over and done," Papa had said. So why did I feel no relief?

Maggie came out with a sweater and slipped it over my shoulders. She sat beside me and together we stared out across the gray, vacant horizon.

Finally, I said, "I keep thinking I should be punished."

"Why, Margaret?"

"I did something bad."

"Was it deliberate?"

"Not deliberate, I guess. The baby didn't have a mother. I wanted to be its mother."

"And weren't you?"

I looked at Maggie. The light from a window illuminated her face, giving it a silvery glow. "What do you mean?"

"Think, child. If you had brought the baby to me and

267

your father, we would have had to turn her over to the authorities. Doubtless, she would have been placed in a hospital. There, small as she was, she would have most likely died and not made a difference to one single soul. But you kept the baby. You comforted her, fed her, and bathed her. You mothered her the best you knew how. She could tell that you loved her. She knew that you cared."

"Oh." I drew a deep breath.

With all my guilt and fear through the years, I had forgotten the part about love. But it was there, too. I had cherished my baby, my Alicia Patricia, most deeply. Surely, that counted for something.

CHAPTER 33

I sat at the kitchen table, eyes barely open, forcing down the oatmeal and milk Maggie had set before me. I hadn't gotten enough sleep because I'd stayed up late, studying for a Latin test.

Sam appeared at the door, his Army surplus jacket buttoned up to his chin and the flaps of his hunting cap pulled over his ears. Papa was out of town on business, and Sam was to drive me to the city stop where I'd catch a bus to school.

"Time to get a-going," he said.

"Hush up, Sam," I muttered. Then louder, "It's over an hour till school starts."

"You got to allow time for them city buses," Sam said.

I gulped down my milk and choked, milk coming out through my nose. I could blame Sam for that. I grabbed my books and dashed from the kitchen. Maggie followed me out with the kerchief I sometimes wore in bad weather.

"Here, child, put this over your head."

"I don't need it," I said. But I took it anyway and stuffed it into my coat pocket. "See you this afternoon."

The morning was foggy and cold. Sam had left the engine running, but since the car had no heater, the engine was the only thing warm. I held my books close to my chest to retain what little heat I'd brought from the kitchen.

At the bottom of the hill, the fog thickened. Sam steered with one hand and operated the windshield wiper with the other. The car crept along slower than a crippled caterpillar, and when we arrived at the bus stop, one was just pulling out.

"Good grief," I said. "Now, I've got to sit here forever and freeze."

"Won't be long 'fore another bus come," said Sam.

But it was. Exactly eight and a half minutes by my watch.

By the time school let out, the day had cleared and turned even colder. But I was in a better mood than I had been in the morning because I had done well on my test. As my bus neared its stop on the way home, I saw Sam through the window, leaning against the car fender, having a serious talk with himself. He held his hunting cap in his hands, and the sunlight had turned his white hair into a glowing orb. It struck me that Sam had grown old.

"Sorry I was such a grouch this morning," I said, settling into the front seat. "I do appreciate your picking me up."

"It be all right," Sam said.

"This weather sure turned off cold."

"Hmm."

We rode in silence until we reached Cardinal Hill Road. Then he said, "Miss Maggie done took sick."

A chill not caused by the weather passed through me. "What's the matter with her?"

"Don't know. Ida say you to call the doctor soon as you gets home."

"When did she begin feeling sick?"

"Not long 'fore I start out to get you."

"I imagine she's coming down with the flu." I looked hopefully at Sam.

"Don't know," he said.

"Well, let's hurry. Can't you make this thing go any faster?"

"You romp this old gal, she lie down and die on you." But he pressed the gas pedal anyway.

I was out the door and running up the steps before the car came to a stop. The kitchen was dark. I flung my books on the table and hurried to Maggie's room. When I opened the door, I was struck by a furnace blast.

"Shut that door quick," Ida said. She was sitting near the fireplace in a reclining chair she'd brought from the hall. "Miss Maggie don't need no draft on her."

Maggie lay in bed, quilt tucked under her chin. Her eyes were closed, her lips were slightly parted, and her white hair lay loose on the pillow.

"What happened?" I asked.

"We was coming from the kitchen where we been folding laundry and was fixing to put sheets in the closet when she start to pitch over. I drops the laundry and grabs her. 'Miss Maggie?' I say, but she don't say nothing. I picks her up and carries her to her bed and makes her snug as I can. You best get the doctor to come see about her."

I switched on the lamp by the bed. Maggie's face was as pale as her pillow. "Maggie?" I said softly. Her eyes moved under their lids as if searching for something.

I went to the hall and rang Dr. Girardeau's office.

"Two more patients and he'll be out," said Miss Browning, his nurse. "In the meantime, keep her warm."

Back in the bedroom, I pulled the rocker over and sat next to Maggie. Ida put another log on the fire, which was already shooting flames up the chimney.

Suddenly, it struck me that the room was too quiet.

"Where's Tamisa?" I asked.

"Sam took her to Momma's on his way to get you."

A log rolled against the andirons, sending up sparks. Ida got up. "Reckon I better fetch in more wood while there's still some light."

After she left, I studied Maggie closely. Her breathing was shallow, a short intake of air followed by an abrupt release. I brushed a few strands of hair from her face.

"Maggie," I said, "I've called Dr. Girardeau. He'll be

here soon. You're probably coming down with the flu like you do sometimes in the winter. Rest now. Everything will be fine."

Her lips move slightly.

Ida returned with an armload of wood. She put one piece on the fire and stacked the rest on the hearth. "It done got colder. Wouldn't surprise me none if everything ain't froze up by morning."

"I wish the doctor would hurry," I said.

"If he going to put Miss Maggie on medicine, he best bring it with him. We can't go out hunting no drugstore this freezing night."

"If she has the flu, he'll probably prescribe bed rest and aspirin. We have plenty of aspirin."

"This ain't flu, Biscuit."

I knew it wasn't flu. But I wanted it to be; Maggie always got over the flu.

Ida took a handkerchief from the top drawer of the dresser, dipped a corner into the glass of water on the night table, and dabbed Maggie's lips. "This heat be drying you out, Miss Maggie." She spoke as to a child.

And Maggie was like a child, so helpless and small, her body barely causing a rise in the covers.

Ida went back to her chair by the fire. I sat on the floor beside her and watched the flames dance and change colors—gold, saffron, ocher, lemon, occasional spurts of pale blue. The hall clock chimed seven.

Ida jumped up. "Lord-a-mercy, it past suppertime, and I ain't fixed us nothing. I'll go whump up something."

"Nothing for me. I'm not hungry," I said.

"Us both got to eat, Biscuit," Ida said and left the room.

We had just finished roast beef sandwiches and milk when headlights swept across the far wall. A moment later,

I went to the front door to let in Dr. Girardeau.

"It's probably a touch of flu," I told him as we walked to Maggie's room. "But she's sleeping so hard, I thought you'd better come take a look."

Ida was smoothing the bed covers when we entered the room. She had twisted Maggie's hair into a ball on top of her head.

"Ida," said the doctor. "I haven't seen you in ages. Must be doing a pretty good job of taking care of yourself."

"I does try and that's the gospel truth," Ida said.

"Well, let's see what Miss Maggie's been up to."

He sat in the rocker and opened his bag. He took her blood pressure on one arm, then on the other. He lifted her eyelids and examined the pupils with a tiny flashlight. He folded back the covers and listened to her heart, shifting the stethoscope from one spot to another. Then he pushed up her sleeve and gave her a shot. Maggie didn't flinch, but I did. And, without thinking, I rubbed my arm a few times.

"Is your father still at his office?" Dr. Girardeau asked without turning around.

"No, sir, he's in Charleston. Uncle Ira's buying a furniture store, and Papa drove over to handle some business."

The doctor faced me. "Can you get in touch with him?"

"He left his hotel number, but I—"

"It be on the telephone table," Ida said.

"Go call him now."

Even under ordinary circumstances, calling long distance made me nervous. I was still trying to dial the number when Dr. Girardeau came into the hall and stood right beside me, making things considerably worse.

Finally, a voice at the other end of the line said, "Ashley Hotel. May I help you, please?"

"Hello, may I speak to my father?"

"Name, please?"

"Pa—Mr. James Boyd Norman."

"One moment, please."

There were five rings, and the operator was back on the line. "Sorry, his room doesn't answer."

"Well, do you know when he'll be getting—"

"Give me the phone." The doctor took it out of my hand. "Operator, this is Dr. Nicholas Girardeau calling from Fredericksboro, Georgia. Get this message to Jim Norman as soon as you can. His aunt is gravely ill. He must come home immediately. Do you understand that?"

Apparently, she did.

After he'd hung up the receiver, he turned to me. "Now, ring up that sister of yours. Tell her to come out here and stay till your father gets home."

I dialed Louisa's number. There was no answer. "She could be out visiting friends," I suggested.

"What about May Belle?"

"She went on a shopping trip to Atlanta."

"Well, who in thunder can you get to come out?"

I put my hand on the table to steady myself. I had known Dr. Girardeau all my life. He was the kindest, gentlest man in the world. This sudden gruffness upset me.

"You call Louisa later," he said more gently. "Tell her to come as soon as she can."

"Yes, sir." I was almost panting with nervousness.

"Now, ask Ida to step out a minute."

I delivered his message.

"She's in no pain," he told us. "All you can do is keep her comfortable and warm." He ran his fingers through his thin gray hair, as though uncertain of what to say next.

"Margaret, you know your aunt is an old lady. She has a tired heart and weak arteries. One of those arteries couldn't hold any longer. It burst. I'll wait with you a while."

"Oh no, sir," Ida said. "No call for that. Me and Margaret can look after Miss Maggie."

"Well, I don't like the idea of just you two handling this, but you're probably right, Ida. There's nothing more I can do." He turned to me, frowning. "You keep trying to reach Louisa. I want her out here."

"Yes, sir, I'll try."

He got his bag from Maggie's room, and I, on unsteady legs, walked him to the front door. When I returned to the room, Ida was straightening Maggie's bedclothes.

"I can't understand it," I said, sitting back in the rocker. "She was fine this morning. She fixed my breakfast. Nothing was wrong with her then. She'll probably feel better after a good night's sleep."

"Doctor say keep her warm and comfortable." Ida reached under the covers to feel Maggie's feet. "Lord-a-mercy, they be cold as ice!"

I drew Maggie's hand from the covers, little fingers curled up like bird claws. "Her hand is cold, too." I started to rub it.

"I gonna fix a hot water bag to set on them feet," Ida said and left the room.

I rubbed Maggie's hand until it was as warm as my own and tucked it back under the covers. I drew out the other hand. "Maggie," I said, "we've got to pray you get well. You pray along with me, even though you don't say any words."

Sliding to my knees, I bowed my head and pressed her hand to my cheek. "Dear God, please let Maggie get well. You didn't give me a mother to raise me. You gave me Maggie, and she's loved me and cared for me better than any mother possibly could. So, please—" My voice caught. I turned my head and kissed Maggie's hand. "Please, God, let her get well. I still need her so much."

Ida's footsteps sounded outside the door. I got off my knees.

"Do you think Maggie can hear us even if she's asleep?" I asked as she adjusted the hot water bag against Maggie's feet.

"I reckon she can. Once my old auntie Florine took a spell. Lay near dead for a week. Then one day she wake up and say she hear everything what been said about her, and some of it she don't like one bit."

Maggie's breathing sounded more natural since her shot. Her hands were warm to the touch. "I think she's going to be all right, don't you, Ida?"

"Don't know, Biscuit. The doctor talk like she pretty sick. But now, you think about it, Miss Maggie done live a good long life. She ready any time to be caught up in the arms of sweet Jesus."

"She's not but eighty-seven. Lots of people live to be more than a hundred."

"Some folks does, not a whole lots." Ida went to the fire and poked it into a roar. I wiped sweat off my face.

"Reckon you ought to try to reach Louisa again?" Ida sat back down in her chair.

"Yeah, I will in a minute." I settled into the rocker.

The hall clock chimed the half hour. I began counting: one-thousand and one, one-thousand and two...I'd see if I could come out even with the clock when it chimed the three-quarter hour. I wasn't far off.

When the clock struck eleven, I yawned. It was too late to be calling Louisa; Ida would understand that.

"You go to bed," she said. "I call if I needs anything."

"I'm not really sleepy, but I might stretch out on the

other side of Maggie's bed a few minutes. You don't think it will disturb her, do you?"

"It won't disturb her one bit."

I took off my shoes and lay next to Maggie where I'd lain so often over the years.

The sound of cap pistols exploding jolted me upright. I looked over at Ida.

"It just be that green log I set on the fire," she said.

"I'll rest a while longer." I lay back down.

* * *

I was awake. A Presence—wondrous, mysterious—filled the room. I tried to move, to speak out, and found I could not. But I felt no fear, only a profound, solemn peace.

I had no idea how long the interval lasted, but when it passed, I fell into a deep, dreamless sleep.

* * *

Gray dawn muted the room, melding the chairs and dresser and wardrobe into the walls.

I was lying under a quilt from my own bed; Ida must have spread it over me while I slept. I sat up and looked across to the fireplace. Coals dimly glowed beneath a coating of ash. Ida was slumped in her chair, head rolled to one side, a shawl covering her lap. Maggie was gone; I knew that even before I became aware that her breathing had stopped. In the dim light, her face appeared to be carved out of stone.

Carefully, as though not to disturb her, I got up and tiptoed to the fireplace. I picked up three sticks of lightwood and placed them on top of the coals. Ida muttered and shifted her head.

I was about to put a log on the lightwood when I heard a car engine. I laid the log back on the hearth, slipped on my shoes, and stole from the room. Halfway down the hall, I started to run—through the back door, across the porch, down the steps—

Papa had just gotten out of the car when I threw myself into his arms. He pressed my head to his chest, and we stood silently for a long moment. Then he released me and walked toward the house, his shoes crunching noisily over the frozen earth.

* * *

Perhaps it was the bitter cold that kept people from attending Maggie's funeral. Besides family, there were a few church elders and their wives, including Hines Stewart's parents; four ladies from Maggie's Philathea Sunday school class, huddled together like blackbirds on a wire; Doreen Hoyt resembling a polar bear in her bulky white coat; and Tallulah Cassels in an old russet suit.

Mr. Harper conducted the service in the chapel of Crawford's Funeral Home in downtown Fredericksboro. Ida, who was sitting behind me, occasionally sobbed. I kept my composure by concentrating hard on a basket of pink gladioli that sat next to the casket. Afterwards, though, in the vestibule when Miss Tallulah gave me a gold ring with a blue stone and said, "This for you rather than flowers," I broke down and could only mouth the words, "Thank you." As I headed to our car for the ride to Walthourville Cemetery in Liberty County, Uncle Ira waylaid me. "Margaret, since May Belle went home after the funeral to nurse that cold she caught in Atlanta, I have plenty of room in my car. Why don't you and Ida ride with the parson and me? We could use some good company."

I glanced over to our car where Papa was helping Miss Doreen into the front seat. "Thanks, Uncle Ira," I said. "We'd like to ride with you."

Walthourville village no longer looked as it did in Maggie's little photograph book. The houses, both those occupied and vacant, had all disappeared. The sandy road where they had once stood was now bordered by overgrown fields and forests of live oaks. Uncle Ira parked under an oak outside the cemetery gate. I got out of the car and my toes turned to ice. Maggie would never have let me wear open-toed shoes on a day like this, even if they did match my suit.

Ida came around the side of the car, and together we walked to the chairs set up under a canopy. Ida sat on the back row; I went up to the front. Louisa and Frank were already seated in the first two chairs. Frank, his face pinched with cold, smiled as I passed. Louisa stared frozenly ahead. I left one chair between her and me. Papa and Miss Doreen arrived, and I slid into the end chair. They took the two empty seats in the middle.

Mr. Harper stood before us in his black robe. "My friends," he began, "we are gathered here to pay tribute to one whose greatness lay in her humility, whose life was spent in service to others."

An Arctic blast swept across us, billowing the canopy, knocking over wreaths, whipping up the feathers on Miss Doreen's hat.

Mr. Harper opened his Bible and, holding down the fluttering pages with one hand, read:

> I am the resurrection and the life: he
> that believeth in me, though he were dead,
> yet shall he live:
> And whosoever liveth and believeth in
> me shall never die.

He prayed a short prayer. People rose and drifted away. I remained where I was.

Two men got out of the hearse. They removed the blanket of flowers from the top of Maggie's casket and laid it on the ground. Then they put straps around the casket and lowered it into a hole that had been dug behind the casket. It hit the bottom with a thud. I put my hand over my mouth to hold in a cry. The men withdrew the straps and folded back a green canvas that had covered a mound of gray dirt. They picked up their shovels—

"So, there you is, Biscuit. Come on now, they's waiting."

I got up and walked to the blanket of flowers, where I pulled out a single white rose. "Goodbye, dearest Maggie," I whispered,s and went with Ida back to the car.

CHAPTER 34

Mumps had been going around Garrett High School since late fall. I thought I'd escaped until one night while brushing my teeth I felt tightness on both sides of my jaw. The next morning it hurt to open my mouth.

"What ails you, Biscuit?" Ida asked after I'd left most of the toast and eggs on my plate.

"A little soreness in the back of my mouth. Must be cutting my wisdom teeth."

She came around behind me and placed her hands on my neck. "Your jaw is swolled up. May as well put yourself back to bed. You ain't going nowhere today."

Nor for the next two weeks. My face puffed out like a blowfish. I could barely mumble my words. The only food I got down was either what I sucked through a straw or slurped from a spoon. Ida wouldn't let Tamisa anywhere near me. Papa would come only as near as my door—except once when he ventured in far enough to put a copy of *The Forsyth Saga* on my dresser. I couldn't read it, though. My head hurt when I tried. I was as cut off from the world as though I'd been dumped into Outer Mongolia.

During the second week of my isolation, Ida pushed the telephone table close enough to my door so that I could talk—no, listen on the phone. Sue Lee Wright wanted to keep me informed about all the Christmas parties I was missing. Hines Stewart had been to a few and had paid special attention to Eva Chatsworth, this tall, snooty girl I'd always despised.

Not that being sick was all bad. I had no appetite and didn't miss eating. Nor did I mind isolation. I needed time to myself. Maggie's death had affected me more deeply than I could have imagined. It was as though some vital part of my being had been ripped away. I hurt, I despaired, and when no one was around, I wailed out in anguish.

After two weeks my jaw was back to its usual size, and the edge of my grief was less sharp. Gradually, I rejoined the world.

The plan for Christmas was for Papa and me to celebrate it at Aunt May Belle's house. Then, three days before, Betsy phoned to say that her mother thought it was too soon after my mumps for me to be around little Milton.

"I'm not contagious," I protested. "The doctor said so."

"I know, and I told that to Mother. But she's stubborn and has to have her way. I did call as soon as I found out, though, so you'd have time to make other plans."

Other plans? The day alone with my father?

The day before Christmas, I sat at the kitchen table, shelling pecans for Ida to toast. But since Tamisa kept grabbing the nut meats from the bowl and popping them into her mouth, I had little to show for my efforts. Ida stood at the counter, stirring up cornbread dressing.

"All this good food better get gone." She turned around to me and frowned.

"You needn't worry about that," I said. "Papa loves your chicken and dressing."

"I ain't talking about your papa. I talking about you. You ain't been eating worth nothing. First that Hope Forest business, then Miss Maggie passing, then mumps taking off what little meat still left on your bones."

"I'm all right, Ida."

"Well, I be over first thing in the morning to fix you and Mr. Jim a hot breakfast."

"No, you won't. You've got to go to your momma's. Papa and I can manage just fine."

I dumped the few pecans saved from Tamisa into a pan and went to Maggie's room with the new *Life* magazine. I'd just settled into her rocker when Ida called me to the back porch. Sam stood at the bottom of the steps, holding up the most perfectly shaped little cedar I'd ever seen.

"Merry Christmas!" he said, extending the tree toward me.

"He found it in the woods when he be out hunting kindling," Ida said. "Ain't it pretty?"

"It certainly is, Sam," I said, accepting the tree. "Thank you so much."

"I'd of brung it sooner, only I just come across it," he said.

After he left, I said, "Ida, you take the tree to your momma's. It'd be a shame for somebody not to enjoy it."

"Momma done got her tree. I done got mine. Sam brung this one to you."

"But Papa and I aren't having a tree this year."

"You is now."

She set it up on the parlor table in front of the window and brought out a box of ornaments. With help from Tamisa—who broke two balls and snapped the wings off an angel—we decorated the tree. That evening, I went to bed early.

Soon, I was in a black lake, struggling to swim to the shore, when I woke up to find myself lying crosswise in the bed, the covers twisted around me. I got up and shivered into my slippers and robe. On my way to the kitchen for a glass of water, I noticed the little cedar silhouetted against the pewter sky. A wave of desolation swept over me. It was all I could do not to cry.

* * *

"You planning to sleep all day?"

I opened my eyes and blinked in the light. Papa stood

283

directly above me, a bemused look on his face. "It's past nine o'clock."

At breakfast, we sat across from each other, crunching Grapenuts in milk and sounding like a couple of mules on their oats. While Papa had his second cup of coffee, I cleaned up from breakfast. Then we went to the parlor.

A box wrapped in silver paper and tied with an enormous green bow sat on the floor near the tree.

"Why don't you open it first?" A smile twitched at the corners of Papa's mouth. "It's for you to take when you go off to Agnes Scott College."

Stooping to tear off the paper, I caught the faint odor of tea roses.

Papa dropped to one knee. "Here, let me help."

While I held the box down, he lifted out a deluxe Remington typewriter, no doubt selected and wrapped by Miss Doreen. I'd told him I'd like to have the camel's hair coat on display in the window at Belk. But of course the typewriter was a more practical gift. And I knew it was given with love.

"Thank you so much," I said. "It's just what I needed."

My present to him was a set of brass bookends: one a lion and the other a unicorn. Their cost had eaten deeply into my savings.

"Handsome, truly handsome." Papa looked from one to the other. "Tha—" Something caught in his throat and he cleared it. "Thank you," he managed to whisper.

We opened the other gifts one at a time until only one box remained. It was wrapped in white tissue and tied with a simple red bow. Since it looked like a shirt box, I handed it to Papa.

He handed it back. "It's for you, daughter. I can tell you it gave her great pleasure to get it for you."

Hand trembling, I turned over the tag. My name was

written there in the familiar spidery script. Carefully, I removed the wrapping and lid. Inside was the royal blue angora sweater I'd admired one day in November while shopping at Goldberg's. It was the most beautiful sweater I'd ever seen and way too expensive to buy. The card read:

To dearest Margaret
On this blessed Christmas Day
December 25, 1947
Love,
Maggie

An odd sound escaped me and Papa looked slightly alarmed.

"Just snuffling like an old dog." I felt embarrassed.

"No, go ahead. It's all right to cry." He fluttered his hand in quick little waves that struck me as funny. I giggled.

He carried the typewriter to my room and set it on the desk. I laid my other presents around it—the sweater from Maggie, the overnight case from Aunt May Belle and Uncle Ira, the Agatha Christie mystery from Betsy and Milton, the bath powder from Louisa and Frank. Gifts now in order, I sat on the bed and thought about nothing.

A clattering of dishes drew me to the kitchen. The squash and green bean casseroles Ida had prepared, the sweet potato soufflé, and the rice and gravy were crowded on top of the stove. Papa stood at the counter, slicing a chunk of Spam and arranging the pieces in a precise row down the middle of a large platter.

"What are you doing?" I asked.

"Preparing our Christmas dinner."

"But what are you doing with that Spam?"

"I thought we should have a little meat with our vegetables."

"What about the chicken and dressing Ida baked?"

"What chicken and dressing?"

I went to the refrigerator and opened the door. The roasting pan was pushed toward the back. I took it out and removed the lid.

"Oh," Papa said.

"Let me finish up, and when everything is ready, I'll call you," I said.

"You know I'd be glad to help," he said on his way out the door.

Ida had set the dining table with a lacy white cloth and the good china and silver. She had placed a bowl of nandina with red berries in the center and silver candlesticks with red candles on either side. She had done all she could to make our Christmas dinner a festive occasion.

After grace, Papa looked around at our bounty and said, "Had I known there would be such a feast, we could have invited a guest."

He searched my face for signs that I, too, wished we had invited Doreen. I managed a slight nod, which seemed to please him.

While I picked at my food, Papa ate lustily and talked about the fruitcake Maggie made every Christmas when he was a boy. The recipe called for, among other ingredients, eighteen eggs, two pounds of butter, and a pint of New Orleans molasses. His job was to cut up the candied pineapple and citron.

After we had finished our meal, he pushed back his chair. "Now, I'll be glad to help with the dishes," he said.

"It's easier if just one person does them."

"Then I'll be reading in the parlor."

I joined him later with my new Agatha Christie. But before I could finish the first page, my eyes started drooping.

I set the book on the table. "Believe I'll lie down a while."

"Oh? Then I might run into town. It must be awfully hard on Miss Doreen being alone this first Christmas since her husband's death."

From my bedroom window, I watched his car disappear down the drive. Two hours later when I woke from my nap, his car was still gone.

Feeling better than I had in a long time, I got up and went to the kitchen, where I poured a glass of milk and cut a large slice of Ida's coconut cake. Every Christmas, even during the war years when sugar was scarce, she had made that cake—three yellow layers with thick lemon filling and all smothered over with coconut icing. It was her love gift to her charges. I remembered, when I was three, using a chair to climb on top of the kitchen table and stuffing handfuls of the cake into my mouth. Ida caught me in the act, but instead of scolding me or smacking my bottom, she hugged me, sticky fingers and all.

I was at the sink, rinsing my plate, when the telephone rang.

"Merry Christmas!" said a young baritone voice.

"And the same to you, Hines!" I replied.

"I heard about Miss Maggie's passing, and I am so sorry. I wish I could have come home for her funeral."

"I appreciate that. It's hard losing her, but people are kind."

"I'm sure that they are. Sue Lee Wright tells me you've been sick."

"I'm well now."

"Well enough for a party? My friend Henry Barton is having one New Year's Eve at his folks' place on the lake. Nothing fancy. We'll build a bonfire, roast hot dogs, play records."

"Sounds like fun. I'd love to go." No apprehension, no hesitation. For once, it was all so easy and natural.

After I hung up the phone, I went to my room, slipped into my angora sweater, and headed outside to the back yard. Mother's old car was parked in its usual spot near the sugarberry tree with its branches like black lace silhouetted against the cerulean sky. I walked on past the clotheslines and chinaberry trees, festooned with their small yellow balls, and around to the pasture. The cows stood near the fence, dining on hay Sam had thrown out. Proud Beauty was no longer among them. Nor was Cherry, Papa's pet Jersey. But Cherry's calf, Blossom, was there with a calf of her own. T-Harry, almost as large as his mother, tried to nurse her, and Blossom kept stepping aside. Finally, she turned and shook her horns at her calf. He backed off and bawled a complaint to the sky.

"Poor T-Harry," I said. "It's hard being forced to grow up."

T-Harry bawled again.

I walked to the front of the house and sat on a step. Seven miles away, the city stretched across the horizon. To the left, amidst the dark trees of Fredericks Hill, Aunt May Belle, Uncle Ira, Betsy, and Milton reveled in little Milton's first Christmas. Urging him to notice his toys, delighting in his every response.

At the bottom of the hill, Papa sat in Miss Doreen's pink parlor, telling corny jokes that caused her to tee-hee and fan her face. "She's a good woman," Maggie had said. "She makes your father happy." Papa, happy at last. I decided I was happy for him, and I would work harder to show it.

Directly ahead in the low hills of South Carolina, Louisa and Frank celebrated the day with Miss Wilfreda and friends. Since her marriage, Louisa had withdrawn more and more from our family circle. But *my* circle still took her in. It always would. I wished my sister great joy.

A blue jay landed nearby on a bare patch of ground. I remembered another blue jay that had once landed nearby. It was summer then, deep in the woods, and a baby lay beside me. And Alicia Patricia was beside me all those years after, when I was trapped in guilt and remorse.

Until Maggie reminded me that what I had done was driven by love. Love made a difference.

I ran my fingers down the length of my sweater and watched the electric blue fibers reach toward my hand. Maggie was with me; her care and devotion embraced me. Maggie. And Ida, too. They were my mothers. I was doubly blessed.

The jay looked all around and settled its eye upon me. It made a soft chirping sound, then pecked a few grains of sand and flew off with a squawk.

Laughing, I turned my face toward the sun and breathed in the fine, crystal air.

THE END